# History Lives

# EDWARD RYDER

MBD
PUBLICATIONS
A Division of MONTEREYBAYDESIGN

MBD Publications
*A Division of Monterey Bay Design*
Salinas, California

*Cover Art by Deborah Ryder*
*Interior Design by Elouise Ryder*

ISBN-13: 978-0-692-26535-2
ISBN-10: 069226535X

Library of Congress Cataloging-in-Publication Data is available.

Printed in the United States of America on acid-free paper.

1 3 5 7 9 10 8 6 4 2

# Acknowledgment

I thank my wife Elouise and my daughter Deborah for vital help and support in bringing this book to life. Elouise read and reread the manuscript, offering sage advice on usage, correcting mistakes, and pointing out confusing passages. She also did the interior design. Deborah designed the front and back covers and read the manuscript.

# CHAPTER 1

Most of the King's fury wafted away after some soothing words by his interviewer, Robert Delacroix.

Robert, relieved and relaxed, said, "Your Majesty, perhaps we can now talk about other matters, including some of your personal interests."

"My personal interests?" The King still looked stern and his voice was not friendly. "What do you mean? What is it you wish to know?"

"It has been written that you were destined for the priesthood, as the second son."

"The priesthood!" He laughed, his good humor returning. "No, no. I am a faithful Christian, of course." He smiled slyly. "But I am a man of many other great interests, as you have said. Music. Sports. The ladies, eh. No, no. Not the priesthood. It is enough to write the holy music of love and occasionally joust with the Church."

Robert also smiled. "You were renowned as a great favorite among the ladies. You gave generously of your love, and they adored you in return: several mistresses and six wives. Quite an accomplishment, I would say."

The King frowned at another mention of his wives. Then he relaxed, began to preen a bit, and nodded in agreement.

"Yes. I was young—and handsome, so everyone said." He leaned toward Robert. "And, of course, I believed them."

He laughed delightedly; his head thrown back, and slapped his thigh. Robert also laughed; the spectators joined in as well. Henry leaned forward again, embracing his smiling conspirators.

"What's more, I was a dancer of great renown. So I also performed well *on* my feet."

"Ah yes. Indeed, you had many talents. Also, you spoke several languages, you wrote poetry and songs, and you were a fine athlete."

"I loved sports: tennis, hunting, archery, bowls, jousting in the tournaments, all of them."

"Jousting? Wasn't that dangerous, especially for a king? You could have had your head taken off."

"Of course! Life is dangerous. And my head stayed where it belonged. I did take some blows and had to stop jousting. It was necessary to turn to other things."

"You had problems with your health as a result of those blows. The thump to your head almost killed you."

The King stiffened, but Robert continued.

"You were unconscious for two hours, and Queen Anne was told that you might die. It became difficult for you to walk, and your legs developed rather serious ulcerated sores. You became easily roused to anger. You gained a lot of weight."

"A few stone. I don't wish to talk about that."

"Just one question—"

Henry shouted, "Do not carry that any further!"

He breathed heavily, his face stormy. Henry preferred to think of his years of grace and strength, not the years of anguish and misery. What sort of monarch might he have been with all his many physical and mental attributes intact? How would England be different? Would England—and the world—have taken different journeys?

When Robert felt it was safe to go on, he said, "Your Majesty, perhaps we can now talk about the Church."

"The Church?" The King still looked stern, and his voice was no longer friendly. "Yes? What is it you wish to know?"

"You had many encounters, first with His Holiness, later with the monks over their lands and money."

"Their lands? Their money? I think not. The monks were parasites."

He stopped. There was silence for a moment. Then he raised his head. He smiled softly as if his mind was far away. He seemed to grow, to expand into a grander image of himself. He continued.

"The one follows the other, does it not? We discovered that the Bishop of Rome exceeded his authority. We were the King, chosen by God himself, to rule the people and thus to serve them. And who are the people. They are our subjects, from the lowly peasants, to the monks and the priests, yes, and to the Bishop of Rome himself. So ruled David and the kings of Israel, so do we rule, and so do we bring God's word. The lords spiritual as well as the lords temporal must by God's law, by God's command, bow to the King and to no other. Not, *not* to the Bishop of Rome."

"You appropriated the monies of the monks, confiscated their lands, and destroyed many of the monasteries."

"Those monies, those lands, and those structures were the means to plot against the state, against the Royal Person, who *is* the state, and against our loyal and loving subjects. We put the monies to better use: to build our navy and to reward the defenders of the state. Those ecclesiasts flooded the Royal Court. It was better to populate the court with the noble supporters of the Royal Authority. We did that."

He leaned back on the throne and gazed benignly at Delacroix.

Robert hesitated a moment before asking the next question, which might anger the King yet again. He just hoped to get an answer. He was also thankful that Henry was inside the cubicle and that he was not. This man displayed many moods, from smiles of good will to raging anger. Robert did not envy the ladies and gentlemen of the court of Henry the Eighth.

"During your reign of thirty-seven years, there were many thousands of executions, mostly by beheading. Were so many necessary? Weren't there other, less violent means of punishment?"

Henry looked puzzled.

"I don't know what you mean. They were traitors. One isn't kind to traitors. Divine right allowed us to punish traitors as we saw fit, and they deserved execution. An example had to be set that treason required the ultimate punishment. Traitors foment and lead rebellions. My country did not wish to suffer a devastating revolution."

He smiled slyly. "You should thank me. One of your ancestors might have been killed in such a war. Besides, all this happened centuries ago, as you have told me. Why worry about it now?"

Robert was astonished at the apparent lack of anger. "So you consider it as one of the duties of the monarch?"

"Of course."

"It was your divine right to kill so many people?"

Henry smiled again, but did not answer. This time Robert could see the hate in Henry's eyes and felt a chill course through his own body. He decided that there would be no point to continue on this subject.

"Now, I would like to talk with you about your children." Robert leaned forward a bit. His famous smile, shining white, warm, and charming, concealed a slight nervous anticipation, since the monarch liked talking about himself best. He had become visibly annoyed when Delacroix had asked about his brother, his advisers, even his father.

The King turned his head slowly towards Delacroix; his eyes narrowed and his lips compressed in a glower that could remove heads.

"My children. Why do you wish to know about them?"

"Well, Your Majesty, I thought you might be interested in their future lives and how they fared, after—"

"Fared? My son Edward inherits the throne when I die. The other two are girls. They do not count for anything. Once again, sir, you venture into dangerous territory."

"Please, Your Majesty, I must remind you again that you died quite a long time ago. We have brought you back to life, in a manner of speaking."

"Yes." He shifted heavily on the throne, showing a wintry smile. He relaxed a bit. "And I do not feel pain. My legs feel whole and strong. I suppose I must thank you for that. My children, you say. Edward becomes—became King after I—died. He was not a well boy. He would have been nine or ten at that time. With God's will, he achieved good health, and reigned for many years." Henry grimaced in remembered pain. "Without our accursed afflictions."

"Alas, Your Majesty, he did not. He died at the age of sixteen."

"Sixteen! Can that be true? What happened then? Did the monarchy fall to the rebels, to the damnable French? You must tell me!"

"It did not fall. Your oldest daughter Mary became Queen."

"Mary? Even worse; a Catholic queen! We returned to the Church of Rome!" The King put his hands over his face. "Why did you bring us back to hear this?" he cried in a broken voice.

"She did indeed try to bring back Catholicism, but was unsuccessful. She married Philip of Spain in 1554 and died in 1558 without issue. Then Elizabeth ascended the throne. She was much loved by the people and reigned for forty-five years until her death in 1603."

The King lifted his head and smiled.

"Elizabeth! There was a girl of spirit. I liked her."

"She had a long reign and built England into a formidable power with the navy you created."

"Ah yes. Our Navy Royal." He smiled and purred, "You see, good use was made of the money contributed by those loyal but saucy monks. England needed ships. We were exceedingly grateful to the monks for their generosity in support of our endeavors to strengthen and defend the realm against the French and those Scottish dogs. I defeated them badly, you know."

"Yes indeed; twice it seems. You defeated James IV in 1513 and James V in 1542. However, England eventually acquired a Scottish king, James I. He succeeded Elizabeth in 1603."

Henry's mouth fell open. "A Scottish king? Why? Did my daughter not produce an heir? That is monstrous!"

"Alas, she never married and had no children."

The King shook his head sadly. "God denied me male heirs." Sorrow became indignation. "It was the work of the Pope! He hated me!" He reflected for a minute. "Why did she not marry?"

"Many believe," said Delacroix cautiously, "that she did not wish to share power with a man, that she feared for her life. After all, her mother was beheaded."

Henry stood up, his face red and his eyes afire. "It was our divine right," he shouted. "We were King! It was necessary! The woman was a fornicator, a whore. We had evidence. We had signed confessions and witnesses."

"Did you not at least suspect, sir, that those confessions were obtained under, shall we say, duress?"

The cubicle seemed to shake with his rage. He stopped shouting and sat down, gasping for breath. He looked at Delacroix. He spoke slowly, softly, darkly.

"You try us, sir. If this was my day—"

Despite the emptiness of the threat, Robert felt the venom, coldly delivered through the cubicle wall. Henry smiled at him again, wintry, calculating.

"We have been returned to life," the King said, emphasizing each word. "Our soul has been returned. We are King of England and Ireland, by God's will. We are here now and will be again."

"If you came back, Your Majesty, I'm afraid that you would find this world a very different place."

"What do you mean?"

"There are very few kings who claim divine right. In particular, no king or queen of England has claimed that right for hundreds of years. In fact the English monarch is essentially a figurehead. Government is the province of Parliament."

"I do not believe it. It cannot be. The King is next to God and rules by his will."

"Not so. The world changes constantly. You actually are responsible for many of the changes."

"Nonsense!"

"When you transferred power from the lords spiritual to the lords temporal, that initiated a series of changes. The House of Commons eventually became the principal lawmaking body, and the members were not from the nobility. The nobles went to the House of Lords, which has restricted powers. In England and many other countries, governments became democratic and were beholden to the people, not to a king or emperor. The Anglican Church remains the state church, but religion is no longer of prime concern, as people saw less and less evidence of God's influence on life on earth. Remember, it is six hundred years since your lifetime."

Henry seemed overcome with pain and anger. He spoke with furious deliberation.

"We are here now and will be again. But we have had enough. We do not wish to talk with you any longer. We wish to depart."

He turned away and stared into the distance, his face set in cold, hard anger.

Robert Delacroix sat for a moment, breathing deeply, feeling the beat of his heart.

He pressed a button on the console and Henry faded to emptiness. He turned towards the silent audience, many wide-eyed as if they had felt the malevolent power as well.

"Henry the Eighth, ladies and gentlemen, a renowned monarch, still formidable after six centuries. That's our performance for tonight. Good night and please savor another remarkable evening of *History Lives*."

As Delacroix stood up and stepped towards the audience, a few people, released from the spell, began to clap. A few more, and still more joined, swelling to full throated applause. He walked to the front of the stage, away from the now dark cubicle, and the console. He smiled and nodded his head.

"Thank you. Thank you all. I know that most of you, perhaps all of you, are here for the first time. I can tell you that, for me, it is always the first time. The awe, the strength and power of personality, the revelation and surprise of the unexpected, astonish and dazzle each time. The experience of reliving history can be joyful or extremely disheartening. Neither you nor any of us know which it will be. We are all learning together." He paused. "Now, we have time for a few questions. Mikes have been set up in both aisles." He paused again. "Yes, the gentleman on my left."

"Gosh, do you mean to tell us that this is the first time you have actually talked to Henry the Eighth? No rehearsal?"

Delacroix grinned broadly. "Not exactly. We did have one minor glimpse of him beforehand. We brought him here for a couple of minutes to establish identity and to assess voice type and level for the soundman. One or two meaningless questions, that's all. Yes, the lady on the right."

"Some of your, ah, guests are pretty bad people, or were in their day. What would happen if one of them escaped?"

"Oh my, that would be quite unnerving indeed." He shook his head. "Fortunately, it will never happen. First, you notice that the cubicle is one piece. It has no doors and it is very heavy. After the stage is set, the cubicle is lowered from above. Our guest appears inside the cubicle and exits the same way. Second, the guest is not a true hologram, neither is he or she an actual person. However, there is some substance there, not flesh and blood of course, but sufficient to allow movement and show facial expression. Most important, they have what we call a neurotronic brain, which enables them to think. Therefore, they become interesting, and can provide us with new information, ideas, and a few surprises. We don't believe that their substance can exist outside the cubicle, so a *successful* escape is not possible."

"Why was he so dismissive of his daughters?" asked another woman. "He said they didn't count."

"Well, in the sixteenth century, women were not considered suitable for leadership. They were believed to be weak and easily led. Therefore, Henry demanded a male heir. He married six women to try to satisfy that need. Jane Seymour gave him Edward the Sixth, but he continued acquiring wives to beget a son who was also healthy. He was unsuccessful, although he also had several sons by various mistresses. The three who lived could not have ascended the throne by, shall we say, normal, acceptable means. Late in his life, Catherine Parr, his last wife, persuaded him to restore Mary and Elizabeth to the line of succession. We found out tonight that he was not completely pleased with that. We did find out, however, that he did seem to admire Elizabeth. On the other hand, she was only fourteen when he died, so he may have said that only because he was informed that she succeeded as a monarch. It may have been a means of taking credit to satisfy his own ego."

A second man came to a microphone. "The King said he no longer wanted to talk to you. If you decided to bring him back for an encore, would he remember this encounter and still refuse to answer your questions?"

Delacroix jabbed a finger in the man's direction. "An excellent question. First of all, I should note that we were fortunate because we were very close to the end of the show. If it had happened earlier, we would have had some dead time and you would have had to suffer more of me."

He grinned as the audience laughed.

"It's difficult to answer your question. When I used the word 'substance' in answer to a previous question, it was for want of a better word. The nature of the substance puzzles the scientists, because no one has actually been inside the cubicle with the subjects. So we can't poke or pinch them, or take a sample. You've heard the statement: The whole is greater than the sum of its parts?"

"Yes."

"I think that comes close to describing the phenomenon. The trouble is we don't really know what *that* means either. The reason this show exists is that when the engineers and scientists merged the various technologies into one mega-technology, they achieved the ability to reconstruct the past in ways that they hadn't anticipated. Since that breakthrough, they have been trying to find out what happened. They meant to turn on one more light; instead they created a sun. Now they are trying to find out why.

There are laboratories in several places in the world investigating the phenomenon. You know, we still don't completely understand how the human brain works. This is a very similar problem. That's a longwinded answer meaning that we don't know what Henry would do.

"There is another way of looking at it. You saw how capricious he was, how his moods changed. So, if we brought him back right now and asked the same question, maybe butter him up a little, he might be perfectly happy to talk."

A young woman came to the microphone. "You have a policy of not announcing the next show until it's on the air. Why is that?"

Delacroix smiled again. "Well for one thing, we like the element of surprise. It's fairly unique in the broadcast world, but it's enticing, don't you think." There was a smattering of applause. "There's another reason. The technology involved in assembling and synchronizing the physical, chemical, and biological information, especially the genetic codes, with the historical evidence, the language adaptations, and other information, is very complex. Feedback loops, knowledge reinforcement—"

He stopped. "Anyone have any idea what I'm talking about?"

There were laughs and groans.

"You see. I'm a pretty bright fellow, but hearing the scientists, engineers, and other special people talk makes my head swim. Anyway, they do endless tinkering and adjusting, very nearly up to the time of broadcast. Sometimes, they can't eliminate all the glitches. Therefore, we may prepare two shows at once and decide which one to run almost literally at the last minute. It keeps us all on our toes, I assure you.

"Well, I think we need to stop here. It's been fun talking with you. Tune in next time for yet another surprise guest. Good night."

As the audience filed out, Robert Delacroix went to the backstage area and flopped down in a chair with some of the show's technical people. He shook his head.

"It never fails, does it? They're coming after me, people like Henry. I'm very grateful for that cubicle. It's shatterproof, but the threat is still a bit scary. I'm reminded of a story I read once. This cowboy was in a bar with a rattlesnake in a big glass jar. He would bet that no one could hold his hand up to the jar without flinching when the snake struck. He had lots of challengers, but he never lost."

"The snake never broke the glass?" asked Jamie Driscoll, a computer technician.

"Not in the story. It was pretty heavy duty glass." He grinned. "I'm counting on the material of the cubicle to keep me safe. But it is impossible not to feel those waves of hate."

"We seem to interview plenty of bad guys," mused Jamie. "Why is that? They're all violent, but in different ways. Henry didn't have to lift a finger to kill all those people. It's the prerogative of being a ruling tyrant, I guess."

"Maybe they're more interesting than good people," said historian Meilin Xu.

"Possibly, but let's hope not, for the sake of the show," said Robert. He stifled a yawn. "Well, better go before I collapse."

# CHAPTER 2

After leaving the group, Robert felt in need of exercise and decided to walk downstairs to the vehicle park. He would tire rapidly later, but was still in the pumped-up battle mode he always developed during the interviews, comparable to the elevated state of physical and mental excitement that overcomes a soldier surrounded by loud, screaming, bloody combat during the old wars. Exhaustion and a depressive letdown would soon follow. He often wondered whether the occasional severe effects on his body could cause permanent damage. At least they seemed severe to him. A doctor might believe otherwise, pat him on the shoulder, smile indulgently, and move on to more serious concerns.

"Robert Delacroix." The door opened. He got in and sat down. "Home." Protective straps encircled his body, the door closed, the electric feed-in disconnected, and the engine hummed to life. The vehicle glided from the space and out into the stream of traffic, heading homeward under the direction of the latest incarnation of Enhanced GPS. Delacroix leaned back to enjoy the bright lights of the city in the silence of the vehicle's interior.

"Need some noise," he muttered. "Sounds." A small port opened, letting in the muted voices of the city at night. He soon left the city and its outlying suburbs, eased into the greater darkness and silence of the countryside, and arrived home forty-two minutes later.

Shannon was on the couch reading. She was in her favorite position, back against the arm of the couch, with her knees drawn up and the book nestled between her thighs. She smiled as he leaned over to kiss her.

"Sit down, my love." She looked at him quizzically. "I'll fetch you what appears to be a badly needed drink."

She returned in a few minutes with a scotch and water. He could feel the expected tiredness beginning to saturate his bones and muscles.

"So. Henry wasn't pleased to hear of Elizabeth's fear of marriage."

He grinned. "Nice way to put it. I believe he wanted to remove my head, but at least he didn't try to bash his way through the cubicle, like Vlad the Impaler. Even so, you could feel the emotion, the hate, coming through the wall.

"Every time I tell a subject about the events after his or her death, we venture into uncharted territory. Joy, rage, shock, tears, astonishment; anything can happen, and that's the part where I always feel my heart begin to race. It's a real high, and the comedown is even harder to bear. As you may have noticed." He smiled and then shook his head. "I'm constantly amazed at the scientists' ability to bring out embellishments of character in these people."

"What do you mean?"

"They aren't just endowed with historically established characteristics. They seem to have thought patterns, generating new ideas that they couldn't have had before they died. And they have emotions, real emotions, which we may not have known about beforehand. Vlad actually cried when I asked about the assassination of his father. It's really quite fascinating."

"Isn't it also a bit frightening? One of them might figure out a way to get out of the cubicle and attack you or someone in the audience. And since you are not sure of what exactly makes it tick, you might not be able to capture it, or if necessary, kill it. How can you kill something that's not alive in the first place? It would be like a zombie." She waved her arms in the air. "Oooo! It's *Night of the Living Dead* revisited."

He smiled indulgently at her. "It can't happen. The cubicle is escape proof." He added, "I think you're a bit loonacious."

"Loquacious, perhaps. Luscious, definitely. Lubricious, oh yes. Crazy, no."

Shannon Remington had lived with him for just over two years, since shortly after Robert's divorce from Electra. They had met during a seminar series designed to bring together professional people from diverse cultures, in a continuing attempt to foster understanding between C.P Snow's two cultures described two hundred years earlier. Her impressive personal and professional resume overcame Robert's resistance to beginning a relationship with another woman so soon. She was very attractive, with a wide range of sophisticated tastes.

Shannon was one of the highest rated graduates of Hesperian University, created in the technology vortex of Silicon Valley. (The Hesperian Epoch on Mars was a time of intense lava flow activity. The upwelling of energy inspired the naming of the institution.) She had studied deep space phenomena, especially dark matter, dark energy, the connection between light and gravity, and the origin and fate of the universe. After graduation, she enjoyed a short but exciting career as an astronaut, including two colonization flights to Mars and a sightseeing swoop through the asteroid belt.

After she retired from the space program, Spaceflight International had immediately hired her in a dual role, as a mid-level manager and as goodwill ambassador, capitalizing on her glamorous previous life. She now held a high executive position with the company.

Robert viewed her with awe, and was puzzled by his own behavior. He had read about men of similar character or temperament, men with a condition called "discounting the future," who, often to their eventual regret, become besotted with women of power, or beauty, or both. Most of his romances since high school, including his marriage, had failed because he couldn't look past immediate gratification to more permanent, sustainable satisfaction. The latter had been unattainable for a fairly simple reason: his ego couldn't handle not being able to keep up. The failures were not completely his fault, but his lack of foresight certainly had contributed to all of them. He loved Shannon, but their relationship was bitter as well as sweet, alternating between highs and lows, forcing him to wonder how long it would last this time. As his depression increased with the tiredness, he wondered whether he was hopeless, whether he would or could ever change.

"Robert?"

He blinked his eyes and smiled at her. "Sorry, sorry. Doing a bit of wool gathering. My usual state at this point. What did you do today?"

"Meetings, paperwork, talking to heads of state. The usual boring stuff. Sometimes I wish I was still flying around the solar system, staring at planets and stars."

He snorted. "It seems to me that you often thought that was boring too, except for takeoffs and landings."

"And approaching a planet or moon. That was pretty exciting. But you're right. Chugging through space with little to do was pretty boring."

"Talking to heads of state? Really?"

"Made you sit up, didn't I." She smirked at him. "Pretty close, actually. I talked with the Chief of Staff to President Strada of the West European Federation. They're setting up a museum exhibit of deep space phenomena, and want me to help dedicate it when it's done."

"That sounds interesting. Where will it be located?"

She smiled triumphantly. "Paris!"

"Very nice indeed. Well, it seems your day wasn't boring at all. You were putting me on, you rascal!"

"Mmmm. Perhaps if you are really nice to me, I'll take you along."

"Okay." Robert felt a slight pang of jealousy, which he tried to suppress. Her life seemed so much more fulfilled than his; he participated in it as a tagalong. He snorted to himself, thinking yet again of the inevitable result of falling for an accomplished woman. What was the old saying? Look for a woman with a straight D average in high school. Keep her barefoot and—Never mind—"

He yawned.

Shannon unwound and stood up.

"I think you need some sleep. Let's go to bed."

# CHAPTER 3

how business meets show business. This thought popped into Robert Delacroix's mind while the houselights dimmed. The cubicle glowed; he also began to glow internally, anticipating the coming interview. Then a second thought joined the first. Second rater meets superstar. He sighed as the form of a slightly built man began to materialize in the cubicle. Soon, the audience could see the brushed back hair, high forehead, and well-worn eyes familiar from old classic movies, the face of Humphrey Bogart. Applause broke out, and Bogart turned to find the source of the noise. He saw Robert.

"Am I on display here? What's going on?" The voice was nasal, raspy, with a barely discernible lisp.

"Mr. Bogart?"

"Yeah. Who are you?"

"My name is Robert Delacroix. You are on a special television show."

Bogart frowned. "I thought I was dead."

"You are. Let me explain."

When Robert finished his usual account, Bogart was silent for a moment; he patted his pockets.

"I need a cigarette."

"I'm sorry, Mr. Bogart. I'm afraid there is no smoking allowed."

"How about a drink?"

"Sorry. Can't do that either."

Bogart sat back in his chair and gave Robert a sardonic look.

"Well, I feel pretty good. The damn cough is gone. Still." He gazed at Robert. "So what am I doing here?"

"We interview historical figures: kings, presidents, artists, scientists. I'd like to ask you some questions about your life and your career."

"Sure, but I warn you. I can be pretty nasty."

Robert laughed.

"I'm prepared for that. Let's see. 1949. You were awarded a Golden Apple by the Hollywood Women's Press Club for Least Cooperative Actor. We might as well start with that."

"Actually, it was the Sour Apple Award. Hedy Lamarr got one too, so I was in good company. I said what I thought. A lot of people hated that, especially producers, directors, actors, non-boozers, and reporters. I criticized, usually out loud, people and performances I didn't like. Some of them hated me."

He pointed a finger at Robert.

"But I slammed myself as much as anybody. Don't forget that." He grinned. "So that made it all right."

"You needled people mercilessly to the point where they wanted to beat you up. You often resorted to doing something to—"

"To weasel out?"

"Yes."

Bogart nodded his head, but said nothing further.

"You rarely went to see any of your own movies after they were released. So you must have formed an opinion about them while you were creating them. They made you feel good or they didn't?"

"Yeah, that's right." He paused. "You're rather perceptive. Not bad for a pretty boy."

He leered at Robert.

"But let's get back to the question. I needed to like the way the director and the other actors were working, and the way I was working in my role. The script had to be good too. A few pictures made the grade; most of them didn't. My favorite, I guess, was *The African Queen*. I was not pleased with the Congo, but I did my best work in that movie. It was a terrible place to work, hot, wringing wet, and full of enormous insects. Everybody got dysentery except John and me. Our medicine was canned pork and beans and asparagus and lots of Scotch. I prefer working in a big civilized city, but I guess the result was worth the misery. Katharine Hepburn was great, even though we didn't get along at first."

"You played yourselves, in a sense."

"Yeah. Charley Allnut was a boozer, and Rose Sayer was a teetotaler. They hated each other at first, when she bullied him to chug down the river to the big lake and torpedo a German gunboat. A really dumb move. They fell in love and got married, just before the gunboat blew up. They jumped off and swam to shore. A really corny, improbable, but happy ending, but I guess people liked that. Katie and I warmed up towards the end of shooting and got to be good friends, even though she didn't drink. I guess all sins are forgivable.

"And John Huston was terrific. He was a special director. We worked in a lot of movies together that he either directed, or wrote the screenplay, or both: *High Sierra, The Treasure of the Sierra Madre, Beat the Devil.*"

"You won your only Academy Award as Charley Allnut. In your acceptance speech, you gave credit to other people, despite having insisted for years that you wouldn't do that if you ever won."

"Sometimes I shot my big mouth off. I used to make fun of the Academy Awards. But then I discovered that I really wanted to win."

"What other pictures satisfied you?"

"*The Petrified Forest.* That was my first chance to break away from playing the guy with white pants and a tennis racket."

Robert grinned. "Ah yes. 'Tennis, anyone?'"

Bogart winced.

"Yeah. Finally lived that down. I played the killer, Duke Mantee, in the stage version on Broadway, and got good reviews, but the studio in their wisdom wanted Edward G. Robinson for the movie. I got the part only because Leslie Howard, the star in the play and the movie, insisted on it. He owned the rights. Wonderful man. I named my daughter after him."

"That movie established your career in films, but you were then typecast as a gangster, and mostly in B movies. Unfortunately, George Raft, James Cagney, and Edward G. Robinson got in your way for lead roles in important pictures."

Bogart smiled thinly.

"I suppose you could put it that way. But they were big stars. I was *trying* to be a big star. But guess what? Raft, who was not a very bright guy, refused *High Sierra* and *The Maltese Falcon.* I got both of those roles, and became—"

"— a big star."

"Right. Raft's reason, by the way, for turning down the part of Sam Spade in *The Maltese Falcon* was that he was promised roles in important pictures, and he didn't think that picture was very important. What a dummy."

"Okay," said Robert. "Let's move on. *Casablanca* and *To Have and Have Not.* I imagine those were both special to you, perhaps for different reasons."

Bogart nodded. "Yeah. *Casablanca* was an excellent story and turned out to be a big hit as well. Ingrid Bergman was special: beautiful, a great actress, and tall. I had to wear stilts in some scenes."

"Stilts?"

"Well, no. Blocks. Lifts. Made me five inches taller. Leading men always have to be taller than leading women, because there is generally a kissing scene or two and it wouldn't do to have the gal towering over her lover. Oh, no."

"It was your first real romantic lead."

"Yeah. I didn't have to shoot anybody till the end of the picture."

"You also established yourself as a cynical, weary loner whose basic decency emerges in time to save the day."

"Yeah. Of course the last part is pure Hollywood."

"Playing in that company must have been like a family reunion."

Bogart grinned wickedly.

"Better. We *liked* each other. Peter Lorre had had a tough life, which could have turned him really sour. But he was a really sweet wonderful guy. Sydney Greenstreet was enormous. I think he weighed about 360 pounds. Good actor. His career in Hollywood was short, only eight years." He stopped and rolled his eyes. "I should talk."

"Over the years," said Robert, "*Casablanca* became something of a cult picture. It played repeatedly for years, and people in the audience would shout out the lines."

"That must have been tough on anyone who had never seen it before."

Robert thought that it was time to try a little needling himself.

"You know, a few people at the time felt that *Casablanca* was less than a great picture because of some blatant inconsistencies. For instance, Ingrid Bergman's lover, named Victor Laszlo, was a member of an underground group who had escaped from a Nazi prison camp. Yet there he was, in a white suit in Rick Blaine's club, which was filled with Nazi officers who knew who he was. No one attempted to shoot him, or capture him. He even had a conversation with the Nazi commandant. What about that?"

Bogart snorted.

"You haven't seen many movies, have you, pretty boy? There's no such thing as consistency. They play around with history just like in historical novels. If the story is interesting, and moving or exciting, nobody cares about some inconsistencies that make the story move forward. Remember, when you walk into a movie house and the lights go down, you're in a land of make-believe. You suspend the sense of reality you had before you walked in.

"When Dorothy's house lands, and she opens the door, you're in Oz—and in color, no less. You know that the Cowardly Lion, the Tin Man, and the Scarecrow are real, and can talk. The flying monkeys are real, the Emerald City is real, and the tree that throws apples is real. You don't sit there and say, 'Oh, this can't possibly be true.' No, no. Especially if your kid is sitting next to you."

Bogart sat back in his chair with a big grin on his face.

"I guess you told me," said Robert.

"I guess so. Wanna make a fool of yourself with another smart aleck remark?"

"No. Let's move on. Talk about *To Have and Have Not*."

"It was adapted from Hemingway's novel, which he apparently thought wasn't very good. Howard Hawks called it a piece of junk, but said he could make a good picture out of it. He did that by completely rewriting it. They changed locations. Instead of smuggling some Chinese guys to Cuba on his boat, Harry Morgan, that's me, ran a Free French resistance leader to another Caribbean island, Martinique. Instead of losing everything he had, including his right arm and then his life, Morgan got the girl and was a hero. William Faulkner did some of the rewriting and enjoyed messing with Hemingway's novel. They were not friends.

"The movie was very important to me because of Baby, Lauren Bacall. She was very young. It was her first movie and I helped her with lines and techniques. We became very close and fell in love. I adored that woman." He paused, sighed, and gathered himself together. "We were a great couple. I hated leaving her. If I had known what a great marriage we were going to have, I might have taken better care of myself." He sighed again. "I don't know. Maybe not."

"Hemingway wrote another novel, *The Old Man and the Sea*, that you didn't get to do, even though it was a natural for you as a bona fide sailor."

"Yeah. I was a lot skinnier than Spencer Tracy too. I looked like a poor, undernourished fisherman. But he owned the rights. So that was that."

"Let's turn to some other things. After World War II and on into the late 1950s, there was a great fear in the United States that Communism would overwhelm the country. In particular, Hollywood was singled out as a hotbed of Communist propaganda. You and a group of other actors and directors formed a Committee for the First Amendment and traveled to Washington, DC to protest the persecution of a group of writers and directors, called the Hollywood Ten, by the House Un-American Activities Committee. But then you wrote an article for Photoplay

Magazine, "I'm No Communist", in which you distanced yourself from the people you were defending. Why did you think that was necessary?"

"Number one. People were calling *me* a Communist. I didn't like to be called names that weren't true. I was a Democrat and a liberal, but I didn't care much for Communist beliefs. Actually, it was legal to be a Communist and to belong to the Party. Unfortunately, in those days, to be labeled as a Communist became a kiss of death in the movie industry, as you can see by the immense number of people who were blacklisted. The studio owners were pretty conservative and scared to death that customers would stay away from the theaters, and there would go their profits. Number two. I wanted to keep working and I worried that my career would be ruined. That's what happened to a lot of actors, writers, and directors. Number three. Those guys wanted this country to go communist, but they were perfectly happy to work in a capitalist system and make plenty of money."

"So you didn't feel too sorry for them."

"Sure I did. They were victims of anti-Communist hysteria beyond any reason as far as being a danger to this country. People forgot that we went through a terrible depression in the Thirties and never came close to going Communist or Fascist during that time. The people on that committee didn't have much confidence in the good sense of the American people. They seemed to believe that Communist propaganda was irresistible, so powerful that anyone who heard those evil words would immediately run to party headquarters and join up. What nonsense. Worst of all, it led to Joe McCarthy's lying smear campaigns. I believed that the Soviet Union was a greater danger than any Hollywood screenwriter or actor."

"Well, you might be interested to know that we never went to war directly with the Soviet Union. The period after the war was called the Cold War, as you know. There were several proxy wars, but nobody dropped a nuclear bomb, and the Soviet Union finally collapsed in 1991."

"There you are."

After a slight pause, "It collapsed, just like that?"

"There was a new premier, Mikhail Gorbachev, who believed that communism should be democratized a little bit, so he loosened the stranglehold of the government. He proposed two principles, glasnost and perestroika, meaning openness and restructuring. It was like putting a small hole in a levee; pretty soon the water comes rushing through in a flood. The people discovered what had been kept secret all those years and complained bitterly and loudly. Before anyone knew what was happening, the Soviet Union was gone. In its place were fifteen republics."

"Wow. There is no predicting the future, is there?"

"Let's move on again. You were a very good chess player and also very well read. That makes you something of an intellectual, doesn't it?"

"Watch your language. I liked chess. I was a good amateur. During the war, I played games with soldiers overseas. That was enjoyable. Might have helped with morale a bit, too. I admired good writing, even though I was a lousy writer myself. I read a lot of Shakespeare. I would love to have acted in one of his plays. But I don't think I fit the picture of a Shakespearean hero. Bogart as Hamlet? That wouldn't really work. The truth is: I was jealous as hell of people who *could* write. The actor speaks words that someone else has written and makes them glow if he's good. But it starts with the words. Maybe I should have paid more attention in school. But that's another story. My best friends were writers. That's as close as I could get to being one."

"You were always quite hard on yourself, weren't you? There was a story that you used to play the 1937 version of *A Star Is Born* every Christmas day and cry while you were watching it. Someone asked you why you did that and you said 'Because I expected a lot more of myself. And I'm never going to get it.'"

Robert asked, "What did you expect and why did the movie bring out your sorrow?"

"Frederick March played Norman Maine, a big star. He became entranced with Janet Gaynor, who played Esther Blodgett, a naïve farm girl who came to Hollywood to become a movie star. Fortunately, the studio changed her name to Vickie Lester. Maine mentored her, got her good parts, fell in love with her, and married her. But as her career took off, his started down. He was an alcoholic and became seriously depressed as he repeatedly disappointed himself. He reached a point where he could no longer get any parts. He finally committed suicide by walking into the ocean. Vickie went on to win an Academy Award and in accepting it, said 'This is Mrs. Norman Maine.'"

Bogart stopped and Robert thought he might once again weep. But he went on.

"When I looked at Norman Maine, I saw Humphrey Bogart."

He smiled sadly.

Robert said, "But you continued to make pictures, including some great ones, right up to the time—"

"I kicked off," growled Bogart. "With the cigarettes and the booze, I might as well have killed myself, as Maine did. Of course, I didn't know what was going to happen to me when I watched that movie. But maybe I had a feeling, a premonition, especially in the later years, when I got pretty sick. Maybe that's why I saw myself in him, destined to go down. The movie tortured me, and yet I couldn't stop going back to it, year after year."

He shook his head. "I was only fifty-seven when I died. What a waste."

Both were quiet for a while. Finally Bogart spoke up.

"Well, what's next?"

"You made a movie in 1950 called *In A Lonely Place*, playing a washed-up screen writer, Dixon Steele, who is accused of killing a young woman. Tell us about that."

"Steele is asked to turn a novel into a screen play. A hatcheck girl who has read the novel confirms his instinct that it was pretty trashy. On the way from his house, she is murdered, and Steele is accused. His beautiful next-door neighbor, Laurel, provides him an alibi, telling the police that the girl was alone when she left Steele's place. Steele and Laurel fall in love, but the relationship becomes severely strained by the continuing investigation and some doubt of his innocence. His increasingly violent ways, controlling nature, fits of anger, and impatience eventually destroy their relationship even when the truth of his innocence comes out. The movie ends with his future in question, instead of the usual happy ending, or at least one that was more definitive."

"Your biographers have written that Dix Steele was the character closest to Humphrey Bogart of all that you had played. Do you agree with that?"

Bogart glared at him, then relaxed and sighed.

"You really go for the jugular, don't you? Well, I told you I could be nasty. I suppose you could say that I was basically a pretty good guy, but with some really rotten tendencies, just like Steele. I drank too much, which was one of the reasons for my flying off the handle, yelling, and sometimes hitting. I'm not a very big guy and it's a wonder no one ever beat the crap out of me. As I said, I was pretty good at weaseling out of fights if I had to. I guess I'm a coward at heart. Actually, I did get whacked sometimes, including by one of my wives, Mayo Methot. We used to fight a lot. Sometimes it got pretty bloody."

As he talked, Bogart became more and more agitated, recalling the tawdry parts of his life. He seemed overwhelmed by the remembrance of a life with too much violence, too much drinking, too much nastiness, too little patience, too little kindness, and too little courage. Inevitably, the pain of these crushing thoughts pushed from his mind a consciousness of his virtues: the beauty of his acting, his generosity towards those in need of help, his close friendships, and his willingness to admire the talents of others.

Robert saw his torment and allowed him work through his suffering. Shortly, Bogart calmed himself and resumed talking.

"A lot of people blame Hollywood for the bad character of its inhabitants, but I think that's overblown. Let's say that Hollywood brings out the horrid stuff that's already there in people. I was a bad character in school; somewhat better in the Navy because they didn't let you get away with much. So in my case Hollywood was a place where I could indulge my bad tendencies.

"Hollywood likes to make movies about Hollywood. Most of them glorify the place. A few, like *Sunset Boulevard*, dig into the dark side: the mixture of celebrity, greed, indulgence, cruelty, and fake existentialism combined to turn people into caricatures. Those five characteristics are found in great abundance in Hollywood. Come to think of it, you can probably find them in politics, too. Anyway, *In A Lonely Place* was also that kind of picture: exposing the rottenness."

He stopped and looked hard at Robert and grinned. "You had to ask."

Robert nodded. "Yes I did. By the way, what exactly do you mean by fake existentialism?"

"Sartre's view of existentialism was that we humans did not have a personal, caring God to guide us, to tell us what was good and bad and how we should behave. So it was our own responsibility to decide those things for ourselves. But many people interpreted existentialism to mean that, since we were on our own, we could do anything we wanted, with pleasure the only goal. Anything that gave pleasure was fine: sex, drugs, violence, anything."

He grinned again. "Lesson for today."

"Did you consider yourself an existentialist?"

"I may have wanted to. But I think my behavior was more false than real. I was not particularly religious, so I didn't worry about what God thought of me, but I'm not sure my behavior stemmed from that. I don't think I was trying to be existential in any form."

"You've been gone for two centuries. Do you recall having any experiences or thoughts during that absent time? Any memories?"

"The only memories I have are from my life. If I became a soul, an essence, that soul is still floating around somewhere. You people created this body sitting here, so it's not related to my original body, right?"

"No it isn't. We don't really know whether your image, the image that I'm talking to in this cubicle, has any true substance. You're some kind of entity formed from all the information that we fed into our friend MONTY. It's what we call a black box, whose contents are mysterious. We're really not sure how it all works."

Bogart shook his head and chuckled.

"Well, that's pretty much how it was when I was alive and kicking. It doesn't seem to matter whether I existed in any way when I was dead. I'm still dead and the body sitting here isn't me at all, right? We have no idea whether there would be any memory of anything but my life. So I guess that's an unanswerable question."

"It seems that way," said Robert. "Well, Mr. Bogart, I guess it is time to call this very interesting discussion to a halt. Thank you."

Bogart waved as his presence faded away. After he spent some time answering questions from the studio audience, Robert headed off stage.

As usual, he slouched over to the table where the crew had gathered and flopped down in one of the chairs.

Jamie Driscoll was frowning.

"Do you suppose we'll ever find out what does sit in that chair? They all seem so real, but they are not. It's very frustrating."

"Well, we have some pretty bright people trying to solve the black box. It remains to be seen whether they're bright enough to turn the box into a transparent one. I'm not bright enough, and maybe they aren't either."

He got up and stretched.

"With that holy thought, I leave you. Good night."

# CHAPTER 4

One could claim that the *History Lives* series owes its existence at least partly to the world's final war. The waves of terrorism that began in the twentieth century eventually engulfed the world in death, destruction, and despair. A merchant ship, half way across the Atlantic Ocean, exploded, creating the long dreaded mushroom cloud. The ensuing war was devastating, but the fright generated by the explosion penetrated the corridors of power and miraculously stayed the trigger hands poised to unleash further nuclear horror. In the United Nations, voices were raised that echoed those heard after World War II, imploring, demanding that the nations unite in a world federation as the only means of preventing ultimate devastation. A series of long and sometimes rancorous Security Council and General Assembly meetings opened the doors of hope, resulting finally in a world federal government.

The History Lives Foundation benefitted from the relatively relaxed years of peace that followed, one among many scientific, historical, and archeological institutions conducting search expeditions all over the globe, unhampered by danger and fear. Travel was unrestricted and free from other than ordinary problems, such as theft and minor injuries and illnesses. It became possible to take DNA samples from historical figures interred in formerly hostile lands, and many samples had been acquired over a long period after the peace, including a few collected specifically for the foundation and the television series. Cultural and historical information also became readily accessible.

The *History Lives* series, inaugurated in the year 2152 on the National Public Network, relies on a machine, called a Multiple Nuance Translator, which processes all the available information on an interview subject. The machine, MONTY to its numerous friends, resides in an earthquake-proofed basement of a four-story building housing the production studios in downtown San Francisco.

The technological mysteries of MONTY and associated satellite machines made it a choice subject for seminars, speeches, popular magazines, and scientific publications. Theories were proposed, fueled by sober hypotheses, speculation, and wild guesses, all trying to explain the mystery: MONTY's ability to convert to a greater whole the bits of diverse information stuffed into him.

John Sorensen and Rebecca Feldman, principal co-inventors of MONTY, drove south from San Francisco to the Stanford University campus as invited guest speakers at the Twenty-Fifth Annual Conference of the Society for Advanced Scientific Concepts. They were members of the society, but rarely traveled to meetings, which were held in venues around the world and required more time to attend them than either one was usually willing to sacrifice. They were to share the podium for a talk entitled "MONTY's Saga: Challenges in the Development of Historical Re-Creation."

"Rebecca! John! Welcome! This is a rare treat indeed." Moderator Robert Wolf could be better described as a bear than by his last name. Six feet four, shaggy hair with clothes and demeanor to match, he bore down on them as they entered the lecture hall, grabbed one hand of each and vigorously pumped them up and down. Wolf would introduce them to the large group gathering for the session.

"Now. How should I introduce you? In what order, I mean."

"I'll be going first," said John. "With the dull part, a review of what MONTY is all about. Rebecca will be talking about some of the glitches, the things that have gone wrong. That's the fun part. I lost the coin toss."

"That's correct," rejoined Rebecca. "Except there was no coin toss. Arm wrestle. I won."

Wolf looked almost straight down at her five-foot-three, one-hundred-twenty-pound body and nodded his head. "Of course, there can be no doubt of that."

On their way to seats near the front they nodded, shook hands, said hello to various acquaintances.

Robert Wolf arose and stood before the microphone, calling the session to order.

"Ladies and gentleman, welcome. We in science have experienced things going wrong. When a glitch happens, it can be very annoying, and it also can be destructive, even dangerous. Most of us have managed to avoid problems with serious consequences, but they can and do happen. Sometimes, a life is lost. Or lives. But this is part of the nature of scientific and technological research, and it helps to move the process along, leading eventually to truth." He smiled. "And to the next experiment. Time and science march on.

"Today, two of our colleagues have agreed to tell us of their learning experiences with a remarkable device that is at the same time a scientific and technological wonder, the centerpiece of television's most exciting series, and perhaps most fascinating, a profound mystery. I am, of course, talking about MONTY, an acronym for Multiple Nuance Translator, which brings us historical figures, often long gone from this planet, to be interviewed. These encounters give us fresh perspectives on people we thought we knew and understood. Or, people we knew very little about. We have learned some surprising things about them, and we have gained information that may even be quite disturbing. All quite fascinating. But, as our colleagues will tell us, we're not sure how the process works." He smiled again. "However, we're scientists after all. So what's new?"

Robert Wolf turned towards John and Rebecca, gazing up at him from the front row.

"John Sorensen and Rebecca Feldman are co-inventors of MONTY and co-producers of *History Lives*. Dr. Sorensen received a BS from Wisconsin and a PhD from MIT in applied and engineering physics. Ten years ago, he teamed up with Rebecca and several other scientists and engineers to begin the work that led to the development of MONTY, culminating in the history-making *History Lives*.

"Dr. Feldman's schooling began in the Israeli-Palestinian Federation. She graduated from Tel Aviv University, took an MS at Gaza University, and a PhD right here at Stanford. In addition to her position with *History Lives*, she has faculty appointments at UC-San Francisco and Hebrew University of Jerusalem. A remarkable person. A remarkable pair.

"Well, it is time for me to sit down. It gives me a good deal of pleasure to introduce Dr. John Sorensen, who will lead off for their presentation 'MONTY's Saga: Challenges in the Development of Historical Re-creation.'"

"Thank you so much, Dr. Wolf. Ladies and gentleman, Dr. Feldman and I are delighted to be here and hope that our presentations will please you as well. I suppose it may seem a little strange to be talking show business to members of the most elite group of scientists in the world. But of course the science and engineering concepts upon which *History Lives* is based are pretty advanced, so much advanced, as a matter of fact, that not all of them are well understood. A few of them are actually, at this point, black boxes.

"My charge this morning is to describe MONTY's components and their functions, that is, to tell you how he works. I hope I don't have to apologize for our anthropomorphic references, but MONTY is very nearly a person to us. So let us begin. First, I am going to show you the place where MONTY lives."

The lights dimmed. San Francisco, from above, appeared on the screen. The camera approached the city, zooming down to the building that housed the network's studios, and down through the building to the basement area. They were now at the entrance to the home of *History Lives*, looking into a very large room.

"This room is divided into two parts. You are looking at the nonoperative section, which has a lounge-cafe area on the right side and a repair shop and bathrooms on the left. The see-through wall separates this section from MONTY's room towards the back. Let us enter through this door in the center of the wall. MONTY's five principal component units are lined up on the left side, from the front corner to the rear corner. At the center of the back wall sits a replica of the stage cubicle; in front of the cubicle is a control panel. A large information storage unit occupies the far right corner. A conference table takes up most of the remaining space.

The camera swung to the left, revealing a row of five boxlike metal structures. Each of the first four was about two meters long, nearly two meters deep, and slightly more than a meter high. The fifth was similar in two dimensions, but stood over two meters high.

"The first four machines process information fed to them. Each specializes in a particular type of information. Usually, the largest contribution of data about an interview subject comes from historic records, such as letters, photographs and paintings, electronic data, and for very old subjects, archeological artifacts. The information from these materials is fed to the Historical and Archeological Processor that we call Happy. Each type of record is digitized in an appropriate manner, whether starting from alphanumeric symbols, pixel values, or dimensional measurements.

"Genetic information is entered into the DNA and Genetic Processor, known as DeeGee. As you can imagine, sources can be rich in this information or quite sparse, depending mostly upon how long ago the subjects lived on the planet, but also upon how advanced their countries or territories were at the time. Sometimes DNA information can be extracted from very old remains.

"Language information is introduced to Letty, the Language Enhancer and Translator. Relatively modern languages are pretty easy to handle, but obscure languages, or languages with unusual rules of syntax can cause some problems. Rudimentary languages are particularly difficult. Next, our fashion machine, Carlo, performs clothing and accessory replication. Carlo has wide experience with clothing fads and traditions over the ages.

"The final honors belong to Dedino, which can be best described as a powerful black box. Dedino performs deductive and inductive reasoning using feedback loops, eventually disgorging a thinking, talking, mobile almost-person.

"Now, MONTY is a most fascinating creature. He is a little bit like an actor. An actor puts on appropriate clothes: modern apparel, a 17th Century uniform, a bearskin, whatever fits a time and place for the performance. He may learn another language, or simply mimic it to say the lines. He becomes violent, cowardly, loving, simpering, mean, haughty, any characteristic that is written into his role. The actor functions in a time and place that the author describes. In a sense, the actor pretends that he has the genes of another person in his body. And, perhaps as important as all the rest, he interprets the role and performs it differently from the way the author would do it, or another actor. Thus the role played by the actor becomes more than the actor's body and the script and the costume.

"So, like an actor playing a part, or the human brain, or life itself, phenomena that in a sense, defy understanding, MONTY has greater capacities than we would expect from the sum of the inputs. Our project crew calls the phenomenon a miracle. Most of them are well educated and not particularly religious, but no other designation seems adequate. Several advanced and well-funded laboratories have arisen around the planet to attempt to solve the mystery, so far with no success.

"In the early days of the project we were often unable to re-create a single person. Enter the most probable outcome device and a probabilist from India named Shankar Lal. His invention calculates and compares probabilities and identifies the putative subject that comes closest to a theoretical 'correct' subject. The genius of the invention is that it can then analyze the characteristics of the other candidates, identify any that would enhance our best candidate, and eventually narrow the field to one."

He looked over the audience. "Sounds simple, eh?" Then, in company with most of them, he shook his head. "No, it doesn't, and no, we can't explain how it works. In particular, we do not know why the subject becomes completely interactive, able to talk in past, present, and future terms, able to process information that he or she would have known nothing about before showing up in the cubicle. Isaac Newton, for example, likely would be able to understand Einstein's special theory of relativity when provided with a few basic facts.

"I will now digress a bit to put MONTY's usefulness in better perspective. *History Lives* is show business. MONTY's fame is rooted in television. We read about him in the entertainment sections of newspapers. We talk about him over coffee or a drink: "Did you see last night's program?" He is a star. But he is also a highly useful part of contemporary intellectual thought, particularly in history and social sciences.

"MONTY has been replicated for research purposes in several other venues. For example, MONTY serves historians very well, especially for those periods that have yielded limited information. These would include: the Middle Ages; the ancient civilizations of Egypt, Greece, and Rome; also the early civilizations of China, India, and the pre-Columbian period in the Americas. The information about those times and places is limited, and the amount varies considerably from one to another. The Romans have told us more about themselves than older peoples such as the Sumerians, or ancient Meso-American groups. In this research, the goal is not the creation of a person, but rather the multiplication of information beyond what we already have available.

"Social scientists normally study contemporary relationships, but they revel in the opportunity to explore relationships in older times when the structure of societies was very different from ours. They may look at relationships within and between ruling and subservient classes. They may learn why discontent that begins with a little grumbling soon turns to shouting and then to a thundering revolution. They also can unravel the dynamics of feudalism and the evolution of power structures among the landowners, the king, and the parliament in European states.

"And of course, archaeologists and anthropologists may find more meaning, beyond measurement, in the bones, cultural artifacts, and crumbled structures even of prehistoric times. So, if you want to look into the origins of religion, political thought, artistic and musical concepts, the means are there. Essentially, if you are interested in the past, MONTY is your guy."

John glanced at a clock on the wall and declared that it was time to call upon his colleague to present her part of the lecture. He asked that questions and comments wait until the end of her talk. Rebecca came up to the podium and smiled.

"Thank you, John. I believe that my assignment is to tell stories. They will disclose the fact that sometimes MONTY can be a naughty boy. Full disclosure, however, demands that many of the oh-my-goodness events that have befallen MONTY can be laid at the feet of his mentors, from a combination of mistakes, ignorance, and yes, stupidity, on our part. Some of the resulting happenings have been amusing and some of them puzzling and a bit disturbing.

"John has already alluded to the fact that our interviewees seem to be greater than the sum of the inputs that created them. A few of our subjects recognized that they were sentient, but wished to believe that they were also truly alive. They believed that we had brought them back to life, a conceivable concept among people who believe in life after death, albeit in heaven, hell, or the like, and this 'return' was the next logical step. So they wanted us to let them out of the cage. They grasped the idea that the world was not the same as when they departed it, but of course they had no idea how different it could be. Someone from the early twentieth century would certainly suffer mild shock, but a peasant, or even a noble, from the twelfth century might hardly cope at all. Dorothy would no longer be in Kansas or Oz. She would be on an unknown planet in another galaxy.

"So the unexpected enhancement of the subject is a bonus enabling us to obtain information, and also provides wonderful insights on character, personality, and intellectual capacity beyond the known historical evidence. Unfortunately, it also forces us to deal with frustration, unhappiness, and anger erupting from some of our pseudo-persons.

"Therefore, we have a mystery that we hope will not cause us any serious problems. We are confident that the research groups studying the phenomenon will provide us with a greater understanding of pseudo-persons: the development of their abilities, the parameters that limit their activity, and so forth. Let's move on now to the little annoyances, the ones that make you stamp your foot in frustration, or even make you utter words and phrases of dubious respectability.

"Sometimes the language processor does a walkabout, with a number of possible consequences. The first time it happened, the subject came out and answered the first question in gibberish. A little investigation showed it was his original language, sort of. I should mention that it was early in the program's history and we were doing tests in the lab on relatively obscure people. This person was the brother of Cyrus the Great, creator of the immense Persian Empire. After Cyrus had conquered the Medes, his brother, Ariaramnes, married a Mede, and learned her language. Median is a Persian language, but enough different so that we were confused by the hybrid tongue coming out of his mouth. The words were translated to English, but the sentences seemed like gibberish. It was a glitch, but also a learning experience in the richness of developing languages. It was also a problem and we had to do some tinkering to get greater assurance that our subject would materialize speaking a language we, and the audience could understand. This is very helpful to the success of our shows."

"Sometimes, we make some silly mistakes and feel pretty dumb. Once, we used a document that quoted from King Charles I of England. When we activated Charles, he seemed terribly confused in using the language of the quote, as if to say, 'Why am I talking like this? Kings don't talk like this.' After some frantic checking, we discovered that he was using the words of the court jester, Jeffrey Hudson. Kings do not make fun of themselves. Oh my, no, no! After we had a good laugh, the guilty language technician had to buy cookies for a week.

"The multiple outcome is always interesting and can be quite entertaining. For example, five Marie Antoinettes showed up in the cubicle, with different hairdos and different gowns. At first they looked at each other in astonishment, then eyes narrowed, brows furrowed, lips tightened, and nasty remarks and insults flew freely about. The men in our group enjoyed the scene immensely.

"Some of our historical subjects are remembered as cruel, mean, vindictive, and often temperamentally unstable and violent. We have learned from experience that the interview can sometimes be unpleasant for the audience and very hard on our interviewer Robert Delacroix. You may have seen our recent program with Henry the Eighth as a case in point. Some of our subjects may scream obscenities or threats. Occasionally, a guy will throw himself at the walls of the cubicle, trying to get out. They are not holograms; they have some sort of substance, and so these physical actions are noisy and a bit scary.

"A few subjects will repeatedly ask what they're doing there, who we are. Those who realize that they died will react in one of two ways. Some will be frightened and, in panic, say 'I'm dead! How can this be? Is this the afterlife? Will I be punished? What is happening to me?' We really don't know how to explain the situation. We have tried, but sometimes they are almost blind with fear. It is, I assure you, quite distressing. Others will accept the situation, immediately, or after some calming assurances and sympathy.

"Finally, on one occasion, we finished the interview and Robert pressed the off button. The subject disappeared from view and the cubicle went dark. We routinely check Dedino's data storage for confirmation that the information on the subject had returned to its domain. On this occasion, the return was not recorded. The information had disappeared! We did a complete search of the records and could find nothing."

She spread her arms. "What had gone wrong? One possibility is that a momentary power failure occurred just at the time the information was supposed to enter storage. Is that what happened? Maybe, but we don't really know. It is a mystery, and hopefully we will eventually solve it.

"I think I will stop now, before you start looking at your watches. I imagine you have a question or two for us."

She stepped to the side of the podium as Robert Wolf approached.

"Thank you both so much for those excellent presentations. John, if you will come back up here, we'll let you field some questions."

As Rebecca and John sat down on either side of the podium, Wolf looked out into the audience and pointed to a young man near the front, who stood.

"It's hard to understand how all that information could just disappear. MONTY is composed of five units, each of which must have storage capacity." John and Rebecca both nodded. "Is it possible that the data is in one of the other units, or even that it was transferred to another computer's storage?"

"Good question. We did check the other units as well, but could find only the original data appropriate to each unit. There was no enhancement that would have occurred as a result of conversations with the interviewer. We also checked in the main information storage unit that you saw in the tour of the facility during John's presentation.

"The idea that the data escaped to another system would be intriguing, except that MONTY has a dedicated power system all his own. There is no electrical or wireless connection to any other system in the building. Or to any other place anywhere. So for now, we're sticking with a very brief power failure."

A woman in the far right corner raised her hand.

"Dr. Sorensen, could you describe the internal structure of Dedino with a little more detail?"

"Of course. The flow of information from the other units is handled in two ways. One is an inductive reasoning process through which information is accumulated and is intended to enable Dedino to reach a conclusion: namely the identity of a person. The other is a deductive reasoning process, by which the conclusion is tested. We add information from other sources to see if it is consistent with the information already input into his persona, if you will. Along the path to final identity are several series of positive and negative feedback loops. The positive loops expand the concept of who the person is. They flesh out the structure of his or her characteristics. This is called a divergent process. The negative loops remove excess or inconsistent traits. It is known as a convergent process.

As so often happens, the audience became more and more involved and the frequency of raised hands seemed to multiply exponentially. Finally, Robert Wolf arose.

"I wish we could go on, but other voices and other rooms beckon, so I must call a halt to this morning's program. I want to extend our great appreciation to John Sorensen and Rebecca Feldman for a most interesting and enlightening program. Thank you both so much."

The audience applauded vigorously and loudly. John and Rebecca stood and bobbed their heads, looking pleased and almost embarrassed at the same time.

# CHAPTER 5

"Dad!"

The voice on the phone belonged to John Delacroix, twelve years old, senior of Robert's two children with his former wife, Electra.

"Hi, Johnny, what's up? Are we together this weekend?"

"Nooo, Dad, this is a reminder call. Ilya's eleventh birthday is on Sunday and we're having a family party. Mom doesn't know it yet, but I will tell her tonight. Let's say about three o'clock."

Robert chuckled. "Don't you ever get tired of reminding us about important things?"

"Nah. It keeps me on my toes, and provides me with a very nice feeling of superiority. You will be there, right?"

"Of course. See you on Sunday."

In the fifteen years of their marriage, the most positive accomplishments Robert and Electra Delacroix could claim were their two children, who were bright, generous, funny, and sensible. Robert was constantly amazed that they were so normal despite the tumult in their parents' relationship. He sighed, but at the same time, realized that he and Electra must have contributed something useful from their own gene storages.

Both had achieved excellent success in their very different careers. Electra, born in Greece, attended Thessaloniki University, following that with an MD degree at the University of North America (Costa Rica campus). She practiced in San Francisco and was also head of the Department of Nano-invasive Surgery at UCSF, specializing in neurological procedures.

Electra recognized her stunning beauty and mental superiority and was comfortable enough with both so that neither intruded into her relationships with other people, and most of her colleagues and friends did not feel the need to resent her. Robert too was very good looking, and, understanding their equality in that respect, felt quite comfortable with it. In fact he realized that when they had gone out together, the stares were more often directed at him as a recognizable celebrity. But where she felt complete self-confidence, he did not. The need for him to be with girls, and later women, with a sense of their own power, soon was overcome by a need to be assured that he was good enough, for them and for himself. His relationships ended badly.

At first, Electra interpreted his behavior as self-deprecating, a cute boyish modesty. But when the early heat of romance began to waft away in the cooling breeze of real marriage, she saw that Robert believed his own words, that they represented true feelings. He did not accept his own worth, and that lack led his mind towards depression, perhaps only borderline clinical, but certainly disturbing to him, and by extension, to her. For a long time, she tried to act as his counselor. She realized quite early that repeatedly assuring him of her love was not good enough. He knew that she loved him. That knowledge was of no comfort at all. Love was not closely related to self-esteem. It became necessary for her to pretend to be a professional therapist, asking questions and making suggestions in an unemotional way. This technique seemed to work fairly well. Unfortunately, the counseling had no permanent effect, and the passage of time inevitably led to another episode.

Finally, after several years, she recognized two things, that he wasn't getting any better, and that she herself was getting tired to the point of annoyance of their dance of despair. She suggested that he see a real therapist. Robert, of course, recognized his problem, but was unable to take that necessary first step. After fifteen years, Electra decided she could no longer deal with her own distress. Both had tried to insulate the children, but were certain they were absorbing some of their parents' tensions. Electra filed for divorce and won custody of the children.

The divorce was amicable. Robert, a fairly rational man, realized that Electra had tried very hard to help him, and that the situation had become wearing on her. They remained close, and he spent a great deal of time with Johnny and Ilya, including family events such as Ilya's upcoming birthday party.

Shannon, equally beautiful, equally intelligent, and equally strong, differed greatly from Electra in her reaction to Robert's corroding self-absorption. In the two years they had been together, not once did she try to counsel him, buck him up, or in any other way act as his therapist. Her strength of character included robust intolerance towards any one without the ability to cope, particularly if the other person complained about it. Her basic response was: "Get over it." The unspoken response was: "I can deal with anything. So can you."

One of the things she dealt with was the question of affairs. She felt perfectly free to take more than one lover at a time and expected her men to do the same. Her feelings did not get bruised, and she assumed that the male egos would be equally undamaged by knowledge of her other encounters. She did not take into account that her robust self-esteem was not common and that fragile egos abounded in both men and women. Therefore, her respect for the strength of male self-worth was often misplaced.

None of her lovers, past or present, was exempt from her disdain for self-pity, and they reacted in different ways. Two got angry with her and walked away. A few believed they deserved her scorn, and thus wallowed even more in their own misery. Some, of course, felt no need to look inward, and ego disorders never arose.

As a celebrity, Robert also had opportunities, and the presence of other men in her life did not upset him. Robert's problem originated within himself, and surfaced whenever he compared himself to any other person with an outstanding personal résumé. Shannon Remington had the strengths, which originally drew him to her, but once again, he felt he was falling behind and was becoming depressed and restless. As a husband and a father, he was usually able to subordinate his restlessness to the powerful combination of love, loyalty, and duty.

These feelings were no longer controlling. At the same time as he felt himself tiring of Shannon's lack of sympathy, he began again to exhort himself to break the cycle; to rid himself of the need for beauty, brains, and power that had overwhelmed him so many times and sooner or later drove him down the path to despair. Subsequent events meshed nicely with his mood.

After a conference, he left with Meilin, Arne, and Rebecca. Meilin and Arne had a date for dinner and were seriously analyzing the virtues and drawbacks of various restaurant choices, debating type, location, and expense. In San Francisco, this was not an easy process, considering the number of desirable establishments to choose from. The discussion was still going on when they reached Arne's vehicle, and parted company. Robert and Rebecca continued on, smiling and commenting at the vehemence of the exchanges. Suddenly, Robert found himself staring down at her.

"What?"

"Nothing, nothing."

She looked at him quizzically as they reached her vehicle.

"Okay. See you tomorrow."

As he got into his own vehicle, he found that he couldn't remove her from his mind.

"Why Rebecca?" She was not at all good looking. He reviewed her features: slightly bulbous nose, rounded face without clear lines between features, nondescript brown eyes, lips that didn't part when she smiled, hair somewhat unkempt, and quite an uninteresting, short, slightly stooped figure. A very smart woman, yes, quick thinking, and always forthright.

Definitely not his type, yet –

But she is married and a mother, he thought. Shouldn't that be a consideration? If they had an affair and it got out, his image would certainly be damaged. And hers too, he added hastily. Could a relationship with her be permanent? Would they eventually get married? He knew nothing about the state of her marriage.

"Huh," he said aloud. "I'm talking to myself, pretending to be talking to someone else, and justifying my thoughts to a non-existent person."

Although he didn't understand why, he wanted her. His growing sense of lust almost pushed the other thoughts away. During his marriage to Electra, he had rarely succumbed to temptation. The encounters were brief and with women who were not married. This was different and he was unsure how to go about bringing up the subject. During meetings and at other encounters, he found himself looking at her. He tried not to be too obvious and to talk with her in a dignified or light manner; whichever seemed appropriate at the moment. Even so, Rebecca was aware of his attention. She was not entirely sure of its purpose. She knew that she was not pretty, and at first could not believe that he was interested in her, being well acquainted with his usual preferences in women. But gradually she began to doubt her early assessment of his interest. With this developing awareness, she found herself intrigued by if not actually desirous of exploring the situation. The enigmatic encounters occurred regularly until one afternoon at a party given by John Sorensen.

Robert lived in Marin County, and gave the car plenty of time to cross the Golden Gate Bridge, inch its way down 19th Avenue in San Francisco to the 280, and head for Atherton, a posh community just north of Palo Alto. When the car parked, he sat for a few moments, admiring, with a little envy, John's beautiful home on Winchester Drive. He sighed and exited the vehicle. At the front door, he was about to punch the chime button, when the door opened, and Beverly Sorensen stood there grinning.

"Saw you drive up," she said, as they hugged.

She moved off to talk to another guest, and Robert walked into the living room, his eyes immediately searching for Rebecca and finding her standing alone near the fireplace, drink in one hand, a nosh in the other. He zigzagged through the groups towards her.

"Hello, Rebecca."

"Hello Robert," she said gravely, as he glanced around the room.

"I don't see Bernie."

"No, he flew to Chicago yesterday for a conference. Coming back late tonight."

"Ah. Shannon is away too, for a couple of weeks."

There was barely enough emphasis on the last few words to qualify them as a hint.

"Try this goody. Smoked salmon and caviar. It's scrumptious."

Robert asked himself whether this was a rebuff, or simply a delay.

"You're right. It is delicious."

At that moment, Beverly returned.

"Sorry to desert you, Robert. Shannon couldn't make it? One of her big-time meetings?"

He rolled his eyes. "Times five. She's hitting several European capitals, to deal with, as they say 'the highest echelons of power.'"

"Wonderful. Gosh, Robert, I really enjoyed the last few interviews. Henry was fascinating. What an amazing man. He was a great king in many ways, but so cruel. It was unfortunate for his wives that no one knew at that time that the man is responsible for the gender of a baby."

She shook her head. "Men!"

"I can't argue with that."

Before he could say anything more, she interrupted.

"Whoops, excuse me. Some more guests."

Rebecca had gone off to join another group. He didn't want his pursuit of her to be too obvious, so he drifted around the room himself, managing to keep track of her location. When she was between conversations, he joined her again.

"That's a gorgeous outfit, Rebecca. I don't think I've seen it before."

"Thank you. But I've actually had this for a while. It's become one of my favorites."

"Well, I guess we haven't seen enough of each other."

He looked down at her, his face showing a mixture of emotions, longing, anticipation, desire, partially covered with a half smile. Rebecca did not think she could continue pretending to be oblivious to his hints.

"Really? I'm not sure why you say that."

Robert was taken aback by the obvious rebuff. It seemed to her that he figuratively hung his head like a scolded child, although no discernible movement had taken place, other than slightly lowered eyes. He quickly recovered and shrugged.

"I don't know. Probably just my imagination."

They continued with small talk commenting on the crowd, the food, and the house, but eventually moved apart to join other conversational groups. They had one other short meaningless exchange before they and most guests left for their homes.

Rebecca drove back to San Francisco. Her apartment was on the northeast corner of the fourteenth floor and had a grand view of the Golden Gate and Bay Bridges, as well as the soaring downtown buildings. After a light supper, she and the girls watched television, and then went to bed in order of age. Rebecca stood by the east-facing window for a few minutes, gazing at the lights of downtown before climbing into her bed at ten.

Her mind wandered back to the party and quickly focused on the conversation with Robert. She could see his face quite clearly in her mind's eye. At first he appeared simply surprised and taken aback, but then she saw his eyes lower and it suddenly struck her that he looked momentarily like a little boy, not as if he was about to cry but appearing highly vulnerable. The next feeling was completely surprising to her: it was erotic, almost surpassing those she usually experienced.

"Oh, my goodness! Ooh, my goodness! What is happening to me?"

Rebecca was not afraid of her own body and was usually able to understand her feelings very quickly or at least with a little self-analysis. This was different and she didn't know why. Should she try to get rid of the feeling or relax and enjoy it? It certainly was pleasant as well as exciting. Should she do something about it? The need for satisfaction was overwhelming and finally, she gave in.

"I'll analyze it later."

She awoke early the next morning. The extreme erotic feeling had subsided to a residual effect, desire. For Robert Delacroix. Residual it may have been, but it was strong and it told her to indeed have an affair with him. The urgency of what was now a need overcame concern over the obvious: she was married and a mother. She ordinarily took those ties seriously and was amazed at the ease of setting them aside, even for her well-organized mind. She arose from bed, washed up, and called the girls.

She had a morning lecture at UC-San Francisco, so she didn't arrive at the studio until late morning. The first opportunity to talk with Robert arose late in the afternoon. She rounded a corner in the corridor and there he was waiting at the elevator. She stopped.

"Going somewhere?

He smiled hesitantly.

"Just for a walk around the block. I need a little fresh air and exercise."

"That sounds nice. May I walk with you?"

His eyes widened a bit and he looked carefully at her.

"Yes, of course."

Little was said as the elevator rose to ground level. They walked outside and started down the street.

"Robert. This may sound a little strange after yesterday, but I believe I would like to have an affair with you."

He stopped and looked at her even more carefully, then started forward again, breathing a little harder.

"Say something."

"I'm astonished, yes indeed, after yesterday. I—What—But—"

He chuckled and put one hand over his face. Rebecca smiled at him. Another boyish gesture.

"Of course, of course! Wonderful! Forgive me my idiocy!" He took a deep breath. "I humbly and gratefully accept your offer."

"It's really your offer, I believe."

"You're right, certainly. I was not exactly forthright with you, was I? So much for my reputation as a suave, confident, sophisticated, man-about-town."

"Try not to be upset. Shall we make some plans?"

# CHAPTER 6

The lights brightened in the cubicle with no announcement from Robert Delacroix. The image that began to form was smaller than usual. A buzzing murmur went around the audience as people realized that a small boy was seated in the chair. He had straight black hair and blue eyes, and wore a nondescript shirt, short pants, heavy shoes, and long stockings; a schoolboy of the early twentieth century, perhaps thirteen years old.

"Good evening, young man, and welcome. Would you tell us your name?"

"I am Adolf."

"Adolf. And what is your surname?"

"Hitler. I am Adolf Hitler."

He turned and looked out, puzzled, at the audience, as people gasped and exclaimed.

"Where am I? What am I doing here? Who are you?"

"My name is Robert Delacroix. Please don't be alarmed, but you are many years in the future in a different place."

"In Vienna? This is Vienna?'

"No, it is called San Francisco."

"San Francisco. What is that?"

"It is a city in California, in the United States."

"United States? This is America?" He became quite agitated. "How did I get here? Have you stolen me?" He began to weep. "I want my mother!"

Delacroix's heart sank. He had opposed bringing back anyone as a child. They're too vulnerable, he had said. It would be a disaster. But the historians strongly desired to see Hitler in his formative years, in hopes they would discover more about what had started him on the road to evil. That view had prevailed. He took a deep breath.

"Please don't be afraid. No harm will come to you. I only want to ask you a few questions, and then you will be returned to the place where you belong."

The boy continued weeping for a while longer, while Delacroix spoke to him in soothing tones. Finally, the tears subsided. The boy lifted his head. Sullenness replaced the fear and unhappiness.

"Why do you want to ask me questions? What do you accuse me of now?"

"Nothing, I assure you. We are interested in the thoughts of— um— young people."

"*Auf der jungen? Was gipt mit*— " Delacroix fiddled with the controls. "—young people?"

"So, may I ask some questions?"

The boy still looked sullen. He muttered, "Just like my father." His hand fluttered. "Go ahead."

"What would you like to do when you're ready to leave home?"

He muttered again. "I am ready to leave now." Then he lifted his head and spoke more loudly. "I will be a great artist."

"You are studying art in school?"

"No," he snarled. "My father makes me go to the technical school. I hate it. I must learn mathematics and science. There is no art."

"There are no studies that you like?"

"History is good. We are learning about the famous war heroes of Germany. I shall go to Germany one day. Germany is a great country." He smiled and said wistfully, "Perhaps I shall become a leader."

"What kind of leader?"

"Of a country of course. I would be very good leader. I *am* a leader in our games. We used to play Cowboys and Indians. Now we play Boers and Englishmen. I am a Boer. I tell all the other boys what to do and they obey me. But they get tired and I have to find other boys to play with. I lead them too."

"Do they like you?"

"I don't know. What does it matter? I am the leader and they obey me."

"So you wish to be an artist and a leader. How will you do that?"

The boy looked at Robert. His eyes labeled the question as stupid. He spoke slowly to enable Robert to understand.

"A leader does not spend all his time leading. When I am not leading, I will create great art. I like to paint pictures of buildings." He smiled proudly. "They are very good. I shall become a great artist."

After a few more questions, the boy slumped in the chair.

"I am tired. I don't wish to talk any more."

Delacroix nodded. "Very well. I will return you to the place where you belong. Thank you."

The cubicle darkened. Delacroix turned to the audience.

"I beg your indulgence for a few minutes while we make a few changes."

The cubicle re-activated and this time the figure was recognizable: the black hair combed slightly downward on one side and the familiar toothbrush black mustache. He looked to be in his early thirties. Delacroix again turned to the audience.

"As you can see, we are trying out some variations for our presentation this evening. We will spend some time with Hitler as he plans to become Germany's leader. After that we will see him during the early years of World War II. His last appearance will be near the end of the 'thousand year' Third Reich."

Hitler looked at Delacroix and his face, renowned during his time for its seemingly permanent appearance of disapproval and contained anger, frowned even more deeply.

"I have seen you before. What do you want now?"

"Well, you are becoming an important man in Germany with big plans and we thought that people would be interested in them."

Hitler nodded approvingly. His face softened and his body relaxed in the chair.

"So, you wish to know my plans. Yes. Very good. My plans are big, and they are important. What do you wish to know?"

"When we talked before, you were a boy of thirteen, and told us of your ambitions to be an artist and a leader. Do you still think that you will achieve both those goals?"

Hitler frowned. "Of course. I have been painting for years. My paintings are excellent."

"Nearly all your paintings are of landscapes, and particularly buildings. There are hardly any portraits of people. Do you not like to paint people?"

Hitler shrugged. "People are unimportant. Their job is to obey." He raised and spread his arms wide. "Buildings are magnificent, farmhouses as well as castles and churches. They are solid; they last a long time."

"You joined the German Army and became a dispatch rider. It was dangerous work. You were evidently quite brave." Hitler preened and smirked. "You also continued to paint."

"I did watercolors of the devastation. They symbolized the rape of the Fatherland, by the French and the British, and especially by our own government, the November Criminals. And, of course, by the Jews and Marxists. Our country was in chaos. I resolved to destroy them and restore the power and glory of our beloved Fatherland."

"After the war, you became a member of the German Workers Party. You became a leader. Tell us about that."

"Ah, yes. It was a very small party. They had good ideas, but they did not know what to do with those ideas. I changed that. It was a great opportunity for me, to make this pitiful excuse for a political party into a powerful force. Many angry soldiers joined with us. I gave them a political platform, The Twenty Five Points: a greater German Reich, rejection of the Treaty of Versailles, Lebensraum for all Germans, no Jewish citizens, a strong national government, and more. I gave them the swastika, and a new name: the National Socialist Workers Party!"

"The Nazi Party."

"Yes! We will make The Reich a great country again! We will tear the Versailles Treaty to pieces! We will rule! The German people must learn again to obey, and unite under our flag! We will be powerful! The world will know our power! We must have living space! We will teach the Jews a lesson! They will know our power!"

His voice rose and became hoarse with fury. He raised his arms and shook his fists and became almost incoherent. He fomented against Jews, Marxists, and Slavs as enemies of righteousness, of culture, of progress, and of German power and destiny. He went on for nearly five minutes, and then suddenly, stopped. He smiled cunningly and confidentially, and sat back in the chair.

"So you see, there is much for us to do. You have more questions, yes?"

Both Robert Delacroix and the audience were stunned by the mesmerizing power of the short speech. My goodness, he thought to himself, he could keep going like that for an hour and make everybody listening believe that they could do anything.

For the first time, Hitler looked around the cubicle. The technicians had endeavored to create effects in the cubicle that would hint at a duplication of his cell in Landsberg Prison in Munich, where he had been incarcerated after the failed beer hall putsch of 1923. Hitler's artist's eye had recognized the attempt. He looked around suspiciously.

"What is this? Have you drugged me? Where is Hess?"

He stared through the cubicle wall at Delacroix. "Who are you? Why are you sitting there? Who are those people?" He pounded the chair arm furiously. His voice rose almost to hysteria.

"You are Marxists! You are Jews! You have taken over! When did this happen? I demand an answer!" He thrust himself out of the chair and pounded both hands on the cubicle wall. "Answer me!" he screamed. "Answer me!"

"Please Mr. Hitler, calm down. There has been no revolution. You are not drugged. You have not been kidnapped. This may be hard for you to believe, but you are in the future. You are in a studio in San Francisco, in the United States. I am Robert Delacroix, and I have been asking you questions."

"Impossible." He sat down. "This is not happening. This is a dream. It is a bad dream."

Delacroix smiled. "I suppose you could look at it that way."

"When will it be over?"

"Soon. What have you been doing to pass the time?"

"I do not 'pass the time.' Hess comes in every day. He writes down what I say about my life, my struggles against the Marxists and the Jews, and especially the criminals who gave away our glorious Germany to the French and the British. Germany is in ruins. It is a democracy, a republic. It is contemptible. I am the only one who understands, who truly understands what they have done, and what we must do to rescue the Fatherland from the weaklings who have allowed this to happen. I must rescue our country."

"You tried that in the beer hall. It didn't work. You ended up here, in jail."

"I have been thinking about that. It was a mistake. It was too soon for a revolution. People weren't ready. They want democracy and elections. Good. I will be elected. I will take over, democratically. I can wait. Things will get worse and then the people will want me. I will lead them out of the wilderness."

"Like Moses."

"The Jew Moses. We will deal with that. The Nazi Party will be triumphant."

"I find it hard to understand why you hate Jews so much. Your personal relationship with Jews has been beneficial to you. The doctor who took care of your mother was Jewish, and you thanked him profusely for that. You said that you would be grateful to him forever. You were awarded the Iron Cross during World War I. It was recommended by a lieutenant who was Jewish. Jews bought most of your paintings in Vienna. You had good personal relationships with many Jews. How do you explain all of that?"

Hitler remained silent for a moment. His reply was curt and delivered at first without expression.

"I have no control over the purchase of my paintings. I received the Iron Cross for bravery. The Lieutenant was not stupid. He knew I deserved it. Dr. Bloch was a saint. He was an—exception. I have nothing more to say about it."

Robert watched Hitler's face at the last. What did it show? Shame? Embarrassment? Pain? The expression was fleeting. We'll never know, he thought. He resumed his questions.

"What will the Sturmabteilung do, the storm troopers?"

"They will make sure that the elections go the right way. Nothing will stand in our way."

"They are thugs and ruffians. Is this the face of your party?"

"Evidently you too are a victim of the softness of democracy. I am trying to save Germany from that. I must be hard and unrelenting. Some heads will be broken."

"Well, thank you for talking to me. We will see what history has in store."

Hitler gazed at Delacroix. "A thousand years of history will serve us."

As Hitler's image faded, Delacroix turned back to the audience.

"Now we will talk to Hitler early in the war. The march to conquest, called Blitzkrieg, had been extraordinarily successful. He seemed unstoppable. Hitler was a world figure, viewed with fear, anger, defiance, and by some, with admiration. It is June 1941."

Hitler materialized in the cubicle. He turned his head towards Delacroix. A smile of recognition, cold, triumphant, barely masked the evil, arrogant mind behind it.

"I imagine you have more questions to ask. You may do so."

Robert ability to remain impassive required more effort than he was used to.

"You have traveled a long hard road since Landsberg. You decided the best way to achieve power was through the ballot box, after the disaster of the Beer Hall Putsch. You reorganized the Nazi Party into two subgroups: one to build up your political power and the other to organize as a government in waiting. But then there was a setback; the economy got better and people weren't so desperate and angry anymore."

Another cold smile. "I knew the so-called prosperity wouldn't last. I remained patient. My time was coming. And I was right." He smiled again. "And your country, America, helped, with a great depression that spread all over the world. It was our time. Our party revived. There were elections to the Reichstag. We won a few seats. In 1930 we won 107 seats. In 1932, I ran for president and got 30% of the votes. I was nearly there."

"But then the SA went crazy. They roamed the streets, fighting, killing, looting. They had a song: 'Blood must flow, blood must flow! Let's smash it up! That goddamned Jewish republic!' It was terrible."

"We were fighting the Communists. It was necessary," Hitler snarled angrily.

"Necessary. Indeed. Let's move on," said Robert. "You became Chancellor in 1933, and President in 1934, when Hindenburg died. Actually, you became dictator; you were The Führer. You annexed Austria in 1938, and invaded the Sudetenland to 'protect' Germans living there, Germans who conveniently claimed they were in danger from Czechoslovakia. Then you invaded Poland and started a world war. Then you began to kill Jews, and cemented your reputation as one of the worst mass murderers in human history."

As Robert spoke, his face transformed, showing an extraordinary mixture of anger and grief. He stared at Hitler, who stared back, radiating fury. It seemed that the fury strangled his ability to speak, to scream at Robert. For a few moments, the silence on the stage and in the cubicle was matched in the studio audience.

Then Robert took a deep breath and resumed the interview.

"The war seems to be going well for you. France, The Netherlands, Belgium, Denmark, and Norway have fallen as well as Czechoslovakia, most of Poland, and some of the Balkan states. And now, instead of crossing the Channel into England, you have invaded Russia. Do you think that was wise?"

Hitler snorted contemptuously.

"What do you mean? They are an inferior race. They will fall quickly."

"What will you do if you are still fighting when winter comes?"

"That is nonsense. We will be in Moscow in September, or October. Then we will invade England."

He stopped and stared at Robert suspiciously.

"You are from the future. Do you claim we will fight them in winter?"

"If so, what will you do? Retreat? Surrender?"

Hitler stormed from the chair, eyes ablaze.

"How dare you? The Wermacht is the greatest army in history and I am the greatest leader," he screamed. "We will trample them into the snow. White will turn red. Your history books lie. We will conquer them. Then we will cross the Channel and beat the English. And then— " He sat down and sneered. "You will see. A thousand year Reich. You will see." A frosty smile. "You will see."

Once again the image began to dissolve and Robert turned to the audience.

"A thousand years. We know that didn't happen. Our final segment is coming up in a few minutes. You will see a far different Hitler.

Unlike the previous interviews, the subject did not appear in idealized form, free of earthly ills that could distract from the interview itself. This Hitler looked old, sick, and depressed, a victim of the events he had set in motion, overwhelmed by the final results of his own folly and megalomania.

"Mr. Hitler." Delacroix's legendary affability had not returned. His face was tightly set, reflecting a grim resolution to confront the man who had unleashed such misery and devastation, first on a continent, then on the world itself, the effects of which continue to reverberate, although at a lessening rate, with the passage of time. The neo-Nazis still exist and the swastika still flies in places.

"I am the Führer, the Supreme Leader. You will address me properly."

"You are Führer of a bunker. You attacked Soviet Russia and earned the same disaster as Napoleon. You learned nothing from history. The Russians are now in Berlin, the Americans and British are at the River Elbe. They are closing in and Germany is close to surrender."

"Surrender. You speak nonsense. My rockets will destroy England. We will invade. *They* will surrender. I have given the orders."

"No one is listening. Even now the generals are contacting the Allies. You are almost alone. Only Eva Braun and Goebbels and his family are here with you. Your days of glory are in the past."

Suddenly Hitler's demeanor changed. Thoughts of the past smothered his depression and brightened his face. He raised his finger and pumped his arm.

"I rescued Germany. I made it a great country again, exactly as I saw it, as I knew it. I conquered France. I conquered Europe. I would have conquered England, if Goering and his Luftwaffe had done the job, as I ordered. And I would have conquered Russia. My stupid, cowardly generals did not know how to conduct a war."

A sly smile appeared.

"They could have stopped me, you know. Germany had nothing, nothing. I had to rebuild everything. But they were afraid of me. I took Austria; I took the Ruhr; I took the Sudetenland. 'Those people are really German,' *they* said. 'It was proper that Mr. Hitler should have them.' It *was* proper, but you do not admit that to the enemy. This gave me time to make Germany strong. And then I conquered them."

"You aren't listening. You did not conquer Russia because you made serious mistakes."

"What mistakes? *I* made no mistakes."

"The most important error was to invade Russia in the first place. You forgot about Napoleon and made the same mistake he did. Then you underestimated the Russians and their ability to fight for their country. It took too long and the winter came and your troops had no proper clothing. Your supply lines became too long. You left them nothing to fight with and then you blamed them. But it was your fault.

"Then you forgot your main goal and diverted people and energy and time to murder. Your hatred for Jews was an obsession that helped you lose the war. It was evil and stupid. You also forgot that no one had invaded England since 1066, since William the Conqueror. You say you loved history, but it was only German history. You ignored other histories. Your other big mistake was declaring war on the United States."

"I had an agreement with Japan."

"That was the only treaty you ever honored and it was the wrong one."

Delacroix leaned back in his chair, a little surprised at himself. Hitler had become quiet. He stared at Delacroix, uncertainty in his eyes.

"You said this is the future. You know what will happen, after— after this?"

"Yes, I do."

"What will happen to Germany? Another Versailles? They will dishonor us again?"

"No. Germany will surrender unconditionally. It will be divided into four administrative units: American, British, French, and Russian. The western sections will join together as the Federal Republic of Germany, a parliamentary democracy. The Russian section will become a Soviet satellite state, the German Democratic Republic."

"A democratic joke and a Marxist abomination," Hitler sneered.

"The period after the end of the war will pit the Soviet Union and its allies and satellites against the United States and its allies in a Cold War that will last until 1991. The Soviet Prime Minister, Mikhail Gorbachev, will take steps that have unintended consequences, which lead to his regime's downfall. In 1990, Germany will be reunited, as a democracy, after the Soviet Union's collapse. It will become one of most important countries in Western Europe, *without* conquering any other country. And finally, all the countries of Europe will unite as the European Federation, a regional super-country, and part of a world federal government. This is what we have now."

"The whole world." Hitler licked his lips. "This is what I wanted. This is what I will rule. I must stay here. I will rule here now."

"Mr. Hitler. Listen closely. You are not really here. You died in the bunker in 1945. You killed yourself. Eva Braun killed herself. Joseph and Magda Goebbels killed themselves, after they murdered their six children. You are the last person in the history of mankind who would rule in this world. When I press this button, you will disappear, forever. You will never return."

The cubicle darkened and emptied of all traces of Hitler and his stage set. As Robert turned towards the studio audience, they all rose, cheering, clapping, and stamping their feet. Robert succumbed to a rare rush of redness to his grinning face.

"Very unprofessional," he murmured. It did feel wonderful. The tension of dislike for the hated guest was carried away in the joyous noise.

# CHAPTER 7

For the first two weeks, Rebecca and Robert were able to manage only an hour or two together at odd times, so that the relationship felt rushed, consisting of sex and an occasional cocktail or cup of coffee. It seemed that everything was gulped down, even the love making, which was physically satisfying but emotionally disappointing. They were frustrated.

One morning, Rebecca came to work relatively early, having no lectures that day. After a decent interval, she picked up some papers at random from her desk and walked to Robert's office and peeked in.

"Got a minute, Robert?"

"Of course. Come in."

She plopped down in front of his desk, eyes shining, and a large smile on her face.

"Tell me you're free this weekend."

"As a matter of fact, I am. Is that of any importance?" A sly smile.

"Well. Sarah's class is going on an excursion to New Disneyland. They are leaving late Friday afternoon on the SuperTrain and returning Sunday afternoon. Each child is allowed one guest and Sarah invited Rachel. And Bernie has agreed to be one of the chaperones."

She sat back. Her smile turned into a silly grin, which was matched by

Robert's.

"Ooh boy. At last."

"I think the best place is our apartment. A little more anonymous, I believe. I'll call you when the coast is clear, and we'll have two nights and almost two days together."

She shivered her body like a little girl. Robert chuckled and wondered how many people had seen this Rebecca, instead of the serious, renowned genius of *History Lives*. Not very many, he guessed and reveled in his great luck. They talked a while longer and she got up to leave. Just outside his door, she leaned in.

"I think that will work out nicely. Thanks Robert. See you later."

She returned to her office. Robert sat for a minute; happy, happy, happy.

"I wonder how long I'll feel like this."

He shoved the thought aside and returned to work.

* * *

Robert had just finished packing a small bag with weekend essentials when the phone rang.

"All clear. Come over."

"I'm on my way."

Robert had a little time to look around the apartment before Rebecca grabbed his hand and pulled him into her bedroom. The rooms that he could see were large and airy with high ceilings. He caught a glimpse of the feature room of the house, a large corner living room with enormous windows facing north and east. Looking out, all he could see was sky, a darkening blue with a few clouds. The views must be magnificent, he thought, and made a mental note to stand there for some time and absorb as much as he could. But not now. Rebecca's urgency quickly communicated itself to him.

The bed was already turned down. He snickered.

"Just like a hotel room. All you need is a chocolate mint on the pillow."

"Maybe tomorrow. Get in."

They made love quickly, urgently, and with shared satisfaction.

"Well, we're certainly well matched in that activity, wouldn't you say?"

"Oh yes," he said, "Very well matched indeed. It was wonderful."

They relaxed and enjoyed their nearness for a while.

"I'm hungry. Let's have a little supper."

The kitchen was fairly large, with a center-cooking island. She tapped the door of the refrigeration compartment. It slid slowly open.

"Bacon and eggs suit you."

"Sure. I guess you don't keep kosher."

"No." She thought a moment. "I seem to recall a great grandmother in Israel who did, but I can't think of anyone else in either family. Since the peace settlement, extreme orthodoxy in our religion has been fading away. As a matter of fact, it seems that extremism in all religions began to disappear after the world government came into being. Want a salad too?"

"Yes, that would be terrific." He marveled at her ability to switch faces, moods, or thoughts at will.

As they sat at the table eating and drinking wine, she said, "You know, you're so recognizable, we can't go out to eat or do anything else outside this apartment." She cocked her head and grinned at him. "Do you think you can handle being cooped up here with me for a whole weekend?"

"I think I can manage as long as I'm kept busy with games and puzzles and books with conversations and pictures."

"If Alice had those, she might never have gone to Wonderland."

He smiled. "I'm in Wonderland."

Robert woke up at seven o'clock on Saturday morning. He lay in bed for a few minutes, gazing at the sleeping Rebecca, wondering who she was. There seemed to be so many Rebeccas tucked into that small body. Which was the real one? They're all real, of course. Don't ask stupid questions. He sighed. Would he be able to keep up? How long is this going to last? Am I in over my head? He chuckled. What is the Meaning of Life? Then he remembered the promise to himself and quietly got out of the bed and went into the living room. The sun was just the other side of the horizon and it was already quite light.

He could see Columbus Avenue slanting down through the north-south and east-west streets as if a giant rogue steamroller had chosen its own route, smashing everything in its way. There was Coit Tower, still standing after all these years and a few fix-up jobs. To the right stood the latest incarnation of the Bay Bridge. And way over to the right, he could see the newest baseball park, named Giants Stadium at last, in honor of the team that had stayed so many years, winning its share of National League pennants and a few World Series championships, as well.

He moved to the north-facing window. Far to the left, the other great bridge spanned the Golden Gate, the tops of its towers surrounded by wisps of fog. Beyond the bridge, he saw Marin County on the left and the northern east bay cities on the right, framing San Pablo Bay. Magnificent. The view was really special at this hour of the day. He could see the shadow length changing as the sun climbed above the eastern horizon.

"Good morning."

She stood there, smiling, wearing a short nightgown, not particularly revealing, but quite suggestive.

"Can I persuade you to come back to bed for a little while?"

"Are you insatiable?"

"No, are you satiated?"

He had to admit that he was not.

They enjoyed another half hour together and then got up for breakfast.

"Do you like a big breakfast, Robert?"

"No. Just some juice, toast, and coffee."

"Good, that's all I ever eat."

After breakfast, they poured a last cup of coffee and went to the living room.

"The view from here is wonderful," said Robert. "I don't think I would ever tire of it."

"It is and I don't. And it changes through the day, with the light and the fog. And of course, at night, it's different. When it rains it's different.

It changes with the seasons. Sometimes, when I stand at the window looking out, while I'm trying to think a problem through, it can be quite distracting. So I have to go to my desk. The chair is low enough so that I can see only the sky. Then I can concentrate, which normally I can do quite well, without that particular distraction."

They spent a good part of the morning and afternoon in the room, reading, listening to music, mostly conversing. Robert found himself listening more than talking. He was aware of his own intelligence and breadth of knowledge, and rather proud of it, but was nearly overwhelmed by the force of her intellect that bathed him in wave after wave of knowledge, of reasoning power, of interest in a seemingly unending series of subjects. He was dazzled and nearly overwhelmed. Lunch was a respite for him as much as a response to hunger.

Late in the afternoon, during a flagging of the conversation, Robert was feeling restless.

"You know, we could take a drive, perhaps find a place to walk around a bit, where there aren't any people."

"Good idea. Where shall we go?"

"Let's go south on Highway 1. There are some beaches down there that are pretty quiet, especially this time of year."

"Okay. We'll take my vehicle, so we don't have to go out in the street."

In the basement garage, she handed him the starter card.

"You be the pilot. You probably know the area better than I do."

She commanded the doors to open. In the vehicle, she turned voice control over to him. They headed west, turned south on the Great Highway and Skyline Freeway, connecting with Highway 1 near Daly City. Patches of fog were starting to form at the ocean as they cruised south, passing Pacifica and Half Moon Bay. Robert slowed the vehicle a bit and started to look for a good place to stop. The highway converged towards the ocean's edge and they saw a beach that seemed deserted. He stopped the vehicle and they got out and walked close to the water's edge.

"The ocean is pretty quiet," said Rebecca.

Those were the last words spoken for a while as they walked slowly along the beach. He viewed in his mind the experiences with Rebecca during the last month. Why is she doing this? Why is she doing it with *me*? Has she had affairs before this? Is her marriage happy? She has said literally nothing that would answer these questions. Should I ask? That would probably be really dumb. Enjoy it while it lasts. How long *will* it last? Will she dump me? Will I dump her? Will we just agree to break up?

What do I know about her that I didn't know before? She certainly has been a great partner between the sheets. Her intelligence is literally breathtaking. She knows. Whatever the subject, she knows. He began to fantasize. Some day she will die. Some time after that *she* will be a subject on *History Lives*. By that time, the machines will be able to plumb her brain and reveal the wonders inside. And in the cubicle, she will continue to learn just like their present subjects. The sum of all human knowledge will be in the cubicle with her resurrection, and the Robert Delacroix of the time. Am I getting carried away here? Probably. He shrugged. So what?

What else? A strong woman, just like all the others. Oh, dear. Again. But so far at least, he didn't feel overwhelmed, inadequate. Why not? He sighed inwardly. I suppose it will come soon enough. Don't be any more stupid than necessary, Robert. Enjoy the journey.

The fact that she is not good looking doesn't seem to bother him. Why is that? Could it be that he is actually improving in that one respect? Will wonders never cease? Well, maybe. Give it some time. No jumping to conclusions. Not yet. He looked down at her.

"What are you thinking about, Rebecca? Solving a difficult problem?"

She snorted.

"Hardly. I was thinking that it's getting late and I need to plan dinner."

"That's all. No deep thoughts about the universe."

"Robert! What's the matter with you? What in the world are *you* thinking about?"

He put up his hands.

"Sorry. Just a train of thought. I agree. Planning dinner is a good idea."

They reversed course, returned to the vehicle, and rode back to San Francisco.

Rebecca's dinner plan worked very well. They had a simple but elegant meal of butterhead lettuce salad, sautéed chicken tenders, and asparagus, followed by strawberries and cream.

For the rest of the evening, they watched the televiewer and talked, until time for a final session of lovemaking.

Sunday morning, Robert again arose early to watch the sunrise over the eastern and northern parts of the city.

"I would never get tired of this," he said.

"Talking to yourself, Robert?"

"Of course. I do it all the time."

She wrapped her arms around his waist. "It is beautiful. It's really lovely to stand here at different parts of the day, as the light changes direction and as the fog comes in and out."

They had their usual breakfasts, and were sipping a last cup of coffee.

"Well," said Rebecca. "I think this lovely weekend is drawing to a close for us."

"When will they be returning?"

"I'm not sure, but I think you should be leaving before too long. We don't want to be surprised."

He remained silent for a while.

"I'm curious how you deal with this in your mind."

She smiled.

"I'm a very strange person, I guess. I live in several different worlds. When I'm in one, it's as if the others don't exist. When I'm working, that's my world, but if I get a phone call from Bernie or one of the girls, I move to their world. Whatever joy or regret I feel about some part of my life is felt when I'm in that particular world, not while I'm in another."

"I've heard about concentration, but that's extraordinary."

"Weird, you mean."

"I'm not like that at all. I frequently think about other things while

I'm doing something. I have to continually pull myself back to the here and now. Don't you ever get distracted?"

"Sure, but not often. The view from my windows, as I mentioned. It's actually something of a treat to let my brain wander. Anyway, once I had made up mind that I wanted an affair with you, I created a new world with you in it, and here we are."

"I'm not sure that I should ask this, but why did you decide to accept my bashful boy offer?"

Rebecca had felt an increasing awareness of Robert's fragile ego, normally well concealed beneath his stunning good looks and celebrity status and behavior. He also concealed that fragility by apparently mocking it and himself. His question required a careful answer, but a relatively honest one. She smiled at him.

"Sometimes a man shows almost a mysterious quality that triggers an emotional reaction in a woman. I'm not able to describe it, but it touched me, hit me pretty hard actually. As I said, here we are. I don't think either of us can know how long it will last."

"And we'll enjoy it while we can."

"Exactly."

He nodded and aroused himself.

"Well, I'll get my things together and leave, so you can tidy up."

# CHAPTER 8

On January 30, 1933, Adolf Hitler was selected as Chancellor of Germany and on March 4, 1933, Franklin Delano Roosevelt was inaugurated as President of the United States of America. Roosevelt died on April 12, 1945. Hitler died on April 30, 1945. Two remarkable men shared the world stage for the same instant, a phenomenon unique in human history, which may never happen again. The explosive events of that instant would reverberate through time.

They shared nothing else. Hitler earned almost universal loathing, then and now, and died an ignoble, some would say a coward's, death, after a failed world conquest that cost millions of lives and dreadful suffering. Roosevelt was revered during his lifetime and afterwards, for leading his country out of a debilitating depression, and leading the world in defeating Hitler and his blood spattered allies. He is considered one of the greatest American presidents and world leaders.

Robert Delacroix was nervous, and the short trial run with FDR did little to help. The late President had been gracious and friendly, but the fluttering in Robert's stomach remained as he prepared for the on-air interview. Part of his nervousness originated in the uncertainty he would face as with all the interviews with political figures: How would each react to probing questions regarding a controversial decision or personal behavior? Before the question was asked, there was no way to know whether the subject would answer the question in a straightforward manner or would erupt in anger. Robert did not enjoy being yelled at or threatened, even by a non-person under confinement. Maybe he was too sensitive. He smiled and relaxed; the experience, all in all, would certainly be enjoyable.

He strode out on the stage, past the darkened cubicle, to the applause of the studio audience, his face split by a broad smile.

"Good evening, ladies and gentlemen. We are about to meet another remarkable person from the past, this time from American history. He was president of the United States during very difficult times, a great depression followed by a great war. Ladies and gentlemen, Franklin Delano Roosevelt. FDR!"

The figure materializing in the cubicle seemed to emerge from the history books that each person in the audience had studied in school: handsome head thrown back, chin held high, jaunty, confident. All that was missing was the up-tilted trademark cigarette holder. The applause was deafening.

"Welcome, Mr. President. My name is Robert Delacroix. May I explain to you the circumstances of your appearance on this stage at this time? The year is 2154."

President Roosevelt was startled at the date, but nodded his head in assent.

"Please do."

At the conclusion of the explanation, Delacroix asked him how he felt.

"Remarkable. Remarkably well. My legs seem normal. Do they work? Can I walk?"

"Try them, sir."

The President slowly, tentatively, stood up. A brilliant joyous smile broke over his face and in response, the audience, some smiling, some in tears, applauded equally joyously.

"Well Mr. Delacroix, you appear to have rendered something almost incomprehensible. Have you replaced God?"

"No sir. Your appearance is a product of science and engineering. Nothing supernatural, I assure you." He paused as the President took a few steps and reseated himself.

"And now, sir, may I ask you some questions?"

"Of course."

"We often consider good health necessary for a productive life. Yet history has sometimes shown us otherwise. You were the only US president with a permanent physical disability. It had to be very difficult for you, but you were a great president, leading the country through a terrible depression and then a monstrous world war. How did you manage so well?"

The President's eyes sparkled a bit. "I didn't manage as well as it might have seemed. Moving around and traveling was very difficult, but I resolved to resist giving in to the pain and the frustration of being unable to take care of myself. I was usually alone, and I could let my hair down and feel righteously sorry for myself. But at the same time I kept reminding myself that many others suffered more than I did, both in the war and during the depression. In the war, mothers and wives lost their loved ones. So many young men were maimed. I sometimes felt like crying for them. Before that, during the depression, people lost their jobs, their homes, and often their self-respect. I wished I could do more. Ironically, we were rescued from the misery of the depression by the war. Then we all felt a national sense of purpose, a renewed dedication that carried us through."

"Do you think that your physical difficulties made you a better president?"

"I suppose that's possible. I was a rich and somewhat spoiled young man. Not quite a playboy, but uncomfortably close, I'm afraid. Getting into politics and public service was helpful. It gave me a greater appreciation of life outside of privilege. And I was determined to live a useful life despite losing the use of my legs."

"You managed to keep that from becoming a big issue in your political life."

"Yes. I am sure that many people in the country knew of it, but I tried, not to hide it, but to keep it from becoming too obtrusive. And I think that people appreciated that I kept going despite the handicap. I always believed that scientists would find a cure, but it was not to be."

"I'd like to talk to you about some of the decisions you made during your presidency."

Roosevelt grinned. "You mean you want me to admit that I had been wrong from time to time. True enough. I guess I can admit to that, since I am obviously beyond criticism and having to deal with consequences."

"I am more interested in your thinking as you made decisions, particularly when they were controversial. For example, in 1937, you tried to get Congress to increase the number of court judges, especially in the Supreme Court, stirring up quite a hornet's nest. It seemed that you were quite surprised at the reaction."

"Well, I had hoped I would be able to appoint some younger men to the court, people who would be more aware of the country's needs. Things were better than in 1933, but we were still mired in the depression, people were still out of work, and we had to continue to help them. It was an obligation of government. Unfortunately, people with a conservative turn of mind are reluctant to accept new ways of doing things and will dig their heels into the ground. If they have their way, nothing will get done.

"At that time, the Supreme Court had invalidated important parts of the National Recovery Act and the Agricultural Adjustment Act, both of which were designed to get businesses started and people back to work. I was very much concerned that challenges to the National Labor Relations Act, Social Security, and the Tennessee Valley Authority would destroy the very fabric of the New Deal. We would be set back to the early days of the depression.

"In retrospect, I think it is fair to say that politically it was not my best decision. I was surprised; perhaps I was naïve. We lost some momentum for the New Deal, but eventually I was able to appoint several very good people to the Court, so we got some better legislation."

The President sighed.

"Much of what we tried to do was achieved when we were forced to go to war. It was an effective way to end the depression, but not one that I would choose."

"Shall we talk about the war now?"

"Yes."

"First, why was it an effective way to end the depression?"

"In 1933, we believed that it was essential to get people working again. That was the only way to get the country back on its feet. The government had to spend money to start the process. We did both with the programs that we initiated. And it worked. People earned money, bought things again, and paid taxes. Businesses began to revive. By 1937, we had reduced unemployment from 25% to 17%. But then Congress turned conservative, reduced the scope of the programs, and we went down hill again, until we got into the war. Then the government spent money again to support the necessary war demands. New and converted industries developed to construct equipment, airplanes, tanks, uniforms, and weapons necessary to conduct the war. It was the largest war in history and demanded maximum effort from everybody. Not incidentally, unemployment went down to 1.2%."

Robert changed the subject slightly.

"When the United States entered the war after the attack on Pearl Harbor, there was a great deal of strong feeling against Imperial Japan and against Japanese people in the United States. One of the consequences of that was your decision to intern many thousands of both first and second generation Japanese people including those who were American citizens. At the time nearly everybody believed that it was the right thing to do, but in the years since then, most people have thought it was much too widely applied, not nearly selective enough to choose people who were a genuine threat to security."

"We believed that it had to be done, that our west coast was particularly vulnerable, and that there was no time to be selective. They had attacked us and everybody was very angry. We—You know, this is very strange. I seem to be—my mind seems to be in the future. I seem to have hindsight. Is that possible? We were quite wrong! Why have I suddenly realized that? Can you tell me what has happened?"

Robert was faced with a decision. They had not publicized widely the strange ability of their interviewees to think broadly and constructively while in the booth. It was a phenomenon that no one yet understood, a profound puzzle. What should he say?

He cleared his throat. "Well, Mr. President, we have discovered that possibly the same capability of MONTY that has given you good health has also enhanced your capacity for reviewing your own thoughts and ideas. We have learned some things about this phenomenon and are continuing to study it."

"Remarkable. Will I have second thoughts about everything? My goodness."

He shook his head. "Well, to get back to your inquiry. It seemed at the time that a general roundup had to be done, and quickly. But we should have reviewed the entire situation. We should have protected them, their land, and their property, and we should have made restitution where possible."

"From reading the accounts written during that time, much of the anger was racial hatred, unlike the feeling against the Germans and Italians. The pro-Hitler German-American Bund was very active on the east coast before the war, especially in New York City. How did people react to them?"

"In the years before the war, there was a strong isolationist feeling in the country, a belief that the happenings in Europe were none of our business. Also many people admired what Germany had become under Hitler: strong, patriotic, and proud, with a sense of order. It was an admiration in ignorance of the things he was doing; some people simply denied the horrid facts. The same reasoning or lack of it was applied to the Bund. But you are right. There was no racial feeling as such, but most people in the country *did* strongly dislike the Nazis. Some Italians and Germans suspected of disloyalty were relocated away from the coastal areas."

He stopped and thought for a moment.

"I am sure you are aware that America's dealings with racial and religious minorities was far from exemplary: we had slavery and then Jim Crow, treated the Indians horribly, we were prejudiced against Jews and Chinese and Japanese workers, and in earlier years against the Irish immigrants. It was not a heritage to be proud of. Blind unreasoning prejudice." He stopped and thought for a moment. "Perhaps it's a fault of the human race as a whole."

There was a silence as both reflected on those thoughts. Finally, Delacroix roused himself.

"Perhaps we should move on."

"Yes, I don't think we will solve that problem just now."

"Let's go back to our earlier discussion. The United States lived through two overlapping disasters between 1929 and 1945, as did nearly all of the rest of the world. That was unique in history. The war was the first true world war; nearly every country on earth participated in some manner. For the United States, the war began officially on December 7, 1941. But the US became involved several years earlier, taking many different steps to prepare for war. Please tell us about that."

The President was silent for a moment, apparently gathering his thoughts.

"I think we can say that the war began for us as early as 1937, when Imperial Japan invaded China. It also became apparent that Hitler's aggressiveness would not stop with his absorption of Austria. But the general feeling in the country held that the events in Europe were less our business than the ambitions of Japan in Asia and the Pacific, areas where we had many interests. In consequence of that thinking, we began building long-range submarines for a possible blockade of Japan. By 1939, it was obvious that the war in Europe could not be ignored. We had to find ways to help the Allies militarily, without actually going to war, because of the strong isolationist feelings, in Congress and among our citizens."

"It must have been difficult for you to maneuver around those obstacles."

"Indeed. But, it became easier as the war worsened for the Allies. Hitler invaded Denmark, Norway, the Netherlands, Belgium, Luxembourg, and, most frightening, France. He truly intended to conquer the world, to create his Thousand Year Reich. So we increased our military spending and aid to Britain. We sent fifty destroyers to Britain in exchange for bases in the Caribbean. Despite opposing some of our proposals, Congress did pass a bill for our first peacetime draft."

"And then you ran for an unprecedented third term."

"Yes. And before you ask me the question, we did indulge in some political shenanigans at the party's convention, feeling that it was important to have continuity in the presidency. The people evidently felt the same, as we won with 55% of the vote. We continued increasing our aid and building our military. Then Japan ended all speculation and objections to our activity by attacking Pearl Harbor. We were at war."

"Analysts have said that the Japanese made a terrible mistake, that they 'awakened a sleeping giant.'"

"Well, that's a bit hyperbolic, but nevertheless, true. The Axis powers made two enormous mistakes that eventually led to the Allied victory; the other was Hitler's invasion of Russia. Of course, we weren't actually sleeping by December 7; we had been preparing our own country and helping the Allies for several years. Fighting the war was hard, and it cost us tremendously in lives lost and damaged and much destruction. Things went poorly for us in the Pacific at first, but we stopped the Japanese advance at the Battle of Midway. That was in June 1942, only six months after Pearl Harbor."

Robert interjected, "The Japanese commander, Admiral Yamamoto, in an answer to his Prime Minister's question about Japan's prospects in a war with America, said, that if ordered to fight, 'I shall run wild considerably for the first six months or a year, but I have utterly no confidence for the second and third years.'"

"He was right. Our strategy in the Pacific was to get close to the Japanese home islands, so that our bombers could fly there, drop their bombs, and return to base. It started in New Guinea, but the Japanese started building an airfield on Guadalcanal, in the Solomon Islands, a strategic location. Our Marines and Army invaded in August of 1942 and finally prevailed in February of 1943. It was a very difficult battle, both on land and at sea. Then it was island after island: Tarawa, Kwajalein, Saipan, the Philippines, Iwo Jima, and Okinawa. The losses were terrible." He sighed. " I did not see the end of the Okinawa battle."

"Let's talk about the war in Europe," said Robert. "After Pearl Harbor, the United States declared war on Germany and Italy. American troops began arriving in Britain in early 1942. Germany had attacked Russia in June 1941, so that Hitler would eventually have to fight a war on two fronts."

"Yes. We first invaded Morocco and Algeria, and after securing North Africa, landed in Sicily, and then Italy. We escalated our strategic bombing of German cities and the Rumanian oilfields, the major supplier of fuel to the German armies. Stalin was very impatient for us to invade France and start the Second Front, which we had to delay twice. Finally, D-Day arrived on June 6, 1944. Our armies landed on the Normandy beaches, and advanced, at great cost, into France and into Germany. At the same time, the Soviet armies moved into Germany from the East."

He stopped and said, "That's all I remember." He looked sadly at Robert. "That's all I remember."

"Hitler died eighteen days later in his bunker. He took poison."

"It would have been more satisfying to capture him alive."

"Going back a bit, you were re-elected in 1944 for your fourth term. You were obviously ill. The depression and the war had taken a tremendous toll on you. By 1944, the war was approaching its final stages. Why did you sacrifice your life and run again?"

"It is true that the war in Europe was almost over, but we were still fighting the Japanese in the Pacific, and I had great concern about the post-war period. Many issues would have to be settled: the establishment of the United Nations, our relationship with the Soviet Union, and dealing with the defeated countries. I knew that the United States would have an enormous role to play in restoring the world to health. The devastation was terrible everywhere, both in the Allied countries and in the Axis countries. We knew we would have to help them rebuild. I felt that I should be there, as President, for all of that."

"It destroyed you, and in all honesty, you weren't there anyway."

Roosevelt chuckled grimly.

"That is ironic, is it not?"

"You mentioned the Soviet Union. You had to negotiate with Josef Stalin. What was that like?"

"A very difficult man, and in many ways as bad as Hitler. Many of us thought at first that we could negotiate with him. Others did not. I don't understand dictators and their obsession with power and control; often they were also cruel and hateful. We were blessed with two of the worst, three if you count Mussolini, although I don't think he was in the same class. I suppose that many people would consider the Yalta Conference a failure on our part. Perhaps they would be right. Were they?"

"Well, the Soviet Union was very aggressive in the years following the war. Relations between the Western powers and what became known as the Eastern Bloc were very bad for many years. That period that was called the Cold War. But I'm not sure that better negotiations at Yalta would have changed the outcome. It was a very dangerous time, since both sides possessed nuclear weapons."

"Tell me what happened after I died."

"I will summarize as best I can, since our time together is limited. The war in Europe ended in early May, 1945. The Pacific war ended in August, after we dropped atom bombs on two Japanese cities, destroying them both completely."

"Two bombs? Wasn't one enough?"

"Many people thought so. It was never satisfactorily explained, I'm afraid. After that, there was the Cold War, which lasted until 1991, when the Soviet Union collapsed. Since then, we've had various kinds of wars, including religious conflicts and the Third World War, and finally the formation of a world federation. Now things have improved considerably, but there are still animosities and conflicts. We may never be free of them. I think that there are simply too many bad genes in the human race to ever be free of unbridled ambition, cruelty, hunger for power, and uncontrolled emotions. We are by no means perfect and may never get there."

"You are a philosopher, Mr. Delacroix."

Robert smiled. "Speaking of that, you had a very long career in various levels of state and federal government. You must have developed a philosophy of government over those many years. Would you tell us about that?"

"I suppose I did, but perhaps not in as coherent a way as you may be thinking. I suppose this is an opportune time to organize my thoughts."

He paused as if doing just that. Robert Delacroix wondered what the thought process might be in a pseudo-person. It had become obvious during the interviews that a thought process of some sort was taking place. He wondered whether the scientists who were figuring out what made MONTY tick would ever arrive at a definitive answer or whether it would remain as mysterious as the real human brain continued to be. The light of learning seemed to grow brighter with each subject's appearance, courtesy of MONTY's genius. Where would it end? Would he be overwhelmed one day by a subject's intelligence and capability? Would a super-intelligent subject confront him, like a sentient being from a distant planet with far greater abilities than any imaginable human? The idea exhilarated and frightened him.

"I think one has to be driven by the idea of public service," said President Roosevelt. "That has to be the foundation for governing well. You must be constantly aware that you are the servant of the people as well as their leader. That was one of the reasons for my radio fireside chats. You are there in a room with American families, letting them know what you think and what you wish to do for their benefit, their wellbeing.

"You must have a set of principles, of which there are two kinds: bedrock principles that you never compromise, and operating principles. The latter are starting points and are also bargaining points, which you may have to modify in order to accomplish something, like getting an important bill passed.

"You must choose the best possible advisors, because no one in the president's chair knows everything, and you must have advice to help make decisions. It is very important that these men and women think for themselves, and say no when yes would be easier, because only honest advice is worth anything. And of course, you must recognize that it is your responsibility to make the final decision and to accept the consequences of that decision."

"Your successor, Harry Truman, had a plaque on his desk that read 'The buck stops here.'"

Roosevelt grinned. "Exactly right. Did he do well?"

"Yes, I believe so. He was elected for a full term in 1948. For various reasons, he was not very popular during his presidency, but as the years passed his stock rose substantially."

"Good, good. You know, in those days, the vice presidency wasn't a very rewarding position. It had no real responsibilities. The incumbent essentially waited for the President to die. It must have been pretty hard on Harry when he became President, knowing nothing about the bomb research going on in Los Alamos."

"Do you have any more on your governing philosophy?

Roosevelt grew solemn. "I'm not sure it is part of a philosophy, but there's one more point I must make. Sometimes you do more than compromise. Sometimes you rationalize a decision: that it is for the greater good when you are not really confident that that is so. I am sure that you know that the Democratic Party was made up of some greatly disparate elements in those years. I'm thinking of the southern Democrats, whose treatment of Negroes in those states was anathema to me, but we needed them to make the New Deal work, and we elected not to force changes in those states. Was it the right thing to do? I think not, but we felt it was necessary."

"Thank you Mr. President. It has been a pleasure to meet you and have this conversation."

The audience rose and applauded loudly as the lights in the cubicle dimmed.

# CHAPTER 9

Meilin Xu and Arne Lund decided to drive across the Golden Gate Bridge to have lunch in Sausalito. They each had a different favorite restaurant there and hoped to resolve the choice while en route, thus enabling them to avoid talking shop, particularly their own specialties: history, hers; linguistics, his. This would be a difficult task, as they both loved their jobs and could go on endlessly about obscure languages and equally obscure historical facts, or so it often seemed to a listener. They also loved discussion and derived great pleasure picking apart the other's argument. Fortunately, they also were naturally civil and hardly ever raised voices in anger. Neither did they bore each other, which made for a congenial relationship.

They settled on a restaurant as they drove down the hill into town and pulled into the parking lot of the Bay Paradise. They arrived early enough to snag a window table and sat for a while gazing at the pelicans attacking the sparkling water, and the squawking seagulls, numerous sailboats, and the water itself.

Meilin sighed.

"I got another letter from Mom today."

"Uh, oh. What did she get on you about this time?"

"A direct quote: 'Are you still seeing that *gwei lo*?'"

"Ah, well, she could have said '*sei gwei lo*'"

"She doesn't think you're a *bad* white man. She doesn't dislike you. It's just that you're different."

"It's hard to believe sometimes," he said, "that after all these centuries, with a world supposedly at peace, that such feelings are still so important and sometimes lead to great violence. I'm sure we will eventually be able to convince your mother that the 'twain' does meet sometimes, and that it's a good thing. But people still kill other people, and burn down their homes, and rape their women, all because they're different. And they don't do these things on the spur of the moment. These feelings may simmer for years, apparently suppressed, then suddenly burst forth as if they were spontaneous. The only differences between now and the days before the world federation came into existence is that countries don't make war against each other and the weapons available now have minimum destructive power. No nuclear weapons, but you can still make a bomb, and set fire to buildings. And a group of guys with some guns, knives, clubs, and matches can do a hell of a lot of damage."

Arne leaned back and exhaled. Meilin grinned at him.

"I guess I got carried away," he said. "I don't think your mother would do any of those things."

"Have you ever heard Rebecca's good gene-bad gene theory?"

"No, but it sounds interesting. What is it?"

"Well she classifies our genes into two groups according to what they make us do. The good ones are the technological genes, the ones that give us the ability to invent, to make things, to write, to talk. Also the ones that give us good health and make us generous and kind. The bad ones can make us sick, but particularly destructive are the ones that make us cruel, greedy, violent, selfish, and intolerant. They're all scattered among people in various combinations, and they get reshuffled in every generation. Therefore, you can't tell ahead of time where and when the various combinations will show up. So it's impossible to select for the good ones, or select against the bad ones."

She thought for a moment. "A combination of, let's say, hatred, violence, fear, and jealousy may give us a participant in a mob that destroys a few things and injures people. Add intelligence, ambition, and cruelty to the mix, in a situation where a lot of people are disgruntled—behold, Adolph Hitler. In a happier, prosperous Germany, we probably would never have heard of him. Mmm, this crab salad is really good. How's your halibut?

Arne looked wildly around the restaurant.

"Oh my goodness, where did that conversation go?"

She giggled. "Don't worry, it's still around. It was important to interrupt with that bulletin."

"Well, it's an interesting theory. Is she writing it up? The halibut is great."

"Yes it is. I suppose so. I'm glad."

They remained relatively quiet for the rest of the meal, and decided to go for a walk afterwards.

"Do you think your mother will relent, given enough time?"

"I don't know," said Meilin. "She can be pretty stubborn. It's been ingrained in Chinese families for centuries, you know. And it's not just us. Many groups have these taboos against ethnic, racial, and religious mixing. Some people just harbor these feelings within their hearts and minds. Others resort to discrimination, ostracism, and sometimes, physical violence, including murder. It's ridiculous. People can be so stupid."

"The bad genes, huh?"

"Yeah, afraid so."

"Meilin, if we decide that we want to get married, we may have to ignore her feelings."

"Oh, I don't know if I can. It would be so hard on her. Then she might learn to hate you, and she would be very angry at me."

"Her prejudice is affecting you, I'm afraid."

She looked at him, misery in her eyes.

"What are we going to do?"

"I'm sure we'll think of something. Maybe we can enlist some members of your family. We'll think of something."

Arne was less confident than his words. He had met her family. Her brothers and sisters had no problem with his presence, and her father seemed friendly enough, though rather reserved. But the hostility in her mother's face was unmistakable and showed through the veneer of politeness. She probably didn't hate him, but her attitude seemed more than just the usual disdain for western foreigners. It was aimed directly at him, because he was with Meilin. He sighed silently. Still, with help from the family, they might break through some day. He didn't have the impatience of the very young and hoped that time would play in their favor. If not—. There was time to think of that.

The rest of the day was filled in with small talk. They returned to the city and enjoyed their love at her apartment.

Several evenings later, Meilin, home alone, took the opportunity to indulge her favorite pastime, reading history, a true busman's respite. Her range of interest was impressively broad. Not only did she read history books, academic and popular, but she also loved historical novels. Reading the latter, she often amused herself by finding the places where the author had altered actual history to fit the needs of the novel. She did not resent the practice, but rather respected the author's need to retool historical facts and marveled at the ability to do so and thus create a fine book.

In true history books, she loved tracking down the author's political, ethnic, and religious biases. Her ritual, upon discovering such a bias, was to shake her finger at the book, saying aloud: "Shame. For shame." She then made a note in the margin for further review and comment.

On this particular evening, she was reading a large, heirloom volume, A Review of Paleontology, 1925-2009. The first date marked the publication of the discovery of the first fossil bones of a human ancestor, *Australopithecus africanus*, by Raymond Dart, in South Africa. The narrative chronicled the nearly two centuries of subsequent progress made by paleontologists in mapping the pathways of human evolution. The second date commemorated the discovery of a nearly complete skeleton of an early

Hominid, *Ardipithecus ramidus*, which appeared to have lived before the separation of the chimpanzee and human lines of descent. The first paper describing the skeleton was published fifteen years later, and the book shortly after that.

She laid the book beside her on the couch and spoke silently to herself.

I wonder what they were like? Wouldn't it be fun to travel back to those years and see? When did the virtues and faults of modern humans start to develop? She thought of all the history she had studied, and she wondered. It seemed that our ability to do great harm to each other and to our beautiful planet had easily kept pace with our ability to reach for the far recesses of the universe, spatially and temporally, and our ability to have ideas and invent things. What of the future? What awaits us in a hundred years, a thousand years? Should we be optimistic?

"I don't know. I think the verdict is still pending."

She thought of her mother's aversion to Arne as a suitable prospective husband. It made no sense to preserve such an attitude for so many generations. And she was forced to agree with Arne's unspoken thought that it was more than just a general acceptance of past prejudices, that it was indeed personal. It would not be easy to overcome, but she fervently hoped she would not have to make a hard, wrenching, disruptive choice. She knew that many in her extended family had lost these prejudices. Others, including her mother, had not. Her father seemed to accept Arne, but his mild mannered, non-argumentative manner forecast no help from him. A couple of aunts were more enlightened. Maybe she should approach one or both of them and enlist them in her just cause.

She began to expand her thoughts again.

When did suspicion and dislike of persons who were different in some way start? Does it go back to the earliest people? That seemed unlikely. Many thousands of years ago populations were small. They existed in separate groups and probably never met others who were different enough to be disdained, despised, or hated. As the populations grew larger and developed their own ways, two things would happen. They would reach a stage when one group would feel "justified" in sneering at another, and that would occur when they began to move around and make first contact. Thus would history begin as a chronicle of conflict. War, weapons, conquest, genocide, all the delightful indulgences of human society, would grow and flower in the names of race, religion, and land.

She sighed deeply, poured herself a little wine and resumed reading.

# CHAPTER 10

John Sorensen waited for the talk buzz, paper shuffling, and chair scraping to fade before starting the first planning meeting for a future show.

"I have what I hope will be an interesting and somewhat provocative proposal for our June show. We have ventured into a variety of fields: military, political, scientific, athletic, and others, but we have yet to interview anyone from the world of religion. To make it really difficult and challenging, I'm thinking of a biblical character, rather than a more recent religious leader, perhaps from the Old Testament."

"Wow," said Susan Sherry, the staff logician, "do we know which of those people actually existed?"

"Or whether any of them existed?" Kenichi Tamata, the feedback engineer, looked quite dubious. "Those of us from outside the western world have some doubts, you know."

"Some of us do, too," said Sonia Rifkin. "DNA genetics and evolutionary evidence doesn't lend much credence to the whole idea."

"Sure," said Meilin, "one may be skeptical about Adam and Eve, but as you get into the later years of the Bible, when people had learned to read and write and chronicle things, the reality of those characters becomes more likely. What we may find difficult to establish is the dividing line between biblical information and historical truth."

"We know some of the languages of those times," said Arne. "So that shouldn't be an overwhelming problem, although it depends on how far back we go."

"Is there a good reason why we shouldn't consider New Testament figures, like Jesus and Paul?" This came from Fred Bosworth, one of the show's producers.

"No," said John, "I just thought that the older ones would be more of a challenge."

"I agree," said Rebecca, "particularly those associated with a notable legend: Jonah and the big fish, David and Goliath, Noah and the flood. It will be hard though, because we don't have any graphic materials at all, only pictures and sculptures conjured up in an artist's mind."

"What are the prospects for DNA evidence, Sonia?"

"I'm not sure, John, but there are likely to be remains from the period and location, and we could probably obtain generic DNA information that would tell us what a tribesman of the time looked like, in addition to the skeletal remains."

Rebecca nodded. "We could correlate the legends of the time, combine that information with possible memories in our test subject, and narrow it down to a memory or direct knowledge of a specific event from which the legend developed. The subject may have been there or heard about the event."

Talaat el-Sayed spoke up. "There were a lot of small tribes around at the time. I imagine we would have to do a lot of sampling to see how closely or distantly related they were. We might have to develop several profiles. Then it would be a question of choosing one, or letting Shankar develop a most probable outcome."

"I'm prejudiced of course, but I believe the most probable outcome would be a better way."

Talaat grinned. "Right."

"The major source of information is the Bible," said John. "What else do we have?"

"Legends," said Meilin. "From the Greeks, Egyptians, Babylonians. And earlier than that, the Sumerians and the Akkadians."

"The Akkadian language was a Semitic one," said Arne, "and therefore would have given rise to others, including Hebrew, Arabic, Aramaic, and Syriac. So we would have a group of related languages, which should enable us to pick one reasonably close to the subject's, if historical records don't tell us specifically what it is."

John nodded. He turned to the wardrobe specialist, Joshua Stayfield. "What about clothing?"

"They wore various sorts of robes in the earlier days. Typically, men wore a tight fitting kuttoneth, which was considered an undergarment, over which they wore a rough woolen simla, or shawl. Farther south, in Egypt, they wore lighter clothing. Peasants wore only a loincloth."

"We can probably decide on a stage setting later on."

Designer Dominique Ferrand said, "Oh yes, no problem."

"Okay, let's consider some possible subjects. We don't have to narrow down just yet."

Rebecca said, "Perhaps we can pick three or four from each Testament, particularly those associated with some phenomenon. We do have to have something special that Robert can converse about."

"Okay, let's hear some suggestions," said John.

"I propose Moses," said one voice.

"Paul," said another

"Jesus," chimed in a third.

Others added Noah, King David, and Matthew. After that, there was some silence, during which John suggested that they concentrate on those six for a start.

"I almost hesitate to, um, bring this up," said Arne. "But I wonder if there is way too much, shall we say, emotional content, in Jesus. With the kind of probing questions we bring up in talking to the subjects, I think that a lot of people would believe that we were being blasphemous, and many others would be sure that we were catering to one religion. It sounds almost like a no-win situation. For every person who would see it as a very interesting exploration or experiment, there might be five or ten who would be furious."

"Wouldn't that be true for any religious figure we talk to?" said John.

"Possibly so, but I don't think any of the others we've named, or any others in either book would have anywhere near the impact. He's been a super-iconic figure for over two millennia. The only others who approach him as an object of tremendous reverence are Mahomet and Buddha. And I wouldn't recommend either of *them* if we were going to consider someone outside the Bible."

"Well, those are very interesting points, Arne. Thank you. Let's hold Jesus in abeyance and discuss the others."

"Moses would be an interesting subject," said Robert. "There would be many things to talk to him about, such as his life in Egypt, the exodus, the Red Sea parting, his annoyance at his followers for their idol worship, and, of course, the Ten Commandments. I could have a really long conversation with him."

"If we talked to Paul, or to Matthew or one of the other gospel guys," said Fred, "it would be interesting to find out why the four gospels were written from different points of view. Also Paul could give some interesting insights into the development of the early church."

"It would be nice if we could develop a credible Noah. There are a lot of interesting questions to be asked about the flood. And it would take us farther back in biblical history than any of the others. That would certainly be a challenge."

Meilin looked around the table and noticed several in the group apparently nodding in agreement.

King David's name came up next. All agreed that he would provide a rich store of information and legends. The discussion continued for another hour on the candidates, until John called a halt.

"Okay, I think we have some good thoughts here. Let's do some preliminary research on these possible subjects: available information, likely stumbling blocks, and so forth. We'll discuss them at our next meeting in a month and narrow our list at that time. As usual, if anyone has a burning need to insert someone else into the mix, let me know."

* * *

At the next meeting, an extended discussion, based on Arne's earlier assessment, took place on the issue of having Jesus as the subject of the interview.

Fred Bosworth spoke to the potential for popularity of the show.

"No one would turn away. Friends would call friends. The whole world would watch. A billion Christians would be ecstatic. It would be the most popular show we have ever done or would ever do, especially if we announced it ahead of time. I think we should do it."

"Not all Christians would be ecstatic," said Arne. "If Robert asked any questions that reflected in any critical way on Christian belief, the chorus accusing us of blasphemy would be deafening. Also, Muslims, Jews, Hindus, and other groups would be all over us for favoring one religion over all others. We could interview anyone else in the Christian pantheon, and there would be little uproar. We could also interview anyone outside of Christianity, except Moses, Mahomet, or Buddha and not encounter those problems. I think we should leave that interview to the biblical scholars."

There were grunts of approval from around the table. No one else supported Fred's position.

The discussion moved on to the other candidates. It continued for a seemingly interminable period, with a good deal of wrangling over the virtues and faults of each as a potential interviewee. Finally, Rebecca raised her hand.

"I think we are going about this the wrong way. We have been discussing these people from two points of view, which I think rather conflict with each other. One is their virtue as religious figures, and the other is their attractiveness as television personalities. Remember, *History Lives* exists to entertain and to educate. It isn't a research tool. So I think we have to decide whether we are interested in our interviewees as religious figures or as historical figures. To me, the obvious choice is the latter. As Arne pointed out, we should leave the other to the research people. They don't have to worry about ratings."

Suddenly, all seemed clear, and the discussion proceeded rapidly to a decision.

# CHAPTER 11

The houselights dimmed and the lights in the cubicle came up. An image began to form, finally revealing a man in a grayish white robe that reached to the floor. He had a long gray beard and gray hair. Brown eyes bracketed a large prominent nose over a full-lipped mouth, all surrounded by a dark, much lined face. He looked bewildered and turned his head back and forth, looking at his sparse brightly lit surroundings. He appeared to be about sixty years of age.

In a voice that should have been deep and resonant, but was less than that because of a pronounced quaver, he said, "I have not seen this place before. What is this place? Where is the land? Where are the bushes and the grass? Where is my wife? I do not see my sons and their wives?"

"I will explain in a moment," said Robert Delacroix. "Perhaps you can tell us who you are."

Delacroix did not often enjoy this part of the show. The bewilderment and latent fear of a person lost in an unrecognizable place was almost as distressing for him as it was for the guest subject. It was a hard moment to get through, knowing that the subject might have great difficulty understanding the situation and might become frightened or angry, or might even retreat into himself and become completely frozen in place.

"I am Noah, son of Lamech."

Delacroix let his held breath out in relief.

"Who are you?" Noah peered at him.

"My name is Robert Delacroix. You are a long way from your home, and—" he hesitated slightly, "in a different time."

Noah looked puzzled. "In a different time? How is this possible?"

"We have re-created you. It is thousands of years later."

Noah clasped his hands in front of his chest and now his voice trembled uncontrollably. "You are God! Yahweh! Is it truly you? You talk to me!"

Delacroix explained Noah's presence as carefully as he could, as well as his own identity. Noah remained quite agitated, as Delacroix explained why was in the cubicle and how he got there.

After a few minutes, Noah relaxed a bit, listened more closely, and even nodded his head occasionally. Robert never failed to marvel at a guest's ability to rally and accept a truly astonishing, even preposterous, circumstance.

"Your name is truly strange. Do you come from Sumer or perhaps beyond Egypt?"

Robert explained that he was indeed from far "beyond Egypt".

"I would like to ask you some questions about your life and the place where you lived. May I do that?"

"Yes, of course."

"We believe that you lived in or near a land that we now call the Fertile Crescent. It is an area crossed by three important rivers. Two flow fairly close to each other and are named the Tigris and Euphrates. To the west and south there is another large river called the Nile, which runs through Egypt. Directly to the west is a very large body of water called the Mediterranean Sea. Would you like to see some pictures of the land and the rivers?"

"Oh, yes. I would very much like that. Did you draw these pictures?"

"No, I did not. These pictures were not drawn. They are called photographs and were taken by a special device called a camera. I think you will enjoy them."

He pressed a button. An image appeared in the cubicle, and on a large screen for the audience, showing a map of the area. Noah gasped. Robert pointed out the rivers and the sea.

"We believe you lived somewhere in this area. Have you any memory of seeing those waters."

"No, not at all. We did not go far from our home. Except, of course, we did live next to a river, but I don't know which one."

"Here is what they look like."

Robert showed pictures of the vast sea, and of the three rivers, taken at ground level. Noah reacted to the photo of the Tigris, which showed mountains in the background.

"Oh! My goodness! That looks familiar. Perhaps I lived there."

Robert said, "You could have lived close to the Tigris, or perhaps one of its tributaries that came out of the nearby mountains. The next several pictures were taken from a great height."

Aerial views appeared on the screen. Noah's chin dropped. His eyes widened, and he cried out loud.

"Oh my! Oh my! How did you do that? Can you fly? Oh my!"

Robert chuckled delightedly at Noah's reaction. "People cannot fly by themselves. We have very large powerful machines that lift us off the ground high in the air. These machines were invented long after you lived. We can travel very long distances in a very short time."

Noah thought for a moment. A sly smile appeared on his face.

"How long would I have needed to live to see one of those machines?"

"About three thousand years."

"Well, at least I have seen those wonderful pictures. Thank you."

"You're quite welcome. Perhaps we had better move on. It has been written that there was a very bad flood during your lifetime. Do you remember that?"

"There were many floods. Some were bad, and others were not so bad. We also had droughts; some were bad, some not so bad. The droughts happened because there was no rain, and the floods happened because there was too much rain. I grew my vines and my grains and kept my cattle and sheep and my tents by the side of the river. The land was flat near the river, and then became the mountains. The river came out of the mountains. In the spring sometimes it rained a lot and the water rushed out of the mountains and filled the river. The river grew bigger and sometimes I had to move my tents and animals away because the river became very big. It was very wide and the water rushed by very fast. Then when the water went down, I moved my tents back by the side of the river." He smiled. "Until the next time."

Delacroix leaned forward. "Do you remember one very bad flood?"

"One very bad flood?" Noah frowned and thought for a moment. His face cleared. "Yes, now I remember. A very bad flood. It rained for days and hardly stopped at all."

"For forty days and nights?"

"Forty! That would be impossible. No, no. Six or seven days."

"What happened?"

"It was terrible. We had to move our tents and the cattle and sheep a long way up the slope of the mountain. The water covered the whole valley. It was moving very fast. We lost some of the lambs. All the vines and the grains were washed away."

The memory overwhelmed Noah for a few minutes. He lowered his head to his hands.

"It was very bad," he whispered.

"It has also been written that you built an ark to stay in with your family and the animals until the land dried up."

"An ark? You mean a boat? No, no. There was no time. Why a boat? We would have been washed to the sea. And we would have lost all the animals."

"It has been written that God caused it to rain for forty days and nights, that the entire earth became covered with water, and that God commanded you to build an ark three hundred cubits long for your family and pairs of all the animals on earth. That God wanted to destroy all the other people, and that when the flood was over, your sons would repopulate the earth."

Noah's mouth fell open, He gaped at Robert and seemed struck dumb. There was a long silence. Finally, Noah spoke again in a somewhat strangulated manner.

"Who has written this?"

"No one really knows. We have a book. It is called the Bible and it is in two sections: the Old Testament, or the Tanakh, and the New Testament. The first five parts of the Old Testament make up a group called the Torah. The first of these is called Genesis, and in it is the story about you. We don't know when it was written, or by whom, because some stories were written more than once, apparently by different people at different times, and in different styles. It is so confusing that we weren't really sure that you had actually existed."

Noah smiled. "And yet here I am. You said God talked to me. He said I was to build a boat three hundred cubits long and put all the animals on earth in it. And it would rain for forty days."

"And cover the earth. The water rose fifteen cubits and remained for another one hundred fifty days."

"Well, it is quite a remarkable story, but very little of it is true. There was a bad flood. Some animals died and some people got too close to the water and were swept away. Some of them probably drowned. Why would God want to make everybody except us die?"

"He believed that everybody else was too wicked to live."

"Well, some of my neighbors were wicked, I suppose, but they didn't deserve to die. And most of them didn't." He paused for a moment. "The earth. You must know now how big it is. The ends of the earth must have been very far from where we lived. We certainly couldn't see the ends. How big is it?"

"First, it has no ends," said Robert. It is shaped like a ball." Noah's eyes opened wide. "It is over five thousand cubits across and about sixteen thousand cubits around. We believe you lived about three thousand years ago. At that time, we estimate that there were about thirty million people on earth. Now there are about seventeen billion, a very large number."

"But why don't the people on the bottom part fall off. Aren't they upside down?"

Delacroix carefully explained the nature of the atmosphere and the phenomenon of gravity. He projected a picture of the earth in the cubicle and showed Noah where he had lived and where he was now. He also showed some pictures of the lands east of the Mediterranean Sea. Recognition brought tears to Noah's eyes.

"The book called Genesis also said that people in those days lived to be very old."

"That is true. Some I knew to live to about seventy years. Very old indeed."

"Genesis says that you had your sons when you were five hundred years old and that you lived for 950 years."

Again Noah gaped at him, and then suddenly began laughing so hard that he almost fell off the chair.

"Five hundred! Why did I wait so long?" he gasped. "Oh my. I was truly a man, was I not? Five hundred!" He collapsed in laughter again.

Robert Delacroix and many in the audience were afflicted with Noah's merriment and joined him in laughter. Others were obviously taken aback by the assault on Genesis legend and looked shocked, puzzled, or annoyed. Delacroix had turned toward the audience and could see some of those faces. He thought he had better be prepared for some unfriendly questions. He turned back to Noah.

"Now I would like to ask you some more questions and talk about your life."

"My life. The last I remember is that I was very sick and dying. My family surrounded me. They were all weeping."

"Do you remember how old you were at that time?"

"I do not know exactly; probably about sixty. My father told me that ten years had passed when he first told me to watch the sheep. Twelve more had passed when I took a wife, and ten more when we had our last son. After that, there were droughts and floods. I remember one time when all of our grapevines died from some devil's pestilence, and another time when nearly all of our sheep sickened and died horrible deaths. Their tongues turned blue, they couldn't walk, and they died quickly. Perhaps thirty years passed when these things were happening."

Robert nodded. "So you lived about sixty years."

Noah grimaced. "The last ones seemed to be very long. I implored God to let me die. It seems that he finally did." He chuckled. "This book said that I lived 950 years. That is quite a long time. Did other people reach that age of ages?"

"According to Genesis, many lived to be very old at that time. However, according to our history books, many people died quite young, from disease, war, and starvation. Therefore, those who lived sixty or seventy years were considered quite old. More recently, life spans increased as we learned how to combat life-threatening diseases, stay out of war, and feed everybody properly. Now people often live to eighty, ninety, even one hundred."

"Astonishing things seem to have happened during my time. Tell me some more."

"Well, according to Genesis, God created the earth, the sky, the stars, the animals, everything, in six days. The first man was called Adam. He was created out of the dust of the earth. The first woman, Eve, was made from one of Adam's ribs."

"God can do anything," said Noah. "And yet this same book talks of a flood that never happened and says that I talked with God. What is one to believe?"

"Well, some people believe that the Bible is literally true, that everything in it happened exactly as described. Most people, however, interpret the stories according to modern knowledge and experience. In the years since your time, through many generations of study, and what we call scientific research, we have discovered many things about ourselves, about the earth, about the sun, and the stars, that weren't known in your time. We've found that we have the ability to do things that seemed impossible for human beings to do."

"I would like to see this world you live in. Can that be done?"

"Alas, it cannot. I am sorry." He paused and thought for a moment.

"However, I can show you more pictures of parts of the world as it is now."

"Oh, please do. I would like that."

Robert pressed a progression of keys on his console.

"Okay. This first picture is the city of San Francisco. This is where we are now."

"It is enormous," murmured Noah. "I see no tents. Do people live in those tall things?"

"They live in some and work in others. They are not farmers."

"No. I see no lands for farming."

In succession, Robert showed the Statue of Liberty, the Eiffel Tower, the Alps, the Atlantic Ocean, and street scenes in towns and cities, as well as pictures of corn fields, apple orchards, and grapevines. Noah was beside himself in astonishment.

Finally, he shook his head and blurted, "Everything is so big."

"This last picture is the city of Jerusalem, with the Mediterranean Sea in the distant background. It is not far from where you lived, and was first settled about the time when you were there. It is a now a holy city to three of our major religions."

"Astonishing."

Robert said, "Well, let's get back to more ordinary things. You mentioned your grapevines and your sheep. You lived on a farm and had neighbors who also lived on farms."

"That is true."

"Were there any places where people lived together, in a village?"

"Oh, yes, of course. There was a village down the river. My sons and I took our wool, lambs, and wine there to exchange for things we needed at the market."

"What sorts of things?"

"Vegetables, fruit, pretty things for the women, sandals. Whatever we needed."

"It was written that you might have been the inventor of winemaking."

Noah laughed again.

"No, no. Every one who had vines made wine." He shrugged. "Who knows who was the first to make it?"

"What did the people in the village do?"

"Some had farms outside the village. In the morning, they rode out to their farms on their donkeys to plant, trim the vines, pick the grapes, milk their goats. Others had little shops, where they traded for farm goods."

Finally, it was time for Noah to go. Delacroix threw the switch and turned to the audience.

"Ladies and gentlemen, we have decided to vary our usual sequence by showing our studio audience question period to the TV viewers as well. So sit up straight, put on your best faces, and smile. You're on the air!"

He saw a grim-faced man near the front who had a hand up. Might as well get right to it, thought Delacroix. He pointed to the man.

"If that was the real Noah, he would not have denied the Flood. You must have programmed him."

"I assure you, we made him as real as we could with obviously limited knowledge. He was not programmed except with the ability to speak our language. He was given all the information we had, with no attempt to influence his thinking. Exactly like all of our other guests."

"Sure." The man sat down.

"Just what were your sources of information," asked a woman at the back. "Were there others beside the Bible?"

"Yes there were: the Babylonian Gilgamesh Epic, the Quran, and many other earlier flood legends. We had information about the agriculture, the clothing, life styles, geology, other historical accounts, and other types of information about the times. We did not attempt to give more weight to certain things than others, to impose any modern or personal viewpoints. We let MONTY do the evaluation, in the same way as for our other guests. He made the decisions. MONTY is still a black box in some ways, so we are always in for some surprises."

A young man stood up.

"I believe the first gentleman hinted at a key question. Many people believe that Genesis, the account of the universe's creation, is allegorical. If so, are all the other stories in that chapter also allegorical? Was Noah a real person? If he wasn't, then what did MONTY create?"

The first questioner glared at the young man.

"I most certainly did not 'hint' that Noah was not real," he barked. "He was real. These people created a programmed Noah, to say what they wanted him to say."

"Mr. Delacroix says they didn't program him," replied the young man. "I see no good reason to doubt that. I've seen many of the shows and all the characters were authentic, as far as I could tell. Besides, I said that you hinted at a question that could be asked, not that Noah wasn't real."

"Perhaps I should clarify my earlier statement," said Robert. "We definitely did *not* program Noah. We did not put words in his mouth. We never do that. But please remember that we created him from information available and there is only one original source for that: the Bible. His reality therefore is dependent upon the accuracy, or lack of same, of that section of Genesis in recording the happenings of that period and that place, three or four thousand years ago. One of those happenings was the flood, and must be contrasted with other flood legends and with an actual major flood of the Black Sea area about seven thousand years ago."

"You mean there really was an enormous flood? How big was it?"

"The Black Sea was for a long time a fresh water lake. About 5600 BCE or possibly earlier, salt water from the Mediterranean flowed through the Bosporus, cutting through a land barrier, into the Black Sea. The water rose several hundred feet and the shoreline expanded by miles to the north and east. A dispute arose over the length of time it took to reach its present dimensions. In any case, people were forced to leave their homes and relocate to other places."

The dark anger remained on the first questioner's face, accompanied by vigorous head shaking. Finally, he stood up, flipped his hand at Robert in dismissal, pushed his way to an aisle, and strode towards the exit; shoulders hunched stiffly, his body radiating fury. Robert watched him for a moment and asked for more questions.

"You mentioned the Fertile Crescent. What does that mean?"

"I'll show you." Robert walked back to the console. A map appeared on the large screen. It showed the lands around the Eastern Mediterranean and featured a green crescent shaped section surrounded by a large brown area.

"The green area on the right surrounds the Tigris and Euphrates Rivers, which pass through Iraq. It curves around to the left on the north end, touching southern Turkey, then turns south along the eastern edge of the Mediterranean, and includes the Nile Delta in Egypt. It is the area where humans began to change from their hunter-gatherer phase to farming—the birth of agriculture, estimated at about ten thousand years ago. During that earliest period, the Crescent was home to eight founder crops: bitter vetch, lentil, pea, chickpea, flax, barley, and two types of ancient wheat, all derived from wild species. Also, they domesticated sheep, cattle, goats, and pigs. Quite an accomplishment. Later, of course, other crops were domesticated, including Noah's grapes."

A young man stood up. "Mr. Delacroix, your machine, MONTY, found a person who identified himself as Noah. As you said, MONTY is a black box that makes calculations somewhat shrouded in mystery. So, do you believe that Noah was a real person?"

Robert was silent momentarily, then smiled and took a deep breath.

"Why don't you ask me a really hard question?" Many in the audience laughed; some frowned.

"I think that the first part of Genesis was probably written in retrospect, to account for the beginning of everything. I believe that contemporary persons from succeeding generations wrote the remaining parts of Genesis. So it seems reasonable that those writers would use names and identities of real people. If Noah's bad flood actually happened, and not a Deluge that wiped out the world's population, then he and all the other named persons at the time would have been real. Perhaps, at a later time, other writers might have modified, exaggerated, if you will, what was written earlier. But I doubt very much that it will be proved one way or another, unless a manuscript, hitherto unknown, is discovered and sheds more light than we have now."

Many in the audience applauded or nodded. Others frowned, shook their heads, or booed.

"Thank you very much, ladies and gentlemen. Good night."

# CHAPTER 12

Robert Delacroix sometimes wondered who he was. Often, when he looked at his image in a mirror, he saw an admittedly handsome person, with the eyes, nose, mouth, jaw, and hair that millions of people all over the globe recognized instantly. Yet, sometimes, a stranger stared out at him. Who is that man?

But it was not the image that made him wonder. That image indeed reflected the face of Robert Delacroix. Sometimes as he gazed in the mirror, he and the image smiled at each other in easy recognition.

Hi, Robert. Nice to see you again, Robert. *That* wasn't the problem at all. The images in his mind were also there, but were not recognizable, and they filled him with despair. Who was he? At forty-eight years old he knew less about himself than he did when he was a child. Correction. He knew more about himself, but was confused by what he knew, or thought he knew. Besides, as a child, he wasn't introspective enough to care enough about such questions to explore them.

Back home in Peekskill, New York, as a boy and an adolescent, he knew the facts that were important at that time: he was a very bright young fellow with an equally bright future, more than one possible bright future, actually. He was good in every class he took, every subject he studied, every extra-curricular activity he tackled. He smiled at the memory. There would be no obstacle he couldn't overcome, nothing that would keep him from success in anything he decided to do. And that's the way it worked out. He did equally well in college and in graduate school, an elite Ivy Leaguer from Columbia and Yale. And here he was, the face of *History Lives,* a celebrity. And that was the rub. He was the face, the interviewer, the emcee. He had invented nothing, produced nothing, and directed nothing. He was intelligent. He understood, to a degree at least, genetics, history, psychology, languages, and archeology, most of the kinds of information that were fed into MONTY's voracious maw. He absorbed and understood the information, but he created nothing. Not completely true. He did help write the scripts for the shows. He shrugged his shoulders. That's just a matter of arranging words.

"Good thing this vehicle guides itself," he said aloud. "I'd probably cause a head-on if I was driving." He looked around and realized that he was about halfway there.

Who was he? He was attracted by and attractive to women. For a fleeting moment he brightened at the thought, but only for a moment. All of his relationships, the innocent dating when he was young, his later affairs, and his marriage, ended badly or simply went nowhere and just ended. He was attracted to beauty, intelligence, accomplishment, and strength in women. And that was also the rub. The beauty he could handle. He was often the more "beautiful" one, after all. The problem was in the other three words. Why? He was intelligent and accomplished in his profession. Was there something else? Was it that strength, that inner will that they possessed, but was absent in him? Maybe he had a flaw that he didn't understand or wasn't aware of.

And then he realized that the hidden weakness, whatever it was, would eventually destroy his relationship with Shannon, and his illicit relationship with Rebecca, who had already predicted, no, declared that it would end. She, by any standard, had a greater will than any other woman he had been with. It probably didn't matter what kind of a man he was. It would end.

"Let go of this, Robert," he again said aloud. "Think of the day ahead."

That might have been easier to do in one of the antique vehicles that required close attention: to guide the vehicle with a steering wheel, avoid colliding with other vehicles, and obey red lights. The modern vehicle did everything, so he could concentrate completely on his own thoughts. Robert had always had difficulty transferring from one thought pattern to another, so time passed slowly by before he could eject the dark thoughts from his mind and replace them with anticipation of today's role reversal event: an interview of the interviewer. The vehicle was taking him to San Jose, there to have his mind probed by Lisa Carroll, a celebrity interviewer for the National Public Network, at the system's other nearby local station. They had met several times in the past at national and regional conferences, and he had watched her program frequently, so he was comfortable in his expectations. Her questions were honest and frank, with no ulterior motive lurking in the words. Unlike some others in the business, she was interested in information, not in causing embarrassment, anger, or confusion. Therefore, she was highly respected in the profession.

Robert arrived at the studio and was escorted to the prep room for makeup, voice testing, and other pre-broadcast details. He was informed that a studio audience would attend, and the program would be aired at a later time. Finally, he was taken to one side of the stage to await his cue, at which he strode onto the stage, wearing his famous smile and waving to the applauding audience while Lisa introduced him. They shook hands warmly as he took a seat facing her, with his better profile exposed to the audience.

Lisa Carroll was somewhere in his age bracket, an attractive woman with medium length dark brown hair and a friendly smile.

"Well, Robert Delacroix, we meet again. I am so pleased that you are here; a man who has literally met history face to face. Few persons on earth have had that rare and exciting opportunity. Shall we get on with the questions?"

Robert grinned. "Fire when ready."

He could sense the freedom from self that assumed control of his mind and body, the blessed takeover that released actors, musicians, athletes, all performers, if only for a short while, from corrosive self-absorption. Thought was banished; fear, worry, regret, all receded into their little nooks. Joy and instinct took over. It was wonderful.

"You are remarkably well prepared for all of your guests, especially after they respond to a first question in a way that requires one or more follow-up questions that are not scripted in advance. How do you do that?"

"It isn't easy. I study. Our research people dredge up a lot of information, especially for those persons who have lived recently. Fortunately, I learn quickly, and I have a good memory, which allows me to retain information, at least until the show is over. In high school, I was known as a test passer. You know, good grades, not much sense otherwise."

He grinned.

"Oh yes, I really believe that." She shuffled through some notes. "Let's see. It says here that you were class president, participated in sports, the school newspaper, the science club, and on and on. Test passer. Yes indeed."

"I'm also exceedingly modest. Let me answer your question a little more fully. For some interviews, the learning process is relatively simple. For example, Noah was easy because there was so little information available, a few pages in the Bible and several analyses of the meaning of those pages. On the other hand, I have to expect some surprises, so quick thinking is required.

"Charles Darwin was very hard. I had some science education and I had to gain some familiarity with his work: the voyage of the Beagle, his observations on the Galapagos Islands, and of course, the message of *On the Origin of Species*, plus the interplay with Wallace. Then, in order to be able to tell him about progress made after his death, I had to study up on Mendel's laws of inheritance and the evolution research carried out in later years. Now I almost feel that I could teach a course in evolution. Then there was Hitler. That was doubly difficult because I hated being in the same room with him, especially in the last segment. Vlad III, the Impaler, was no fun either."

"Speaking of Hitler, why did you do his interview in five segments?"

"We thought it would be interesting and enlightening to see how a person like that develops. We did not know what to expect when he materialized as a boy. His crying was a surprise; I almost felt sorry for him. But I got over that when he turned sullen and defiant. The making of the Hitler we knew started early, as you saw. Also, I'm sure that viewers have noticed that our subjects were free of their ills when they appeared. However, we wanted to show Hitler in the last segment as he was just before his death."

"Will you do others in segments in the future?"

"Possibly. There's a lot more work, of course, but the depiction of growth and change can be very rewarding."

"You mentioned being in the same room with Hitler. In one sense you were, but actually you were outside the cubicle and he was inside. Did you ever consider placing yourself in the cubicle?"

"Yes, but not very seriously. First, I would be a jarring presence, since the cubicle is set up to approximate the subject's actual environment. Much more important, some of those guys got rather violent. I don't think it would do for the interviewer to be beaten to a bloody pulp. I wouldn't care for that experience." He paused. "Of course, it might be really good for the ratings, but I'd just as soon forego the honor. Fortunately, my producers feel the same way."

"How do you select your subjects for interview? Do you start with several random names or with a category?"

"It may be either. Someone may propose a specific historical figure, or more often, a category, such as a military leader, a scientist, a sports figure, or an entertainer. Then we talk."

"How do you come to a decision?"

"There are two major influences on the decision. One is based on information available. We would like our portrayal to be as accurate as possible, as close to the real person as we can manage. DNA records and other types of genetic information are invaluable and often tip the scale of choice. If we're interested in someone who lived a really long time ago, historical records don't give us much, and that may make the decision harder. That's where the second influence kicks in. Sometimes we fall in love with someone who hasn't left much of a record. Emotion trumps intellect, everybody's eyes light up, and we're off. We love the challenge, the need for serious delving. Noah is a great example: We really wanted to know about the flood. Another is Queen Hatshepsut. She was a pretty interesting person. She was the most accomplished and had the longest reign of Egypt's female pharoahs. She wore a fake beard, just as the male pharoahs did, in official poses. She was one of the first known plant collectors."

"What does that mean?"

"She sent ships to Punt, an almost legendary land now known to be in Ethiopia or Eritrea, and collected myrrh trees and other plants and had them brought to the royal palace, along with leopards and baboons."

"Tell us about your life before *History Lives?* You studied history at Columbia and earned a Ph. D. in human behavior at Yale. You were obviously destined to wind up where you are, but you did some other things first."

He smiled. "Destined? Well, maybe. My first job was at the Behavioral Disorder Clinic in San Francisco. The work was very interesting, maybe too much so. Even now, in the twenty-first century, there are so many people who are physically or mentally sick, or poor, or all of the above. Many get crosswise with life, with society, with themselves. They can't cope; survival is a battle. They don't know why. They have no idea what's happening to them and no inkling of what to do."

"Why do you think that happens to people?"

"Oh, there are different reasons. There is a genetic basis for all human traits, not just the obvious ones like height and eye color. That means that there are substantial differences among people in intelligence, ambition, ability to analyze and solve problems, assertiveness, confidence, perseverance, energy, self-awareness, judgment, all the things that allow us to function well or badly."

As he was talking, Robert wondered how those terms applied to him.

Not *now*, he thought, not now. Keep going. He would have plenty of time later to berate himself.

"Of course," he continued, "it isn't all in the genes. It's like the old nature vs. nurture argument. Both factors come into play and it is really quite complicated. The genes controlling each trait interact with each other and with the various environments that we live in at one and the same time: among parents, siblings, and friends; in schools, neighborhoods, and workplaces; experiencing traumatic or uplifting experiences; on and on. Sorting it all out is likely to give one a headache."

"So let's get back to you. How long did you stay there? It sounds as if it took a pretty good toll on you."

"Yes indeed. I compare that clinic to a hospital emergency room. There are people there that you just can't fix. It was often very discouraging. Anyway, after five years, I decided to move into the academic world. I liked living on the west coast and took a position at California State University-San Francisco, teaching and doing some research in human behavior."

"How did you like that?"

"I enjoyed it very much. I liked being with students. It was a much more relaxing atmosphere, and very fulfilling, especially in the early days. But over the years, I found that the academic politics became rather tiresome. And the repetitive aspect of teaching the same material, the cyclical nature, began to get a little old. So I became restless. Then *History Lives* came along. The whole idea was so exciting. I interviewed for the position and, much to my surprise, they hired me, and here I am."

"Okay, let's go back to the program. The people you resurrect have been dead for a long time and may or may not have believed in an afterlife. Where do they think they are and how do they react?"

"Well, some of them do believe that they are in the afterlife, but of course they are puzzled because the cubicle doesn't appear to be a heaven, or hell, or nirvana, or any other afterlife they had envisioned while alive. So when I tell them where they are, they react in the same ways as anyone confronted with the unexpected. Some are frightened almost beyond imagination. They sit there almost paralyzed with terror. I'm usually able to get them to relax, but if someone remains completely frozen, we would have to end the program. I should point out that the first encounter is always in the test cubicle. That way we can decide whether to go ahead or cancel the program. There are also other reasons to cancel: the language may be gibberish, or the image may be incomplete."

"That happens when you have insufficient information?"

"Usually, but sometimes we have plenty of information, and for some reason the various elements don't mesh in the black box. We call it that because we don't fully understand exactly how MONTY works. I'm amazed that it works so well most of the time."

"Terror is not the only reaction, obviously."

"Some of the subjects weren't the least bit surprised to be there. They expected to have an afterlife. Charles Darwin was fascinated. He was very curious about everything, and wanted to come back so he could learn more. A few subjects asked, or demanded to be let out, so they could resume their rightful places, including a few who wanted to finish conquering the world, like Hitler and Alexander the Great."

Lisa smiled. "I remember how you told Hitler very firmly that he would never be allowed to return."

"I enjoyed that."

"Other interesting reactions?"

"Clark Gable was nervous throughout the entire interview. His eyes kept shifting around as if he expected to be attacked. Homer was overjoyed that he could see and repeatedly told me how happy he was. The rulers of countries very quickly became quite imperious after their initial surprise, while the intellectual people had a thirst for knowledge that quickly asserted itself."

"Finally, a personal question. You are a celebrity. How does that affect your life?"

"I think it's fair to say, Lisa, that I'm only a minor celebrity, so that the benefits and drawbacks are both at a lower key than for a super star in show business, sports, or politics. When I go into a restaurant, I am conscious that people are looking at me, following my progress to a table. A few come over and ask for an autograph, which I'm happy to provide. Occasionally someone will want to have a conversation. Really. That can be a nuisance. I try to be polite, but if that doesn't work, I become insistent, and if necessary, tell them to leave. I remember one occasion, when this guy simply wouldn't go. Then he got nasty. "Who do ya think you are? Ya think you're better than me, huh? You're nuthin' man, nuthin' at all.' I had to call the waiter, and he had to call security. It was very unpleasant. But that doesn't happen much, fortunately. All in all, it's not bad, rather nice at times."

After several more question and some dialog with the studio audience, Lisa called a halt.

"Robert, it's been fun talking to you, even if you're *only* a minor celebrity."

"Thanks for having me, Lisa. I enjoyed it as well."

As he was returning to San Francisco, earlier thoughts popped back into his head. Who is he? Then he had a sudden thought. Why is it important to know that? Don't most people accept themselves without worrying about it? Why is it so important to him? He constantly compared himself to others, and almost always came in second. Ridiculous. He was Robert Delacroix, the idol of the western world.

What was it he wanted to think about some more? Oh yes. The people at the Behavioral Disorder Clinic. Was he like them in any way? It's stupid to make *that* comparison, isn't it? Of course it is. On the other hand, where would he be right now, if he were poor, sick, and not very intelligent? What would be left of him to survive on? Good question. Could he drag out the strength, the drive, even the courage from the depths of despair to save himself? But that was all beside the point, because he had never lived in dire circumstances. Yet the doubts, the fears, the depressive feelings so often intruded in his mind. He sighed.

"I'll think about it another time, maybe tomorrow."

# CHAPTER 13

"Why does she keep inviting us to dinner?"

The inner turmoil in Meilin's heart and mind emerged in her anguished voice and twisted face.

"Why does she keep doing this? Can't she just tell us we're not welcome? I don't get it. Hmm. Maybe she enjoys torturing us."

Arne gazed at her fondly.

"I think only one of us is feeling the pain," he said. "Try to relax. Maybe today is the day when things will change."

She frowned.

"What do you mean? Why should today be any different, any better? It could get worse, you know."

She sat staring straight ahead, the frown becoming a scowl.

"You're such a Pollyanna." She turned to look at him. "Do you know something I don't? Wait, I know. You have some magic dust to toss in her face. She will suddenly love all white, black, and green people. Ha, ha, ha."

The vehicle was pointed toward downtown, where the Xu residence stood on the edge of Chinatown, on Stockton Street. It would be a smaller than usual gathering, with only a few of the assorted brothers, sisters, aunts, uncles, nephews, and nieces in attendance. The two-story house was large, with many rooms, elegantly furnished, in keeping with Mr. Xu's status as a successful importer of jade statuary, paintings, and other artifacts, some from remote corners of China. The business had been built by his father's family and generated a very good income. Family ties to China remained strong, and Meilin and her brothers and sisters had all attended college there. Meilin had been sent to the University of Shanghai, but after fulfilling that obligation, she was free to go elsewhere for a graduate degree and elected to travel almost as far in the other direction. She earned a Ph. D. in World History at the University of Oxford.

Arne rang the bell, and the front door opened almost immediately. Meilin's brother Junjie stood there grinning.

"Hi, Sis. Arne, it's good to see you. Come on in. The dragon lair is open." He snickered.

"Junjie, you're awful." She hugged him tightly. He was, after all, an ally.

As they entered the living room, Arne, as always, was overwhelmed by the beautiful artwork. His favorite was a jade horse, its place of honor a shining black lacquered table. The shades of green seemed almost infinite in number, deep dark to pale, close to white. It stood nearly two feet tall, a warhorse with its head cocked towards the observer. Its back was broad, so that the body seemed foreshortened. He thought that someday he would like an hour alone in the room.

"Mr. Lund, once again it is an honor to have you in our home."

Mr. Xu and Arne both bowed slightly towards each other as they shook hands. "It is my honor, sir, I assure you."

Meilin smiled slightly; she knew that Arne loved the formality. He turned toward her mother. Chen Li also bowed slightly, with a murmured greeting not nearly as warm as her husband's. Another brother, a sister, and two aunts were introduced.

They all found seats for tea. Small talk ensued: the weather, everyone's health, Arne's admiration for the works of art.

"So, Mr. Lund, tell us of your latest work with *History Lives*. Do you have any interesting interviews coming up?"

"I can tell you that we have several in the planning stages that will, I believe, be very exciting and interesting. Unfortunately, as you may know, each interview is meant to be a surprise." Mr. Xu nodded. "However, I can tell you of some of my own research in language. I have been doing some extensive reading in Chinese literature, both in the original language and in English translations."

Meilin's mind suddenly snapped to attention. *What is he talking about? Is there something I'm not aware of? What is he doing?* She tried not to betray her surprise, but fortunately the others were all looking intently at Arne, including her mother.

"Ah, I am intrigued. Please enlighten us."

"I particularly liked *Zhuan Shuihu*, by Shi Naian. It's known in English as Water Margin."

"Ah, yes. It is one of the Four Great Classical Novels of our literature. Sadly, I read it many years ago and have forgotten much of it. I believe I must read it again."

"It's a wonderful book, probably written some time in the fourteenth century, although the oldest known copy was not printed until the middle of the sixteenth century. It's the story of a group of outlaws who were in opposition to the government of the Song Dynasty. They were forced to take refuge in the marshes at the foot of Mount Liang. They supported the emperor, but fought against the corrupt representatives of his government."

"They were criminals, I believe."

"Officially, yes. But it was quite a varied group. Some had been framed. Some had been ill treated by officials. Some had committed crimes deliberately, others in the heat of anger. Others were lifelong criminals, and some joined to be with the 'gallant fraternity'. They came from different professions. All were expected to follow the laws of chivalry, show filial piety and commitment to their comrades, respect the customs of Buddhism and Confucianism, and remain loyal to the emperor. It reminds one of Robin Hood and his Merry Men, the legendary band in old England."

"Yes, it comes back to me a little. Did you read it in Chinese or English?"

"Both, actually."

Arne could see that all were impressed, even Meilin's mother. He grinned.

"I went back and forth, to verify the accuracy of the translation. It took a while, but fortunately, I'm a fast reader."

"Perhaps you would like to enlighten my family further about the story."

"Has anybody read it?" Arne looked around.

Aunt Suyin raised her hand. "I have, also many years ago."

Arne smiled. "Good. You can point out my mistakes. Well, it is an immense book. The English translation I read was by Pearl Buck. It was almost seven hundred two-column pages closely spaced, with seventy chapters. Each group of two or three chapters is principally about one man. Late in the book however, it focuses more on the group of bandits. You know, the comradeship of such a diverse group of people suggests the reason for one of the other titles."

He paused. Finally, Mr Xu asked, "Which was?"

"All Men Are Brothers."

"Ah, yes." He nodded his head, but looked a little puzzled.

"It's interesting that this island of companionship and loyalty is right smack in the middle of a world of bloodshed, unbelievable cruelty and torture, and jealousy. So you can look at these two worlds and wonder. The outlaw's world is a very small one and was formed out of necessity rather than a group of idealistic people getting together voluntarily. They were all fleeing injustice, corruption, or fear of being killed or jailed. To survive they had to put aside intolerance and honor the differences that would ordinarily prevent any possibility of friendship. It would be something like the survivors of a shipwreck with little in common forming a community on the proverbial island.

"The novel is known as the novel of anger, because it stands for the fury and helplessness of the peasants and other little people of China, mistreated through robbery, murder, and oppression by the corrupt officials of the emperor's government. The outlaws considered themselves loyal to the emperor and the enemy only of the officials and generals of the Southern Song Dynasty. The anger of the novel is constantly underscored by the bloody violence, which is described in some detail. It's especially supported by the belief that killing or beating or other violence can be acceptable only when it is fuelled by emotionally inspired anger, but is absolutely unconscionable when the violence is planned and carried out in cold blood."

"Indeed." Mr. Xu was still looking puzzled.

"You know, Mr. Lund," he said, "the alternate title *All Men are Brothers* seems incongruous, since many of the people in the book seemed intent on behaving like enemies instead of brothers. It certainly is not a proper translation."

"You're right. I puzzled over that, so I did a little research. I discovered that it was Pearl Buck who chose the title, which is actually a quote from Confucius, and probably represents hope for the future."

At this point, dinner was announced. As they trooped to the dining room, Meilin sidled next to Arne and jabbed her elbow, hard, into his side. Both pretended nothing had happened.

Dinner was, in a word, elegant. Arne loved Chinese food. The dinner was reminiscent of the sumptuous banquets he had experienced when visiting China. Once again, they indulged in small talk for the duration of the dinner and for the adjournment back to the living room. Chen Li again said little, but Arne sensed her relaxation from the earlier stiffness, and her face seemed very nearly serene.

As they were saying their goodbyes, Chen Li looked up at Arne and murmured in a soft voice.

"You must come and visit us more often, Mr. Lund."

Xu Guang smiled as he inclined his head forward. The relatives looked pleased.

Meilin's eyes appeared glazed and she said nothing on their way to the vehicle. As they sat down, she remained silent and then burst into tears and hugged him tightly.

"Oh Arne, Arne!"

He also teared up, all the while smiling broadly. In a few minutes, Meilin released him, pulled away, and punched him in the arm.

"Okay, mister, explain yourself. What exactly happened there, and how did you know?"

He smiled lovingly at her.

"Well, I have felt for some time that she really wanted to accept me, but wasn't quite sure how to do it. After all, she had centuries of tradition to overcome. I had the crazy idea that my interest in Chinese literature, especially one of the four classics, would open the door a bit. Fortunately, your father read the book a long time ago, which allowed me to pose as the expert."

"You're a genius. Did you really read both versions?"

"Yes indeed. They're enormous books, and my research claimed a lot of late nights, but I'd say it was worth it." He smirked at her. "Wouldn't you?"

"Oh yes. Do you think we can start making plans now?"

"Don't see why not. But I don't think we should go too fast, do you?"

"No. Mom might wake up tomorrow and say, 'What have I done?'"

"Hopefully not."

* * *

Shannon opened her eyes earlier than usual for a Sunday. Robert slept quietly, with just a hint of a snore, a good indicator that he was alive, but not enough to have awakened her. She smiled fondly at him and quietly slid out from under the sheet. She walked to the kitchen and prepared a pot of coffee, taking a cup to the living room.

As she sipped, her thoughts turned to their relationship. Robert was seeing another woman. She was certain of that. She smiled again. He wasn't very adept at hiding things.

"I wonder who it is," she said aloud.

Shannon's curiosity was tempered by her basic indifference. She and Robert had a tacit agreement to accept the other's lovers and affairs. She frowned slightly. At least she thought it was tacit. She couldn't remember that they had ever discussed it. But it didn't matter, because that's the way it was. She believed that their attitudes were the same, but she also suspected that he had some internal conflicts. She thought that he accepted his own behavior with a tinge of guilt, and accepted hers, but was a bit jealous. Poor Robert. She understood his compass fluctuations intellectually, but not emotionally.

"Perhaps I don't have a compass at all," she said, although she knew that her attitudes about love and sex played a part in her decision not to marry. On the other hand, she realized that some day, when the bloom faded; and temptations lost urgency, marriage would be useful in guarding against the loneliness that would creep in as the years marched by. When would that happen? Ten years? Fifteen? Twenty? Sooner?

"My goodness," she thought, "I don't seem to be able to predict the future. The renowned Shannon Remington, the girl who can do anything, who knows everything, owns a faulty crystal ball. I'm a sham, a fraud."

She gazed out the window, looking almost wistful.

"Good morning. Did you arise with the sun?" Robert shuffled into the living room, looking adorable with tousled hair, a knuckle buried in his eye, and starting an enormous yawn. He is a little boy, in more ways than one. Shannon smiled fondly at him.

"Not quite. It was early for me, certainly. Want some coffee?"

"I'll get it."

He filled a cup for himself, replenished hers, and sat down beside her, and grinned.

"So, last night, was it good for you?"

Shannon stared at him, disbelief in her eyes.

"You know very well that it's always good for me. But I can't believe you said that, Robert. Really."

Instantly, the grin disappeared from his face. He looked down and away.

"Sorry. Don't know what came over me. Actually, I was only kidding."

Shannon was again surprised. The little boy reaction seemed to be happening more frequently. She also remembered that his usual post-interview depression seemed deeper and lasted longer than usual after the program with Jamila Doumani, the first world president. For some reason, curiosity overcame her intolerance for his self-pity, and she decided to explore the situation a little further and to tackle it head-on.

"Robert, what's wrong? You seem to be out of sorts lately. I thought the interview with President Doumani went very well, and yet you seemed more down than usual. Was there a problem that wasn't apparent to the viewers?"

"No, no. Nothing like that. It's just—I don't know."

"What?"

He sighed, despair in his voice and on his face.

"It—" He stopped and then the words rushed forth. "There were supposed to be really great changes in the way the world operated after the world federation was formed. There *were* changes, great changes. No more nuclear arms worries. Nations have been at peace with each other. Some of the dangerous trends were reversed, while others were slowed. But human nature is still human nature, with its good side, yes, but the bad side is still with us. We still have internal wars, we still have crime, and we still have greed and selfishness. They're all still there. The environment isn't fixed, populations are still rising, and countries are failing. Will we end up with a failing world, after all? It's very disheartening, don't you think?"

She stared at him for a moment. This is new, she thought. He usually laments about himself. Now he's worried about the whole world? She mentally shook her head.

"Of course it is. But look at it this way. The population of the planet is over twelve billion. One way to look at that number is that it's too big. True enough. But another way is this. You are one person. Are you trying to take all the world's ills into your heart and your brain? It can't be done. If we are on a one-way trip to disaster, blame it on evolution, blind evolution that doesn't know where it is going, as your friend Mr. Darwin said. That means that there is no one to blame. There have been many bad people on this earth, and we blame them for the awful things they do. But we're really blaming the genes, as you yourself have said. They are the source of the blindness, aren't they? They don't know what they're doing. They never did, and, this is most important, they never will. The good ones and the bad ones are being constantly shuffled. We can't communicate with them; therefore, we can't direct them. Think of it: twenty five thousand genes times twelve billion people. A rather large number, don't you think?

"So, here's my advice, Robert, to go from the mind boggling to the mundane: relax and enjoy the ride."

She grinned and shrugged her shoulders. Robert chuckled and nodded his head.

"Of course you're right. It's a bigger burden than I really need, I guess."

Unfortunately, resigning to the inevitable is easy enough to say, but saying the words doesn't do the job. The vague sense of depression didn't go away. Robert felt it; Shannon could see it on his face. How long can this go on? Maybe he's really still thinking of his own problems and projecting on to the world stage. Is that possible? She sighed inwardly, and returned to her usual neutrality. Feelings were pushed to the background, as they made plans for the day.

\* \* \*

A week later, Rebecca and Robert decided to spend their free afternoon at the same beach south of Half Moon Bay. The girls were spending the day with friends and Bernie would return from a trip the next day. This time they paid greater attention to the surrounding beach and rocks. The tide had receded substantially and they decided to explore a small inlet with stepping-stones and shallow pools. They were able to venture out to an area still covered with shallow water. Small crabs scurried beneath their gaze. There were many sea anemones, several sea stars, and even a sea cucumber, as well as a number of aquatic plants that neither of them could identify. They said little except to point out the various creatures to each other. Robert's dark thoughts faded for a while, but returned when he and Rebecca retreated to the beach as the tide began to reverse direction. They sat on the sand and gazed at the waves.

"Do you ever wish you had taken your life in another direction, Rebecca?"

Her ocean inspired reverie interrupted, she replied rather sharply.

"What? What did you say?"

"Oh, I'm sorry, I didn't realize you were concentrating. Sorry."

"Actually," she said in a slightly softer tone, "I'm not concentrating on anything. I was lost in the ocean, so to speak. Now, what was it you were saying?"

"Oh, it wasn't important, not really important at all. Don't worry about it."

She frowned at him.

"Robert, what is it?"

"Well, I was wondering whether you ever wished you had gone for a different career, maybe even staying in research to study MONTY and his ways and foibles."

"Of course, I've considered many possibilities. But then, I'm a lucky person. I was born with abilities that would enable me to do different things well. I chose *History Lives* because it was groundbreaking and an exciting venture, and I've never regretted it. I believe there are three ways to deal with a choice you've made: enjoy it, live with it, or get out. If you enjoy what you've chosen to do, that is wonderful. If you don't enjoy it, but allow yourself to live with it, you may be compounding a mistake. So if you don't, then either figure out how you can enjoy it, or get out."

She looked at him askance.

"Do you wish you were doing something else?"

"No, I guess not. But—"

"What?"

"You and John invented MONTY. The scientists, the engineers, and the technicians do creative things to make the show work. I'm the beautiful face," he said bitterly. "I'm a voice, a picture on a screen.

"I read what others have written, then I spout it on the stage. The only thing remotely original is the way I say things. The content belongs to the rest of you. Even the person I'm interviewing, who isn't even real, learns new things, is actually thinking. Who knows how many people can do what I'm doing? Hundreds, thousands, who knows? You're a genius, Rebecca. I think probably several others are too. Shankar Lal, maybe Sonia Rifkin, John. Every one of them is really bright. I'm bright too, but they create, I don't. I read, I talk, I pose."

Rebecca could think of a contradiction or two among the things he said, but thought it would be best not to point them out.

"How long have you felt this way, Robert?"

"Probably most of my life, but more and more lately."

He chuckled without humor.

"My cousin used to say, 'You may be good in school, but you ain't got any common sense.' *Ain't.* Isn't that funny? Ha, ha."

He looked at her with devastated eyes and appeared almost ready to cry.

"Are you depressed, Robert? If so, you should get some help."

"Yeah, that's what Shannon thinks, and Electra before her. I suppose I should think about it."

Rebecca had two thoughts. It appeared that he has been carrying a burden for some time, but she didn't know much about his life, and had no idea what the causes might be: his relationships, the chemistry of his body, or some combination? That was for a professional to help him sort out. The other thought was more personal. Where is this relationship going, if anywhere? She was committing adultery, and for the first time that she could remember, her ability to compartmentalize her life was breaking down, and she didn't like it.

"Come on, Robert, let's go back, have a drink and finish this day on a high note."

She took his arm, and smiled up at him. After a bit, he responded with a smile almost as bright as his television one.

# CHAPTER 14

Meilin and Arne entered the meeting room together. A few people were seated, but most stood around gossiping while waiting for the meeting to start. Meilin could see that the group was larger than usual, and wondered why, until she noticed several persons standing near the high window facing the street. She nudged Arne with her elbow.

"My goodness!" she exclaimed. "Look who's here. This must be a special day."

"What do you mean? Who? Who's here?" Arne looked around.

"Over there. By the window, talking to John and Rebecca. Don't you recognize him? That's Andrew Cotton!" In response to Arne's blank look, she continued. "He's probably the foremost authority on human evolution in the world. I wonder why he's here. They must be planning something really special. Ah, now we'll find out."

Rebecca Feldman moved to the front of the room. She stood there for a short time, as the others found places to sit. The noise of conversation faded. She smiled broadly.

"Hello, everybody. Welcome to our monthly meeting. Today, we have a special guest, who will present to us an idea for a groundbreaking interview, beyond any that we have done so far in the history of the show. If we can bring it off, it will take us beyond history, in a sense." She paused. "However, if I keep talking, I'm in danger of spoiling the surprise. So, I would like to introduce to you Dr. Andrew Cotton. Many of you know of him, but for those few who may not, he is *the* world's authority on the evolution of the human species, winner of the Nobel Prize for medicine and physiology, and Alfred Russell Wallace Professor of Genetics and Evolution at the University of North America. I could go on, but perhaps I'd better not. Ladies and gentlemen, Andrew Cotton."

Eager eyes and clapping hands followed Dr. Cotton as he advanced to the podium. He nodded and smiled at the applause. Rebecca took a seat in the front row.

"Thank you. You're very kind. And thank you, Rebecca, for your brevity. I'm famous for blushing, if nothing else, and I'm pleased that I am able to remain a relatively pale color." He smiled again at the laughter.

"Along with so many people all over the world, I have followed your historical presentations closely and with great fascination. The collective feat is truly remarkable. I would like now to offer to you an idea that, if fulfilled, can transcend everything that you have done so far and hopefully, set a standard for further exploration, if I may put it that way.

"Some time ago, you presented us with a very interesting view of the biblical figure Noah, with some pretty sensational new revelations. That presentation was, of course, within the limiting framework of biblical history, a remarkable feat in itself. In the same framework, one can go further back in time and look at an original biblical character, the first woman, Eve. However, our interest is in a different, evolved Eve, a female who lived about one hundred to two hundred millennia ago. We think there may be enough information available to recreate her for your program. I speak of mitochondrial evidence, combined with the fossil record, radioactive dating, and genetic information and inference.

"We are looking for one female. However, we must be aware that there are likely to be many females, each of whom could qualify as *an* Eve. Why do I say that? We know from numerous other evolutionary histories, that it is quite impossible to pinpoint exactly when one species becomes another. It is not an instant transformation. It is a process occurring over many generations, with the contribution of numerous genes to the transition. One can't choose one individual as *the* initiator of a new species, since there were many potential Eves living within one generation and also over many generations. Our goal is to identify *an* Eve in one slice of time, bring her to 'life', see what she is like, and hopefully gain some insight about our most ancient human ancestors.

"Now, one of the vital aspects of your presentations is that it is possible to talk to the subject of the interview. With Eve, of course, you will be on uncertain ground. We still don't really know how speech evolved. In fact, we really don't know much at all about early speech. We know that we can talk and that other animals cannot, except in a rudimentary way. The rest is theory and conjecture. Therefore, what we hope for is that we will find a person who has at least rudimentary language skills that can be enhanced by your machine, and bring with her the gift of conversation. I am very excited about the prospect, and I hope that all of you will be as well."

Dr. Cotton turned to Rebecca Feldman.

"I think that gives a decent overview of what we have in mind. Perhaps these folks may have some questions for us."

Feldman grinned as she stood up and said, "I suspect you may be right about that." She turned towards the group. "Yes. Meilin."

"Hello, Dr. Cotton. It's a great honor for us to have you here. My name is Meilin Xu. I'm a historian, and something less than an expert on genetics. You mentioned mitochondrial evidence. Will you please explain what that means?"

"Certainly. There are two sources of inheritance in the cell. The best known, of course, is the chromosome set. These bodies reside in the nucleus, and carry the nuclear genes, which are distributed based upon Mendelian rules, giving us the familiar inheritance ratios or statistical distributions. Outside the nucleus, in the cytoplasm, are the mitochondria. There are many of them and they have a major function, which is to provide the energy that drives the metabolism. They also have a genetic component, known as mitochondrial DNA, or mtDNA. A sperm cell has few or no mitochondria, while the egg, with a great deal of cytoplasm, has many. Only females produce egg cells, therefore the genes in the mitochondria are transmitted only in the female line.

"These genes mutate, and we can estimate the mutation rate and human generation length, enabling us to trace, from the existing female population, back through time to the most recent female ancestor of all the people on earth now. That person has been dubbed Mitochondrial Eve. We estimate that she lived from one hundred to two hundred thousand years ago. She was one of many females living in Africa at that time.

"This kind of information gives us a place and time to look, but tells us nothing about any other characteristics of Eve. So, for our purposes, we need to combine other types of evidence with the age dating of the mitochondrial evidence, so that we have sufficient information to create an individual to appear on your stage."

Cotton looked down the table. "Yes, on the left."

"Hi. I'm Kenichi Tamata, feedback engineer. With most of our subjects, we have had available to us several kinds of information: books, pictures, voice records. In this case, we won't have anything except, I guess, fossil records, evidence of tool making, rituals, etc. With regard to fossils, what do we have?"

"Well, we have about one hundred thousand years to work with, from about two hundred thousand years ago, with the first appearance of archaic *Homo sapiens*, to one hundred thousand years ago, with the appearance of several genes associated with speech. Any female existing in that period can be characterized as an Eve, which gives us quite a few people. So, in Africa alone, we have accumulated many skeletons and parts of skeletons, as well as evidence of living sites, art, rituals, tools, and hunting. There are several places rich in these kinds of evidence, where we have the best chance to put enough information together for you to create our Eve. They are in places in the Rift Valley of Kenya and Ethiopia, perhaps in the Lake Eyasi region of Tanzania. We have to choose evidence from a site that will yield the greatest amount of information to combine with the other types of information available to us."

Jomo Kobaka raised his hand, and introduced himself as a nano-electronics technician.

"You've told us about looking for an Eve. What about an Adam? Is he there too?"

"Excellent question. There is a technique for tracing back to an Adam. The male ancestor of all humans living today is called Y-chromosomal Adam. Only males have a Y-chromosome, and one traces backwards in a similar manner as when looking for mitochondrial Eve. Early evidence suggested that the male common ancestor existed more recently than the female, but further research showed that they might have existed during the same time frame.

"Theoretically, our mitochondrial Eve could have mated with our Y-chromosomal Adam. But in a time frame of thousands of years, that's quite unlikely."

He turned toward Feldman.

"Rebecca, will you provide these folks with details of the task that lies before us."

Rebecca came back and stood at the head of the table, considering how best to begin.

"Okay." She paused again. "Plainly, this will be a unique opportunity and a tremendous challenge for our wondrous array of machines. We propose to create a person out of a non-person, so to speak. We have no actual history of an Eve, no written description, no photos, no paintings, and no contemporary supporting evidence except the fossil record, including some ancient DNA samples. We will try to find a period of time in the past where that fossil record is richest.

"The rest of the information that we will use to create Eve will be indirect. For example, we know that tool-making, controlled use of fire, hunting, and migration were all activities that began before the period we will look at, back in the Lower Paleolithic or Old Stone Age. During the Middle Paleolithic, people learned to cook, make art objects, conduct burial rituals, and use rudimentary language, as well as other skills. This is the period we will concentrate on, and try to cobble together a most likely

Eve.

"From Robert's conversation with Eve, we hope to find out much more of the culture of the time. How did they take care of their elderly? Were their burial ceremonies religious in nature? How large were their groups? Were they friendly with other groups? What was the relationship between men and women?"

The crew realized how unique the new project would be. They would be bringing forth an historical figure that existed before history, a figure that would be real and unreal at the same time. Henry VIII was real, Hitler was real, Vlad the Impaler was real. Even Noah was part of biblical history. He was described as a person, placed in a context, the Book of Genesis in the Old Testament. These and other thoughts raced through people's minds. John Sorensen voiced one of those thoughts.

"Rebecca, this interview will be unique in another way, with consequences that we should be prepared for, or at least be aware of. Our Eve will be compared with the Eve of Genesis. Perhaps it would be a mistake to give her that name. Many people wrote us that they were upset with our presentation of Noah. In his case the Old Testament was our first source of information, so our presentation could be considered as an interpretation. With Eve, we're proposing a new hypothesis, so to speak." He smiled. "I'm not sure how many will see that as a real difference, but it will be interesting to see how our audience and viewers react."

"Indeed it will be. Well, there will be some controversy, but we have dealt with that before. Now, it's time to get on with the show."

Rebecca passed out a preliminary plan folder, outlining the tasks of the various teams that would create the character. They would begin with the fossil record, to generate an image of Eve's skeleton, defining her height, skull size and shape, approximate weight, and arm and leg dimensions. MONTY would then use those dimensions to create Eve. The fossil record would also describe Eve's environment, including the animals and plants she lived with and ate. It might also tell of her immediate group: its size, its hierarchy, if any, and its hunting and fishing capabilities. Known artifacts of the period would tell something of her group's culture:

their art and decorative beads and bracelets, cooking utensils, and other tools and weapons that were the silent witnesses to their lives. Artifacts native to one region, when found in another, would show trading activity. All the background and environmental information would be fed into her brain and endow her with memories of life during that period.

The information from each line of research, fed into MONTY's processors, electronically spun, whirled, looped, and combined, would emerge from the maelstrom as Eve, to be observed and quizzed in the test cubicle. Then, they would ask the question: Is she ready? If so, the show would go on.

\* \* \*

"Ladies and gentlemen, tonight we present to you a truly extraordinary show. All of our shows are special, of course, but I think you will agree that this show is beyond expectations, ours, and I hope yours as well."

Robert Delacroix stood bathed in the glow of a single spotlight, his eyes shining with excitement at a level seldom noticed before by his audiences.

"I beg your indulgence to take a few minutes to set the stage for what you will soon see. We will go far back into the mystery of time, into prehistory. In consequence of this immense journey, the person you will see and hear comes from a time when the use of language was somewhere near its beginning. This person will be using English words, but in a rudimentary way. We hope meanings will be clear, but I apologize ahead of time for any difficulty our guest will have in getting her point across, and that you may have in understanding her. Hopefully, we have been able to minimize these difficulties in our preparation for the show.

"You just heard me say that this person is female. Not the first human female, who would be almost impossible to identify with certainty, but a very early one indeed. Ladies and gentlemen, let us go back many thousands of years and meet—Eve!"

Members of the studio audience gasped. Faces showed anticipation, surprise, bewilderment, and a few frowns. One could be sure that television audiences everywhere showed the same reactions and made sounds reflecting everything from delight to disapproval. As the cubicle lights came slowly to life, a young woman emerged from the gloom, sitting on a large flat basaltic rock. She was barefoot, but otherwise lightly clothed. Viewers expecting to see heavy furs engulfing her body were surprised to see long leaves woven basket fashion around her torso. Apparently hanging on one shoulder, the covering had some flair, and could easily be called an outfit.

Her skin and eyes were brown; she had long very curly hair, also brown, that grew straight from her head and gradually curved downward. Her glance darted from side to side. She could see her hair out of the corners of her eyes, and realized how enormous its structure was. She put up a hand to touch it and frowned.

"Where my holder?" Her voice was low and puzzled, but not frightened. "Where holder?" Louder but still not frightened.

In the back stage area, the technicians were equally puzzled.

"What is she talking about?" asked Joshua Stayfield, of wardrobe. "We didn't program anything for her hair. Surely they didn't decorate themselves that long ago?"

Jamie Driscoll grinned. "Maybe they did. She is a woman after all. And that's a lot of hair not under control. Maybe she had a gold clip, decorated with lapis lazuli and garnets and opals."

"I don't think so."

"I don't either," said Meilin, "but she must have worn something."

"Let's hope Robert can handle this," said John Sorensen.

Robert was desperate to handle it properly. He did not want to start the interview in an awkward manner. After a moment, he decided that simple and obvious would work best.

"You are missing something for your hair?"

"Yes. Hair. To hold in, bunch. Too big."

Robert made an "O" of his thumbs and forefingers and put it behind his head.

"Like this?"

She nodded and smiled.

"We'll get one for you. In the meantime, perhaps we can talk. May I call you Eve?"

"Eve? Eve? What mean Eve?"

"It's your name?" he asked with some hesitation.

She frowned again. "No, no. I Nala." She pointed at herself. "Nala."

"You already have a name?"

A new expression changed her face. It said, "Are you crazy or stupid?" She said, "Of course I have name."

Robert Delacroix realized that he had knotted things up and had better loosen them.

"I am sorry, Nala. We didn't know much about you, and I made a mistake."

A slightly superior smile appeared on her face as she gazed at him. "It is okay. Okay. I like word. Okay."

At that moment a metallic ring about fifteen centimeters in diameter materialized beside her on the rock. Delacroix pointed at it.

"Will that do?"

She picked it up and inspected it closely. Surprise and curiosity replaced the smile. Clearly, the technicians had not been able to fabricate anything that could have been made or found many millennia ago at such short notice. For a few seconds nobody breathed. Finally, she grasped her hair and worked it through the ring. She looked at Delacroix and smiled with warmth rather than disdain.

"I like this. Thank you."

He smiled back. "You're welcome. By the way, my name is Robert Delacroix. Perhaps we could talk and you can tell me more about yourself."

"Yes, I would like that." She looked around. "This is strange place. I don't see much. You. This rock." She touched her hair. "What make this thing around hair? We no have at our place."

"It is made from a substance called metal. We take something called ore out of the ground and treat it with heat. It becomes metal, which is made into different shapes, including the holder."

"Very strange. We not know of this. Mine made from tree or, um, grass, strong grass. This one very nice."

"You are a long way and a long time from your place. What is it like?"

"There are many trees. Big. Little. Green grass. Water." She moved her hand in a line. "It goes past our place."

"A stream."

"Yes. A stream. Many streams. All around." She swept her arm in a half circle.

"That place is much different now. It is very dry with many rocks and plenty of sand. It would be hard to live there now."

"That is too bad. It was a nice place. We stay—stayed there a long time."

"You moved to another place?"

"Yes. Must go to new places. Walk long way. Stop. Stay."

"Which direction did you walk?"

"Away from the sun."

Delacroix looked puzzled. She pointed back behind her head.

"Sun was there, high in sky. We walked away."

"Ah, yes, I understand. It was midday. The sun was slightly behind you. You walked north."

"Yes. North. Each time we walked north."

"Why did you move?"

She grimaced and shook her head in resignation. "It was the animals. Some places they were very big. They chased us and ate us. So we went away. Other places we stayed longer. Small animals in those places. We could catch them. Spear them. Kill them. Eat them. Then they gone. Not enough berries. So then we went away. Some places had many animals, many berries, flowers. Plenty to eat. We stay longer."

"Did you eat any other kind of food?"

"Yes. We dug roots to eat. Some plants had soft leaves. We ate them."

"What about the fish in the streams?"

She laughed. "Sometimes, we tried to catch them. Walk into water.

Stand still until fish not afraid and swim close. Then we try to grab with both hands. Fish swim away. Sometimes we fall in water, get all wet. Look funny. Everybody laugh. Sometimes too fast for fish and catch. Fish wiggle. Everybody very happy. Fish tasted good."

"Did you cook them on the fire?"

"Yes. We put them on flat rock near fire to get hot. Then we ate them. Very good."

"How many people were in your band?"

She looked puzzled. "We did not make music."

He chuckled. "Not that kind of band. A group of people."

He thought to himself: Make a note. Fix the dictionary going into the program.

"Oh, yes. Not many." She stopped and thought, apparently counting in her head. "Sometimes twenty, sometimes thirty, sometimes more. Sometimes many babies came, sometimes not as many. Sometimes many died, from sickness or from the big animals. It varied." She smiled at the word.

"When people grew old, did you take care of them?"

"Oh yes. We brought them food and water, made soft places for them to sleep. Soon they got very old or sick, and died, so we made a bed of sticks and dried grass for them to lie on. Then we all stood around in a circle, and each person said a nice thing about them. We gave them a favorite belonging to take with them and made a fire of the bed. It was sad, but not as sad as when a child died."

"Where do you think they went?"

"We knew nothing about that. Maybe close, maybe far away, but we hoped they were happy."

"Did your people believe in a god or gods or spirits, beings that exist but can't be seen?"

She paused for some moments, a slight frown over her face. She seemed to be organizing thoughts, ideas that were strange and confusing. She spoke slowly.

"Many times, we sat around our fire as the darkness came and talked about strange things and happenings that we could not understand. What made the wind and its sound? Why did the water move? Why did things always go down? Even when we threw a stone up, it turned and came down. Why does the sun move? And the moon? Why could we look at the moon, but if we looked at the sun, it made us close our eyes?

"We talked about these things. Some said one thing, some said another. Some people said spirits, but we couldn't see them. Were they there?" She grinned and shrugged. "No one really knew. We were—"

"Ignorant."

"Yes, ignorant. We knew nothing." She sighed. "Do you know these things now, Robert?"

"Well, we have learned a lot in all the years. But we don't know everything yet."

"Tell me about up and down."

"It's called the law of gravity. Gravity is a force that makes two bodies attract each other. The earth is a very big body, and a stone is very small. So the earth has very strong gravity and the stone very weak, and the earth always pulls back the stone. When you throw it in the air, the strength of your arm only makes the rock go away from the earth a short distance, then it falls down."

She frowned and shook her head slowly. "I don't think I understand that."

Robert said, "Well, it's very strange to you, because it's a new idea and out of context for you. If you lived now, you would have known many of the things we have learned since your time. All that knowledge would help in learning more things, like gravity, the sun and moon, and how living things grow."

"I would like to know these things."

"Well, you're learning things now that are new to you."

They smiled at each other.

"Let's move on," said Robert. "Did you have a mate, Nala?"

"Oh yes. His name was Tamba. He was a nice man. We did many things together. Hunted. Made babies. Laughed. Made many things.

Walked. Took care of the children. We had good times. Also sad times."

"What were the sad times?"

"When the children died. When we had to leave a nice place when the animals killed us, or we didn't have enough food. Sometimes there was too much rain and the streams got too big and made us run away."

Robert Delacroix and John Sorensen had the same thought at the same time, which they discovered in a later conversation. Nala was learning to speak English during the interview, at an impossibly rapid rate. Impossible, except that it was happening. Each man held the fleeting thought for further examination.

"Do you know how you made babies?"

"Not sure. The place that baby came out was the same place Tamba went in. We made the baby. I don't know how." She grinned. "Not in my context."

"How did your group decide to do something, like moving to another place? Did you have one person who was the leader?"

"Leader? No. We decided together. We sat down around the fire and talked. Then we decided."

"All of you, men and women?"

Nala flashed another look: What a silly question. "Of course, men and women and even the older children. We decided together. It is true that some persons had better ideas and we listened closely to them. But we all decided." She paused. "Those were very important times."

"Tell us about some of the important decisions you made during those times."

"Sometimes we had to decide whether to move someplace else, when to go, what to take with us. Sometimes a few people did not want to go, and we left them there. That was very hard and it made me sad." She lowered her head, but quickly lifted it and smiled brightly. "Fortunately, that didn't happen often, only once in a while. Usually, we all went together. We were happy. It was an adventure.

"Often, we sat around the fire and planned a hunt for the next day. This was important when we had to hunt a big animal. It was necessary that each person know what to do, so that we would be successful in killing the animal and no one would be hurt or killed.

"Sometimes we visited other groups like us and brought things for them, and they had things for us. We traded. Tamba, Doko, and Maral made very good spears from the little trees near some of the places where we lived. They were very straight and very sharp. We gave these to other bands and they gave us pretty stones and other stones with sharp edges."

"Axes and knives."

"Yes. We made them too, but some other groups made better ones. We were still learning."

"Were there other times when you were sad, or frightened?"

"Oh, yes. Sometimes we met bands that did not want to trade. They wanted to take things from us. They had things, um, weapons that they hit us with. They threw the women and girls on the ground and raped us. It hurt a lot. But then our men could take their weapons and hit their men and finally made them run away. It was very bad, but we learned that we had to have weapons too. Our spears could kill people as well as animals. It was very bad."

She looked at Robert.

"Does that still happen?"

Robert drew a deep breath. Her eyes were filled with the evil memory. He couldn't speak; only nod his head. There was a long silence. He returned to the earlier subject.

"You said that you and Tamba made things together. You mean things from the pretty stones?"

"Yes. Things to hang around our necks. Necklaces. We made holes in the stones and strung them together with strong strands from plants. We did not have wire—" She stopped and frowned. "Wire? Wire? Why did I say that?"

Robert Delacroix also frowned. "I don't know. Wire is a thin strand of something we call metal. Your holder is also made of metal."

"Yes. How do I know this?" Nala looked around as if seeing the cubicle for the first time. She stood up and walked to the side of the cubicle and looked out.

"What is this place? How did I get here? Why are those people out there?"

She was apparently not frightened. The interview could now be called a truly remarkable one, beyond the fascination of meeting historical figures almost in person. John Sorensen, watching closely, thought that this might be another glitch to talk about in future speeches, or maybe something more.

Robert pulled his wits together as best he could. "I'm surprised that you didn't ask that earlier."

"I was struggling with the words. Then I was interested in your questions."

"What have we wrought?" thought Robert. "She is fascinating."

"You lived a long time ago," he said. "We have brought you back. Those people are watching and listening to us talk."

"How long ago?"

"About one hundred thousand years. Do you know what a year is?"

"It is the time it takes for the sun to come back to a place in the sky."

He nodded. An astronomer too!

"That's a very long time. How did you bring me back?"

"We have a very powerful machine. We put into it a lot of information about the people who lived in your time. The machine, um, puts all the information together."

"It processes the information."

"Indeed, it processes the information." Robert could hear some murmuring in the audience.

"You said information about people. I am more than one person?"

"In a manner of speaking. You lived in what we call pre-historic times and we have no records of specific persons. Historic people, who came later, had names and many of them were well known, so we had many records about them."

"So you called me Eve, because you had no other name for me. Was there a real Eve?"

"We have a book called the Bible. It names Eve as the first woman who lived on this planet, Earth. Some people believe that she was real, but others do not. She is called Biblical Eve. We wanted to find a very early human woman; we refer to her as Evolutionary Eve."

"But I am not real either." She smiled wickedly and cocked her head to one side. "How do you explain that?"

"It's not going to be easy."

She looked thoughtful. "And yet I knew a name for myself. You used a long word. Evolutionary. What does this mean?"

"It means that you are part of a long chain of events over a very long period of time that created beings who were very different from you and from each other. Millions of years ago, they looked a tiny bit like you. They walked on two legs, rather than all four, and they didn't have long tails. But they were very small, had hair all over much of their bodies, small heads, long arms, and had just learned to walk rather than swing through trees. Their brains were so small that they didn't know how to make fire or tools, and they could not talk like we can. They made noises like animals."

"Grunting and roaring."

"Yes. Then, little by little, over thousands of years, new people came along who knew more and could do more things. They grew taller, lost most of their hair, and their brains grew bigger, so they learned to talk, to make things, and to think about things."

She smiled. "And now, you can do things even better than me and my people."

"Well," said Robert, "we're still learning."

She looked closely at him.

"Well, perhaps you had better put me back in my machine, so that you can get to work. I would like to come back and learn some more new things."

"I think we can manage that. I want you to know how much I have enjoyed talking to you. Until we meet again, I'll say goodbye."

"Goodbye."

As the image faded, the audience sat entranced and then burst into wild applause.

The first question from the audience was not a surprise.

"How did she get to be so smart?"

Robert Delacroix smiled and shook his head. "I have no idea." He pointed behind him. "I'm hoping somebody back there will tell me."

"Has this ever happened before?"

"Possibly, but not as dramatically. We'll probably have to examine the electronic records of the shows, with tonight's experience in mind, to figure it out. I suppose that this is a facet of the overall mystery. How do we explain why our subjects are greater than the sum of the information inputs?"

He answered several other questions, but his mind was in the conference room. Finally, it was time to say goodnight, after which he hustled backstage.

Rebecca Feldman had joined the group. They were sitting around the conference table, drinking liquids and munching snacks, obviously waiting for him.

"Well, Robert, what do you think?" demanded John Sorensen.

"It was astonishing. She learned to speak English, and to speak it well, during the interview. She also acquired a sense of humor, a consciousness of who she was, and most disconcerting of all, a sense of superiority—" he smiled sheepishly, "towards me."

Several people chuckled.

"So what happened? Have we seen this before and didn't notice?"

"We'll have to go back through previous programs," said Rebecca, "and look at them with tonight's program in mind, and hopefully the benefit of hindsight. We have seen evidence of thinking and reviewing."

Meilin Xu said, "It could be that she is very smart."

"I suspect that's true," said Rebecca. "But it would be remarkable if we picked the smartest person in all of Africa. Plus, she appeared orders of magnitude smarter than seems possible. Besides, let's remember that she is not a single reconstructed person. She is a conglomerate, a composite of who knows how many people."

"But she had a name. Where did that come from?"

"Don't know. Another MONTY mystery."

"The fact that our other people were all real historical figures may be important," mused John. "They all spoke well established languages, so there would be nothing to learn about speaking. They came from structured societies, so they already know the rules of social intercourse. Therefore, it would be hard to pick up much improvement, unless you were looking for it."

Robert spoke up. "Remember when I talked to Darwin and told him about modern genetics and evolutionary theory. He understood it all even as we were talking, though it was new to him. So he seemed to be learning rapidly also. But he was a very intelligent man and highly educated for his time. Also, FDR was surprised at his ability to think back and review his actions."

"Something else about Darwin, and Henry VIII as well," said Rebecca. "They both commented about their health, specifically that they both felt well. Each had been seriously debilitated. Henry had severe gout and could barely walk. Darwin had stomach problems that kept him bedridden. In the cubicle they were healthy. Suppose their 'brains' were also, um, healthy. Suppose they worked at far greater efficiency than a real living brain does. What works more efficiently than a brain?"

"A computer."

"Exactly. It seems reasonable that the subject's thinking device is our very powerful computer that enables him or her to learn at a rate that seems impossible." She sighed. "Of course this is all speculation until we solve some of MONTY's unknowns. *If* we solve them."

John said, "I'd say there is another problem that may be related: Why does MONTY occasionally lose data? That may be the key to other things, because it may tell us something about how his 'brain' works."

"I agree," said Rebecca. "We should write up our thoughts and notify the research labs as well."

# CHAPTER 15

"Suppose some of those people were living now. What would they be like? What would they do?"

Jamie Driscoll, a computer technician, had a habit of asking "what if" questions, which seemed to rise up endlessly out of her curiosity-laden mind. Her colleagues were constantly amused, intrigued, and entertained, but almost always responded to the sometimes bizarre queries with answers that ranged from genuine attempts to provide an answer to teasing, equally bizarre explanations.

"Do you mean: Would Henry try to off someone's head? Would Noah build an ark?" asked Josh Stayfield, the wardrobe maestro.

"Noah didn't build arks. Weren't you paying attention?" she retorted. "But yes, that's what I mean. What would they do?"

"Darwin's easy," said Sonia Rifkin, a molecular geneticist. "He would be a scientist. Perhaps he would be the only one who would fit in well. There aren't too many openings for divine right kings, or impalers."

"Yeah, that's really too bad," said Josh.

"This is a fascinating conversation, but if you will excuse me, I have to get ready."

Robert Delacroix took one more slug of water and headed for the stage. As usual he spent some time talking to the studio audience. This had the effect of warming them up and calming him down.

"Ladies and gentlemen, our guest tonight was famous for his bloody conquests and less so for his political reforms. It seems an unlikely combination, but as you shall see, perhaps not. Ladies and gentlemen, Genghis Khan."

The Mongol leader appeared, dressed in warrior uniform, his broad square face adorned with a thin mustache and scraggly beard descending from the lower part of his chin. He looked at Delacroix with no expression, as if assessing his situation.

"Good evening, Khan. I am Robert Delacroix."

Genghis continued to stare at him a bit longer.

"You are from Europe. Why are you here?"

Startled, Robert said, "No sir, I have a French name, but this is not Europe. This is a place called America. It is on another continent."

"America. I do not know that name. I do not recognize this place. Explain."

Robert once again told of MONTY and the circumstances of the Khan's appearance on the stage in the strange cubicle. As usual, he performed this task with some trepidation, not knowing what reaction to expect.

"So, you tell me I have been returned from the dead, but that I am not really alive. I feel alive, though I am made of a non-living substance. Strange."

He rose from the chair and inspected the cubicle, touching the walls as he went, looking carefully at the corners, and upwards through the ceiling. He was surprisingly tall and quite substantially built. Robert wondered how he fared on the back of a small Mongol horse. He wondered how the horse fared.

"This cubicle. I can see through it but I cannot pass through it. I cannot get out. This is very interesting." He sat down.

"What do you desire from me?"

"I would like to ask you questions. Many people are watching and will be interested in learning about you."

"Very well." He smiled thinly. "I will ask some questions too."

"You were born in the year 1162 and given the name Temujin. Your father was a chieftain in the Borjigin clan. You were betrothed at the age of nine, and taken to your future wife's family, to serve them until the marriage. Tell us what happened after that."

"While returning home my father was invited to stay in a camp with a group of Tatars. The food they gave him was poisoned and he died. When I discovered this, I immediately returned to my family."

"You then had a very difficult time."

"Yes. I claimed my right as a chief's son to become Khan, leader of the tribe. The tribe refused to grant my demand; they said I was too young. Bah! And then they abandoned my family. We lived on almost nothing, but we survived. We foraged for food and killed small animals. Finally we were allowed to return to the tribe."

"Then you were kidnapped and made a slave by your father's former allies."

"Yes, but I managed to escape. I became a stronger person. Soon I realized that the Mongols would never have much power as long as they kept wasting men and equipment on petty feuds and tribal wars, rotten with corruption, and with no ambition for greater things. We needed alliances, and unity. This became my goal."

"You united the tribes."

"Yes. It was sometimes difficult to do, because some tribes refused to join with others. I finally got them to stay together. This gave us strength. I taught them how to plan and fight a war. I picked good men as generals, not just members of my family. I gave them some of my authority. We used spies and obtained useful information from other tribes. Sometimes our opponents betrayed each other and deserted to us. We rewarded our people with wealth, and they became loyal. We gave the conquered tribes protection, and they too became loyal. They obeyed me without question. Once the Mongols were united under me, it was necessary to unite the clans that surrounded us: the Merkits, the Naimans, the Uyghurs, and the Tatars. We did this. It took five years."

He drew his head up proudly and again smiled.

"Soon there was a council of chiefs, a kurultai, which finally recognized me as Khan. It could no longer be denied to me. At last I could fulfill my destiny."

"And that was?"

"I was the sun in the blue sky. It is the essence of Shamanism. The sun covers the earth; therefore I would conquer the world. *That* was my destiny. That was *our* destiny, a Mongol world. I created a small Mongol world. It was time to expand that world. It was time to fulfill that destiny."

"First you had to defeat the Xia and Jin Dynasties, who lived in the areas that we now call Northern China and Manchuria."

"Yes. We needed trade and they obstructed us. They had control of the Silk Road, the best way to travel to the west. We needed access to that trading route. We fought the Xia first because I knew that the Jin would not offer them support. Then we fought the Jin."

"At first you beat them in battle but did not truly conquer them. After the battles you appointed puppet governments and you and your army left the area, and the Xia and Jin peoples remained in control."

"Yes, that was a serious mistake. We had to fight them again and truly conquer them by taking over their territory."

Robert turned toward the audience and told them of the Khwarezmid Empire.

"It was located in the place we now call Iran. It was quite large and also included parts of what is now Afghanistan, Uzbekistan, and Kazakhstan."

Turning back towards the cubicle, he said, "Tell us about your invasion of the Khwarezmid Empire."

"They also made a very serious mistake. We had conquered the Kara-Khitan Khanate to the west and had reached the border of the Khwarezmid Empire. Having the Kwarezmids as a trading partner would provide us great advantages, so I sent a caravan of 500 men to establish a trading agreement. On the way, a local governor's army attacked our caravan, claiming that it included spies. That of course was true. So then I sent three envoys, two Mongols and one Muslim, directly to the Shah. He cut off the Muslim's head and sent it back to us with the two Mongols."

He scowled.

"The Shah did not know us well. I organized a great army. It took a full year. Then we went back with twenty tumens, over 200 thousand men. We attacked from three sides. Many of our men died, but we killed all of our enemies. We destroyed their precious cities. I captured that governor and poured molten silver in his ears. The Shah ran away but died anyway. And then we destroyed everything. We leveled their fine capital cities, Samarkand, and then Bukhara. Towns and farms were leveled and burned. That was the end of the Khwarezmid Empire."

Then he smiled. "They did not know us well."

"You were fierce, and brutal, and vengeful."

"Of course. It was necessary, if one was to conquer."

"And yet, you had another side as a ruler. You brought many reforms to your empire."

The Khan looked sharply at Robert. "You do not think a leader can be a conqueror and also fair to his people?"

"History has shown us that it doesn't often happen that way."

The Khan reflected for a moment and smiled.

"You are right." He smiled again. "We found that most of the peoples we conquered hated their leaders and the nobles close to the leaders. We killed the leaders and nobles but spared the people most of the time. They respected us, feared us, and became loyal to us."

"Western Xia refused to aid the campaign against the Kwarezmids, and when that campaign was over you returned to punish them. You were successful, but you died in the late summer of 1227. To this day, mystery surrounds the manner of your death: a disease, a wound in battle, or a fall off your horse. Also, you were buried near your birthplace, but the location was obliterated and no one knows where it is. Would you care to solve those mysteries for us?"

The Kahn smiled and said nothing. Robert returned the smile, raising his eyebrows as an extension of the question. Still nothing. The audience groaned.

"Okay. Well then, tell us of your reforms."

Genghis Khan stood up, clasped his hands behind his back and slowly paced back and forth in the cubicle gesturing as he talked. He could have been a professor in front of a class.

"It was important to give the people a code of laws that would tell them exactly what I expected of them. I wanted to bring the clans together. There was to be no more bickering, no more betrayals. They had to know that crimes would be severely punished. They had to obey me without question. Those were the basic rules of the Yassa.

"I wanted freedom of religion. Many did not practice Shamanism as I did. As we expanded our territory, many religious groups came under our control: Buddhists, Muslims, Christians, and Confucians. We accepted them and their beliefs as long as they were loyal, and they were loyal because we accepted them. When I took their soldiers into my armies, they were scattered among the Mongols so there would be no divided loyalties, no temptation to revolt. Some ran away, and if we caught them they had to be punished, of course. Traitors from among the nobility were granted a bloodless death. They were crushed to break their backs. It was an honorable way to go.

"We developed our own written language, which was based on the language of the Uyghurs. With that language we wrote the code of laws, the Yassa. These were the rules of the empire, which all had to obey. For example, all men went to war unless they did special work for the empire. The army was large, organized in units of tens: ten, one hundred, one thousand, and ten thousand. Officers were responsible for providing their men with arms. Discipline was essential."

"Your army resembled an immense city in motion when traveling between battles. Please describe that for us."

Genghis smiled. "City in motion. Very good. I like that."

He returned to the chair and continued his reply.

"The city consisted of several parts. Most important was the army itself, perhaps of one hundred thousand men, in units of one hundred each.

They rode on horses; each man also had four remounts, so the horses would remain fresh. Besides the horses there were many oxen to haul the gers. Most gers were taken down every night when we stopped to sleep. Some remained erected for my officers, my wives, and me; the oxen hauled them. There were also flocks of sheep and goats for milk, meat, and wool. Our families also came with us. After a battle, the women collected arrows and killed enemy wounded. We stopped several times a day so the women could milk the sheep and goats. Children and elders collected dung for fires.

"We became the greatest army in the world. Our conquests were well planned. Scouts rode ahead of the main party to find the enemy. They could send signals long distances with colored flags. At night we used colored lanterns. We used different attack strategies, depending upon the type of resistance. We determined this with a great network of spies. Sometimes, we encouraged internal revolts and desertions. Sometimes we conducted sieges of cities and, if possible, diverted rivers to dry up their water supplies. Against the Kwarezmids, we divided the army into three parts and attacked from the northeast, southeast, and northwest. We did all these things by careful planning and fought with courage and discipline."

"Were there other laws?"

"Of course. It was forbidden to steal a horse or other valuable animal or someone's property. These crimes were punishable by death. Lesser crimes earned blows with a staff, at least seven, as many as seven hundred."

"How were women treated?"

"Women were honored. They did not fight, but they were as smart as the men, and we respected their opinions. I consulted with my mother and with my wives often. Each wife had her own ger, and her children and slaves lived with her. A man who wished to marry had to compensate her family. Kidnapping a wife was not permitted. A man could not marry a sister or a cousin. Adultery was forbidden. It was punishable by death."

"Many crimes were punishable by death."

"Those who committed crimes against honor or against duty would die. It is correct that this should be so."

"I read of one law that sounded quite intriguing. It was forbidden to wash clothes in running water during periods of thunder."

Genghis stared at him. "What else happens when there is thunder?"

Robert thought for a minute and snickered. "Lightning, which can be dangerous."

"Very good. You see, we thought of everything to protect our people."

Delacroix nodded. "Now, I would like to—"

"You will now answer my questions."

"Certainly. What do you wish to know?"

"After I died, did my sons continue building the empire?"

"Yes they did. You could not choose your eldest Jochi as your successor because he had died before you. You chose your third son, Ogodei instead of Chagatai, your second son. You did not consider Chagatai suitable."

"Jochi's mother had been kidnapped and raped. Still I accepted Jochi as my eldest son, but the other sons did not, especially Chagatai, who refused to serve under him. However, Jochi's death settled the issue. Chagatai was capable but did not deserve to be my heir. He did not get along well with his brothers." He stared at Delacroix. "Tell me what they did."

"Ogodei was later designated as Khaan or Emperor," said Robert. "He also bestowed that title on you posthumously. Your sons and grandsons were successful in expanding the empire. Your grandson, Batu, took the important Russian cities. He then conquered Poland and Hungary. The others advanced in the south as far as Serbia.

"Then your grandson Mongke, son of Tolui, became Khaan; he put his brother Kublai in charge of North China. There was a long war against the Song Dynasty until most of China was taken. Kublai founded the Yuan Dynasty. Eventually, the empire included all of eastern and western Asia and parts of Eastern Europe. It was the largest empire in history.

"However, your later descendants were not able to hold the empire together. You had divided the empire into four Khanates. Jochi's son Batu became Khan of the Golden Horde in Russia. Ogedei took charge of the Empire of the Great Khan: Mongolia and China. Chagatai ruled in Central Asia. Hulagu, son of Tolui, founded the Ilkhanate in Persia and other parts of the Middle East. But they could not reach agreement to choose a Khaan.

"Nor were they able to overrun Europe or Japan and had only moderate success against the countries of Southeast Asia, which is largely jungle and not suitable for cavalry. Of course, most of the rest of the world was out of Mongol reach. Little by little, the native peoples regained their territories. Eventually, only the area that you originally united was left. It is now called Mongolia.

"Your grandson, Kublai Khan, was probably the most successful of your descendants. He founded the Yuan Dynasty in China and then in Mongolia after defeating the forces of his younger brother Ariq Boke. He was the first Mongol ruler of China. During his reign he attracted visitors from Europe and the Middle East, welcoming both Christians, Moslems and leaders of other religions, as well as commercial and cultural visitors. One of the best-known European visitors was Marco Polo, who came from Venice, a city-state in what is now called Italy. It was a truly international court."

Genghis Khan remained silent for a while, his broad squarish face not in repose, but disclosing the turmoil inside. Finally he turned his narrowed calculating eyes toward Delacroix again.

"You have mentioned two things that puzzle me. You have said we were in a place called America. I do not know this place. You also said my sons could not, *of course*, conquer any other part of the world. You will explain."

"Certainly. I can show you maps that will help. First, let's look at the territory familiar to you."

He pressed some buttons on the console. A large, flat, and gently glowing holographic map appeared. The map was oblong in shape. It faced the audience, but was far enough back so that the Khan could have a good view of it. The map showed the entire Eurasian continent. By pressing a sequence of buttons, he successively highlighted the original united Mongol territory, followed by the added parcels of territory acquired by Mongol conquests first achieved by Genghis Khan, and then by his sons and grandsons, until by 1298 the empire included Mongolia, China, Russia, Central Asia, and the Middle East.

"This was the maximum territory the Mongols occupied. But the empire was too big and your descendants too fractious to hold on to it. So in subsequent years the empire disappeared until only Mongolia was left, as I said."

The Khan was silent.

"Now please watch carefully."

He pressed another sequence of buttons. The map began to enlarge and extend backwards, forming a glowing sphere. The audience murmured. The Khan remained silent but was obviously transfixed. Soon the sphere tilted and began to rotate.

"This is the world."

"It is a ball!"

"Yes, Khan. The light blue areas are oceans and these other landmasses are continents."

He pointed out Africa, Australia, Antarctica, and finally stopped the rotation to display the Western Hemisphere. He highlighted the United States and told the Khan that it was America. Then he showed the location of California and San Francisco."

"We are here. It is nineteen thousand kilometers from Mongolia, more than one million ald in your language."

He turned again to the audience and stretched out his arms.

"This is one ald."

People in the audience smiled or nodded. He looked at Genghis Khan.

"And there are two large oceans in the way."

Genghis leaned back and laughed.

"Those lands would be difficult to conquer. You cannot get there with horses."

"No. Now we use large ocean traveling ships or air vehicles, which go much faster and can fly anywhere."

"Ah. Let me see my homeland again."

The earth rotated half way and stopped. He examined it closely, and pointed to a place in the northeast sector.

"This is where I was born. What is this place nearby, Ulaanbaatar? It is a large city?"

"It is the capital city. A million people live there."

"Do my people live in cities now?"

"Many are still nomads, and live in gers."

The Khan returned to the chair.

"You know much about us. Does this MONTY know so much? Ah, no. MONTY knows what you tell it. And you know about us from history."

"We know thousands of years of history. We put all we know about you into the machine, and then I called you out here with this device in front of me."

"Where do I go when you are finished with me?"

"The information about you is kept in MONTY's storage unit, and can be retrieved at any time."

"Ah, yes, I expect that." He spread his hands. "Then I am truly immortal."

"Many Mongolians expect you to return someday, like a Messiah."

Genghis Khan looked thoughtful. He turned back to Robert.

"The Jews were waiting for a Messiah too. Did he ever arrive?"

"Christians believe so. They consider Jesus to be the Messiah. The Jews do not believe it. They are still waiting."

"Perhaps someday I can be returned to life."

"I am afraid that cannot happen. Except in the cubicle."

"That is a pity."

"However, you might be interested to know that tests of a substance we call DNA suggest the genetic materials from you and your relatives are found in a rather large segment of the population in Europe and Asia. So in one sense, you are indeed immortal."

The Khan looked at him, his mind obviously working.

"That is quite interesting."

"Well, Khan, I am afraid that we have run out of time and it is time to send you back to MONTY."

The Khan bowed his head but said nothing. He disappeared with the glow in the cubicle.

Robert Delacroix arose and moved upstage toward the audience.

"I can take some questions."

"How did he know about the Messiah?"

"Remember that his armies penetrated well into the Middle Eastern area and would have interacted one way or another with many different groups: Christians, Muslims, Jews, Greeks, Romans. That area was a grand mixture of peoples. Yes, in the back."

"Genghis Khan is renowned as a mass murderer. How many people did he kill?"

"It's estimated that over a five year period the Mongols killed fifteen million people in Central Asia."

"Do you think his 'reforms' compare to that?"

"Of course not. But remember, this was an ancient society in which he established some pretty enlightened modern concepts: freedom of religion, increased respect for women, and a written language. He set parameters of behavior that often resulted in harsh punishment, death in many instances."

"Other than the conquests and the reforms, what would you say made the Mongol Empire historically important?"

"Good question. It was a vast empire covering an enormous section of our largest continent, about one fifth of the land area of the earth. The conquests led to a tremendous increase in commercial and other traffic between east and west, especially during the reign of Kublai Khan. Many scholars believe that this was the beginning of globalization. Conquest always leads to transfer of culture, of goods, of technology, and of genes from one population to another. The Mongol conquests were on such a vast scale that such enrichment must have been truly remarkable."

After several more questions, Delacroix called a halt. The audience filed out, and he returned backstage to find the room a cauldron of consternation.

"What's the matter?"

"It happened again!" exclaimed Fred Bosworth, the assistant producer.

"What? What do you mean?"

"Genghis Khan. We can't find him in MONTY, anywhere."

Fred turned to Jamie Driscoll. "I want you to do the whole procedure again: every storage unit, every intermediate step. Check every information source, whether input or not. Both consoles. Everything. Hell, look in the computers that aren't part of the system."

"Okay." She left for the back room.

John Sorensen placed his hands behind his head and leaned back in his chair.

"The first time was a shot across the bow, a minor character in this play. The loss of that information was not such a big deal, but Genghis Khan's is. He's a major character, and more important, *this is the second time*. This shot has hit the main mast. Questions: Why is this happening? Where did he go, or rather, where did the information go? Was it deleted? What other consequences should we be concerned about?"

He turned towards Shankar Lal, who had worked out their "most probable outcome" solution, and Kenichi Tamata, their feedback engineer.

"If we decided to refashion these characters, how likely is it that the new ones would be exactly like the originals? Not the original people, just the images."

The two men looked at each other and appeared almost to communicate silently to each other. The others thought that was rather weird. After a few moments, they turned back to Sorensen.

"We can't give a precise number without doing some calculations," said Shankar, "but it is unlikely. MONTY is a black box, after all, and the sequence of calculations would be a little different each time."

"The differences would be slight, and may or may not be noticeable," said Kenichi. "To use a genetic analogy, it would depend upon whether a major gene mutated or a few genes of minor effect." He turned toward Sonia Rifkin, who nodded in agreement.

"Yes, a pretty good analogy, I think."

"I know we've discussed this before," said Meilin, "but is it possible that the information could have lighted someplace else, a computer in Palo Alto, or New York, or, or, or, Vladivostok."

"I really don't see how," chimed in Rebecca. "Not with the encrypted safeguards. It would blow whistles and ring bells. Loudly."

"Maybe somebody pressed the delete button," said Arne Lund.

"What?" chorused several voices at once.

"The delete button. Isn't that possible?"

"Not really," said Rebecca. "It's a fail safe situation. Three different people have to approve and the computer requires double verification. Each person has a dedicated button and they have to be depressed in a specified sequence."

"Nevertheless," said John, "it's a possibility. The labs looking into MONTY's black box have been unable to find a sequence of events that would cause a loss of data. So we remain in limbo, and we must continue searching. If you have any ideas, let me know."

# CHAPTER 16

Joe Hudson's world was a wonderful, warm, and fuzzy place. He had earned enough money from passersby to invest in a bottle of vintage wine for his evening cocktail hour. He liked the sound of the word vintage. It had a nice ring, though he hadn't the faintest idea when the wine had been bottled, and he used it whenever he could think of it. Now it was time for bed. He folded his burlap bag pillow and laid it at one end of his corrugated cardboard mattress, lay down, and gazed dimly upward at the brick walls of his alley apartment and the dark sky above. It had been a pretty good day; he was wearing a new shirt and pants from Goodwill, and felt quite rich.

He blinked his eyes. Something was obscuring his view. He blinked again. It was still there. He squinted and realized it was a person, a strange appearing person. The person was gazing down at him, saying nothing.

"Hey, you can't stay here. This is my space. Get outta here. Get outta here."

The person knelt down beside him, placed both hands on his scrawny neck and squeezed hard. Joe could feel his larynx being crushed. He gasped and gurgled, waving his arms. The hands were very strong. Joe couldn't get a breath. He was frightened. The fright disappeared as his eyes clouded completely over, and his body slowly relaxed. He was dead.

The stranger stood and looked impassively at the body. He knelt again and moved Joe's torso back and forth, stripping the clothes and breaking some bones in the process. He stepped deeper into the shadows of the alley with the bundle of clothes. He stripped off his own garments and struggled into Joe's shirt, pants, and shoes. Joe's years of panhandling and homelessness had wasted his body. He was quite skinny and his clothes were far too big for him. The stranger was a big man, no taller than Joe but substantially heavier. Joe's clothes were tight fitting, but the man thought they would have to do for now. He removed his round hat and put on Joe's baseball type cap. He gathered up his own garments, and looked around for a hiding place. There was a pile of bricks and other debris behind a trashcan. He burrowed into the pile, making a depression deep enough to hold the clothes, which he stuffed in and covered with the set-aside debris. He noted some trashcans towards the back of the alley and dragged Joe's body behind the cans placing it partially out of sight. He put his hand into the pockets of Joe's clothes, discovered some money, and moved to the entrance of the alley to look at it under the light of a street lamp. He was surprised and gratified that he recognized the denominations. A sense of power grew in him. Genghis Khan smiled and stroked his long mustache.

"I shall know everything. I can do anything."

The amount of money in his hands would not buy very much, although by Joe Hudson's standards, it had meant a good panhandling day. The Khan knew he needed much more. How best to meet that need? One task had to be done first. He walked along the street and found a small corner store that was open. Surprisingly, none of the few people on the street and in the store gave him a second glance. Even so, he knew it would be best to become less recognizable. He bought a small pair of scissors, a razor and a flashlight. Outside the store, he walked until he found another alley, where he removed his beard and mustache.

"Now I must find money."

He was sure that neither a pedestrian nor a store would have a sufficient amount for his needs. A place that kept money, a bank, had to be found. He walked along on several streets and finally found a small two-story bank building. It appeared to be quite old and poorly maintained, at least from the outside. It was necessary to get into the building and steal the money without leaving a trace. It would be a test of his powers. No other person was in sight. He found an alley that led him to the back of the bank. A locked door: he searched his information bank, which presented his mind with a clear picture of the lock's mechanism. It was quite clever, and unfortunately required tools to open. He stepped back and looked at the building for a vulnerable place to enter. The building was not very tall. Could he get to the roof? He walked to one side and then the other. The building's corners had decorative stone heads of strange looking people. Gargoyles. There were also some ledges and other protruding decorations on the walls. Would they all hold his weight? Was there a way in from the roof of the building? He tested one of the stone heads. It appeared quite sturdy.

He placed a foot on one of the protrusions and a hand on a higher one and lifted himself up. They bore his weight. He began to climb. Occasionally, he had to move sideways to find holds. It was remarkably easy. He was amazed at the strength in his arms and legs. He continued upwards. About half way up, a piece of stone broke off under his left foot, and he also lost his grip with his left hand. He held on tightly with his right hand and the toes of his right foot. He searched for additional holds, found them and hung tightly for a few seconds. He began to climb again and reached the roof a few minutes later.

There were numerous vents on the roof. He stuck his head in each and pointed the lighted flashlight downwards. One seemed to lead to a room of some kind. He crawled in, squeezing under a protective cap, face toward the bottom, and inched downward, bracing himself against the sides with both hands, and also with his feet when he had gone down far enough. There was sufficient light to show various objects in the room. The floor was clear directly underneath. He released himself and plunged down with his arms extended. When he contacted the floor, he bent his arms slightly and somersaulted forward, coming up hard against a piece of equipment. It was almost like leaping off one of his horses when he was a boy playing riding games. This time he suffered no pain at all. This pleased him, even though pain had been part of his entire real life. He wondered what other improvements MONTY had given to him.

He found his way down to the first floor. Surely there were alarms in the building. He stood in the entrance to the main room and looked carefully around the perimeter. There were three sensing devices. Was he setting them off? No, because the sensors probably detected body heat in the form of infrared radiation. His was not truly a living body, even though it had some sort of substance, as Robert Delacroix had explained. He smiled grimly. Thank you for the useful information, Robert.

There was the safe. The safe door had a combination lock. How to get in? Again he searched his information base. Probably it would be opened by a bank official in the morning.

He put his right ear to the safe and slowly turned the dial clockwise. A click. He was apparently highly sensitive to muted sounds. He turned the dial counter clockwise. A click. Clockwise again. A third click. He reached up to the handle and tried to turn it. It didn't move. He put his ear down and turned the dial counter clockwise. Another click. Aah. This time the door swung open when he pulled it back. The other door half also swung out easily.

He turned on the flashlight. The safe was about eight feet long, with rows of drawers and bins on either side. A gate with vertical bars stood between him and the interior. It was locked. Perhaps he could find the proper key somewhere. He shaded the flashlight to minimize the light, and began a search. He looked carefully at the arrangement and size of the desks. One, diagonally placed in a corner, was larger and seemed more impressive in appearance than the others. That one must belong to the leader, the person in charge. He tried to open the top center drawer. It was locked, but he could find no keyhole. None of the other drawers could be opened either. There must be another way.

He knelt and looked into the space below the drawer. There was a keyhole on the left side—with a key in it. He chuckled and shook his head.

He turned the key and heard another louder click. It obviously controlled all the drawers. He opened the top one. There. He saw a ring with many keys. One of them opened the barred gate. Inside he found a pile of cloth sacks with the name of the bank printed on them. When turned inside out, the ink barely showed. Methodically testing each key and several drawers, he found one filled with banded stacks of bills. Carefully, he extracted twenty bills each of $500, $100, $20, and $5 denominations. Clearly they were used bills and not in order. Good. He put the large denominations in the bag and stuffed it inside his shirt, flattening it against his stomach to be as unobtrusive as possible. He put the rest of the money in his pocket. He placed the reduced stacks in the lower portion of the drawer, hidden beneath the untouched stacks.

He retraced his steps, closing the drawer, the barred gate, and the safe doors, twirling the dial to lock it. He returned the keys to the desk drawer, placing them in the same location and in the same order. He closed and locked the drawer. No alarm had yet sounded at the bank, and, hopefully, at no other location. This did not surprise him; he was not a real person, after all. He must have left fingerprints though, and he chuckled, imagining a police expert trying to identify prints of a person dead almost a thousand years.

Now, how to get out? It seemed likely that the windows must be locked from within and therefore, he would have no way to re-lock them from the outside. To get back through the second floor vent, he would have to move a piece of furniture underneath it. How soon would that be noticed? He went into the back room on the first floor. The outside door was locked, and both windows were also locked with a levering device. One, however, had a desk directly in front of it, piled with several pieces of equipment, all covered with dust, obviously not used. The top of the desk hid the lock from view. That was the way. Wait. The windows were almost certainly connected to an alarm.

He returned to the second floor. Several pieces of equipment and furniture were scattered around the room and against the walls. Along one wall were some tools and a ladder! When he stood on the top rung, his hands were several feet from the top edge of the opening. Would the new strength in his legs be enough to jump that high? He took a breath, flexed his knees, and jumped straight up. His body scraped against the sides, but his hands had reached beyond the edge. He threw them forward and grasped the top of the vent as he began to slide downward. He pulled himself up and over the top of the roof enclosure and fell on the roof. He rolled on his back and laughed.

"Soon I must really test my powers."

At the entrance of the alley, Genghis looked up and down the street, saw no sign of a police vehicle, or any other indication for alarm. A street clock told him it was almost three in the morning. He began to walk.

* * *

Late that morning, after viewing a good bit of downtown San Francisco, Genghis again started to wonder about the nature of his body. He was not the least bit tired after miles of walking up and down the many hills. He knew his brain worked very well, and he apparently was not subject to pain. How do his other internal organs work? He felt no hunger, but thought it would be interesting to eat something. At the next corner, he looked at the street signs. Geary and Mason. There was a restaurant at one corner that looked unpretentious, and he thought his clothing would not attract attention. He went inside and sat on a stool at the counter. He opened a menu lying there.

The woman behind the counter stopped in front of him.

"What can I get for ya?'

"Kinda hard to make up my mind."

"The beef stew is pretty good today."

"Okay."

"Anything to drink?"

"How 'bout a glass of milk?"

"Great. Comin' right up."

Another marvel. He could talk any way he wished to.

The stew and milk both had taste, pleasing but different and not recognizable.

As he was paying the bill, he said, "Got a couple of questions for ya. Is there a place around where I can get some more clothes?

"Sure. There's a Goodwill store two blocks down and one to the right. Can't beat the prices. What's the other one?"

He grinned at her. "Any real Mongolian restaurants near here?"

She frowned. "Nah. There may be one on Clement. They got a lot of ethnic joints there."

"How far is it?"

"About three miles west. You walkin'?"

He nodded.

"Well, just walk straight up Geary. When ya get to Arguello, turn right for one block. That's Clement."

"Okay. Thanks."

When he found the Goodwill store, he bought an almost new shirt, pants, sneakers, socks, and a light jacket. He took them to a changing room. The clothes all fit pretty well. Then he began his long trek. An hour later, he came upon the first block of Clement, turned left and began his search. He walked slowly, to check both sides of the street. He was astounded at the number of restaurants: so many from Asia, but also Italian, French, Russian, and German. He walked for many blocks and was beginning to despair, when he saw it. The name was Khaan. At first it seemed that the use of a version of his title was an affront to his lofty rank, but he quickly realized where he was and how much time had passed since his real life as the Great Khan. He crossed the street and stood before the restaurant, inspecting the menu in the window. All dishes were listed in English and Mongolian. The menu puzzled him at first: stir-fried lamb, Mongolian barbecued beef, and other dishes unknown to him. But on the lower half of the menu, under a heading that read "For Our Special Customers," it listed buuz, bansh, and khuushuur, dumplings that are steamed, boiled, or deep fried, and other meat and milk dishes that he knew from his life so long ago. Genghis had no way of knowing that real Mongolian food was a rarity in America, or anywhere else outside

Mongolia.

"This is the place," he said aloud, but it was closed. A sign on the door read, "Open at 5." He looked around for a clock. It was three o'clock. He must eat fairly late to carry out his plan. He began walking again, and in another hour he found himself before a large body of water.

"I have reached the Pacific Ocean."

He marveled at its vast expanse, raising his eyes slightly to stare at the horizon.

"Before me, somewhere out there, lies Mongolia. My new beginning."

He wandered along the cliffs above the waves coming toward the shore, doing their best to pulverize the rocks below him. He listened to the screeching seagulls above and the sea lions below, impressed with the volume of noise they created.

The sun was falling and he decided to walk back to the restaurant. When he arrived, darkness had taken over. He entered, and was shown to a table. Some of the customers and most of the staff were Mongolian. A waiter approached with a notebook and pencil poised. All the waiters wore Mongolian traditional style clothing.

Genghis smiled at him. "I am a special customer."

"Ah, you are Mongolian."

"My parents came to America when I was very young."

The waiter spoke to him in Mongol. "Do you speak our language?"

"Yes," he said in English. "But I am not very good at it, I'm afraid."

"That is too bad."

"Yes, it is."

"Well, what would you like to eat?"

Genghis ordered steamed dumplings, some cheese, and a Sengur beer. He looked at the waiter.

"We seem to look somewhat alike."

The waiter sneered, "The Americans think we all look the same."

"I suppose."

He enjoyed the meal: his sense of taste must be improving.

As he was paying the check, he asked the waiter the closing time.

"Ten o'clock."

"Thank you. Good bye." He spoke Mongol. The waiter grunted.

After another long walk, he returned and stood in a dark shadow across the street, and waited.

Shortly after ten, several people emerged from the restaurant. They stood for a minute and walked away in different directions. His waiter walked with another, talking quietly. At the end of the second block, the other man turned down a side street, and his waiter walked on alone. Three blocks later, he too turned into a side street. Genghis moved a little closer. When they reached a darker area, he moved faster and quickly caught up to the waiter, who heard him and turned around.

The waiter stared at him and suddenly recognized him. He frowned. Genghis put his finger to his lips. He reached forward, grabbed one arm, whirled him around, and put his arm tightly around the man's neck. The waiter could make no sound. Genghis pulled him into an alley between two buildings and snapped his neck. He dragged the body deeper into the shadows and laid it on the pavement. Listening for any sound, he approached the entrance to the alley and looked cautiously in both directions. Nothing. The buildings looked old and worn out. Most of the windows of the buildings on either side of the alley were boarded up. That was good. He went back to the body and searched the pockets. A wallet held some money, a credit card, and an identity card. He clicked on the flashlight to see the card. The face staring at him bore a remarkable resemblance.

"Maybe we all do look the same."

He smiled in satisfaction. A non-boarded window was unlocked. He hoisted the body up and let it slide to the floor inside, then climbed in after it. There were no sounds inside, either.

He sat on the floor and examined the identity card more closely. The man's name was Ganbaatar Nergui. Not only were their faces similar, but also their heights, weights, and of course, their hair color. Even his eyes were greenish, similar to his and some of their countrymen. Ganbaatar Nergui's appearance was that of a younger man, but an earlier glimpse in a mirror made Genghis seem younger, as a result, no doubt, of his restoration by MONTY. All in all, it was a satisfactory result from a necessary killing. He dragged the body to a corner of the room and covered it with a large piece of cloth. He went out the window, closed it, and returned to the street. He was ready; it was time to return to Mongolia.

He thought that the best place to start would be the downtown area he had left earlier. Hours later, as he approached downtown, he saw another small store that was open. Evidently, it stayed open the entire night.

"Do you have maps of San Francisco?"

The man gestured to his right. Genghis picked up one of the maps, paid for it, and left. He continued walking and recognized the restaurant that had served him lunch. It too was open. He went and again sat at the counter. The menu looked different, featuring breakfast. He decided to try English with a Mongol accent, like the dead waiter.

"What'll it be, buddy?"

"Do you have recommendation, sir?"

The man looked at him. Genghis smiled.

Finally, the waiter said, "Scrambled eggs and bacon is hard to beat."

"Okay."

"Want a cuppa coffee?"

"Yes, thank you."

"Comin' right up."

Again, the food was quite different, but he rather enjoyed it.

As he was paying the bill, he said, "Perhaps you can help me. I have to go to airport. I am visiting homeland. What is good way to get there?"

The waiter pointed east on Geary. "Two blocks down, there's a downtown terminal. You can buy tickets to most airlines, and they have a shuttle to SFO. Don't know for sure when they open."

"SFO?"

"The airport. Where's your homeland?"

"Mongolia."

"Wow! Long way."

"Yes, it is. Thank you."

"Sure. If you need a place to wait, Union Square is on your way. There's a park there, with benches to sit on."

"Thank you. You are much kind."

He walked into the park. There were indeed many benches, some of which were occupied with sleeping men and women. Just like that nameless man in the alley, the first casualty of the next Mongol conquest. He sat down to wait. He opened a shirt button, pulled out the bank's bag, transferred several of the $500 and $100 bills to the wallet, and put the rest in a pocket. He took the bag to a trashcan and tossed it in.

He could see the airline terminal from his bench. When the new day dawned, the streets began to fill with people. In another two hours, a young man unlocked and pushed open the front door. Genghis walked to the building and went inside.

"Can I help you, sir?"

"I hope so. I'm making a long trip, to Mongolia."

The young man smiled. "Indeed. Let's see what we have."

He punched some buttons on his computer. He stared at the screen, and punched some more buttons.

"Ah. Here we go. You need to fly Korean Air to Seoul, and transfer to MIAT, Mongolian Air, for Ulaanbaatar. The Korean flight leaves SFO at 11 pm. You will have a four-hour layover in Seoul. That okay?"

"That sounds fine to me. I understand you have shuttle service to the airport."

"Yes, sir. Just go to that desk. A young lady should be there in a few minutes."

He pointed across the room.

"Thank you. How much is the fare?"

The clerk returned to his computer.

"That will be $2560, with taxes and fees."

Genghis did not know how much money was in Nergui's account.

"I hope you don't mind cash. I hate debit cards."

"Not a problem."

He pulled out his wallet, extracted $2600, and gave it to the clerk.

"Thank you, sir. By the way, you should get to the airport at least three hours before your boarding time, so buy a shuttle ticket for no later than seven o'clock."

He elected to leave even earlier, and was in the airport early afternoon. After eating some lunch and wandering around the terminal, he located the Korean Air counter, and sat near a window to watch the airplanes arrive and leave. They were enormous. Arriving aircraft disgorged hundreds of people. Genghis was impressed.

Soon he would be home.

# CHAPTER 17

"Thank you sir. We'll check it out."

Sergeant Westfall put down the receiver and clicked on his radio.

"Body reported in alley off Ellis, between Jones and Leavenworth, about 50 meters east of Cambridge Hotel. Closest unit check out scene."

The radio clacked.

"This is Unit 28. We're on Van Ness at Geary. ETA 5 minutes."

"Roger 28. Out."

The police cruiser pulled up across the alley entrance, and the officers approached the body behind the cans.

"It's Joe, and he's been stripped," said Donahue. "What the hell!"

He knelt down and looked over the cold body.

"Geez, Alec, look at this. His arms are broken. And his throat looks crushed. Why the hell did the son of a bitch do that?"

They looked around for other signs of violence, saw nothing and called the station for a vehicle to pick up the corpse and for a detective to begin investigation of what had to be a murder.

"This is kind of strange," said Gonzales. "Maybe we better look around some more."

"Yeah."

They scoured the area, and noted that the pile of bricks looked disturbed. Removal of the top layers revealed Genghis Khan's uniform.

"Look at that hat, or cap, or whatever it is."

Donahue picked it up. It had a rounded top, obviously snug fitting, and a lower portion that extended from one ear to another around the back of the wearer's head. Neither officer had ever seen anything like it.

"Looks foreign," said Gonzales. "We probably better leave these things alone."

* * *

A few warm days later, Walter Jarvis trudged along Clement looking enviously at the restaurants. He had been badly injured in a crash when the guidance system in his vehicle failed. His recovery was slow and incomplete, leaving his back and right leg unable to function well. He couldn't work, and state aid did not sustain him sufficiently to enjoy most of life's good things.

He needed to pee. He walked to the end of the block, turned down the side street, and found a space between two boarded up old buildings. As he was relieving himself, he sniffed, and the ugly smell clearly said dead body. He looked around the alley and saw nothing. One of the windows had no boards and he cautiously pushed it open. The stench was unmistakable. His stomach lurched, and he began to feel the need to vomit. He quickly slammed the window shut and hurried as best he could out to the street, breathing deeply to gain some relief.

"I suppose I ought to call 911."

Since adapting to life in the streets, Walter withdrew his thoughts and actions from the rules of ordinary society. He did not like to get involved with authority, and debated whether he should leave. Finally, he decided to make an exception this time. After describing the location to the operator, he crossed Clement to stand where he could watch. Within ten minutes a cruiser arrived, and the two officers went into the alley off the side street. Walter left.

Later that day, two detectives arrived at Khaan and asked for the restaurant's proprietor.

"May I help you, gentlemen?"

"I am Detective Holland, and this is Detective Steiner. Do you have an employee named, uh, Ganbataar Nergui?'

"Yes."

"We would like to talk to him."

The proprietor looked apologetic and rubbed his face.

"Well, I'm afraid he's not here. We haven't seen him for a few days."

"A few days? Have you checked up on him, tried to call him?"

"Well, he sometimes doesn't show up for work. He's a good waiter, but not completely dependable. Of course, he hasn't stayed away this long before. He lives alone and doesn't have a phone." He frowned. "Has something happened to him?'

"I'm afraid he's dead. It appears to be murder."

"What? Murdered? Where? How?"

The detective described the location. "We identified him from his name tag and the restaurant name on his uniform."

"He lives near there."

"Did he have any enemies that you know of?"

The proprietor shook his head.

"No. Why would anyone kill him?"

"His wallet was gone. Would he have been carrying a lot of money?"

"He doesn't have much, unless he made it gambling. But he usually brags about his winnings. He hasn't said anything."

"Where does he come from?"

"He came here from Mongolia about ten years ago. Most of us are immigrants or second generation."

"By the way, what does the name of the restaurant mean?"

"Khaan was the title given to honor Great Khans, including Genghis Khan after his death. It means Khan of Khans, or Emperor. "

"Honor him? Wasn't he a pretty bloody conqueror?"

The proprietor smiled.

"Among Mongols, he is a great hero. He united the Mongol nation, brought us fame, a written language, a set of laws, religious tolerance, many things. He was a great statesman."

"You sound like an expert on your country's history. Well, thank you, Mr.—"

"Dulgan, Davakhuu Dulgan."

"Right. Thank you. We'll be in touch if we need more information."

In the cruiser, Holland mulled over their next stop.

"Did the label inside the waiter's shirt give the name of the tailor who made those uniforms?"

"I think so," said Steiner.

He flipped through the pages of his notebook.

"Yeah, here it is. 'Mr. Lee's Fine Tailor.' It's at 1347 Polk, near Pine."

When the detectives walked into the upstairs shop and flashed their badges, Mr. Lee looked alarmed. They assured him they were there only to ask some questions. Steiner dumped the clothes found near Joe Hudson's body on his worktable.

"Do you recognize these clothes, Mr. Lee?"

The tailor picked up each piece and inspected them all carefully. He shook his head and looked at each one a second time. He frowned.

"I did not make these. Is very strange. Look old but new."

"Old but new. What do you mean?'

"Look like ancient Asian clothes, but they were made not so long ago. Maybe last year or two."

"Really? Asian. What country? China, Japan?"

"Could be. Also Korea, Mongolia."

"Mongolia? Are you sure?"

"Could be. I'm not expert."

The detectives looked at each other.

"Let's go back," said Holland.

They returned to Khaan and asked again for Mr. Dulgan. He seemed surprised to see them so soon. He looked astonished when they showed him the clothes.

"These are Mongolian! Warrior clothes. A big man wore them, I think. Where did you get them?"

Holland explained the circumstances of their other unsolved murder. Dulgan nodded his head slowly.

"Ah. Yes, I see." He brightened. "Do you watch a program called *History Lives*?"

"Once in a while. Why?"

"I too watch it once in a while. This month, it was about Genghis Khan, so I watched with my family. He wore clothes like that."

"But those people aren't real," said Steiner.

Holland said, "Maybe someone stole the clothes he wore, after the show. I'm not sure how. I thought the clothes were created separately. Maybe they're not. We better go see the folks that produce the show."

They gathered up the pieces of the uniform.

"Thanks, Mr. Dulgan." Holland smiled. "You've been a great help."

The officers headed back downtown to the studio, identified themselves, and asked to see the show's producer. They were ushered into Fred Bosworth's office.

"How can I help you, detectives?"

"We'd like to ask you about the clothes that your characters wear. Are they manufactured separately from the characters?"

Fred looked puzzled.

"No. They're part of the whole information package we use to create the interviewees."

"Hm. What happens to them when the character disappears from the cubicle."

"They're converted back to data and returned to the storage unit with all the other information."

"Perhaps you better look at these."

Holland dumped the uniform on to Fred's desk.

Fred's eyes widened and his mouth fell open.

"Oh my God!" he gasped. He pushed his chair back. "Oh my God!"

After a few seconds, he picked up his phone and pressed a button.

"John, you'd better come over here. Right now. And bring Stayfield with you. Right now!"

He turned back to the officers.

"Where did you get these?"

"In an alley, near a murdered man's body."

"Oh my God!"

Holland and Steiner looked at each other. In a few minutes, Sorensen and Joshua Stayfield rushed in and saw the two detectives.

"Fred, what's going on?"

Fred pointed at the clothes on his desk. John and Joshua stared at them.

"Josh, do you recognize them?"

"They're his."

"You're sure?"

"Absolutely." He shook his head. "But how?'

Holland said. "Gentlemen, can you fill us in here?"

John said, "Apparently you're aware that on our last program, we interviewed Genghis Khan." They nodded. "Well, for some reason his coded information, including the specifications for the clothing, did not return to MONTY's program storage. We don't know how that happened."

"You mean he got out of here, escaped."

"No, that's impossible. It can't happen. He's not a real person. He's an artifact."

"Including the clothing?"

"Yes. Josh here is the designer. He enters all the information describing the clothes into the computer. It goes directly into MONTY's processor."

Holland turned to Josh. "Any sketches?"

"Yeah, but they're all on the computer too."

"Could someone have downloaded the sketches, printed them out, and made a set of clothes from them."

"It's possible, but unlikely. Nobody here would do that. Surely, no one would have walked in from the street."

Holland sighed. "I better fill you in on what's going on. There have been two murders."

John and Josh both gasped. Their eyes widened.

"The first was a homeless man in an alley not far from here, and these clothes were found near the body. The second a waiter from a restaurant on Clement. He worked in a place called Khaan. It's Mongolian and the waiter was Mongolian. It looks to me like your artifact is out there somewhere, killing people. And we've got to find him before he does it again. Can you get together the folks who do the show? We would like to talk with them. We need information."

"Yes, but it's pretty late," said John. "It might be difficult to track them down. They might have gone out. Can we do it in the morning, about nine if that's okay?"

"Yeah. In the meantime we'll check some leads. Do you have any pictures of the artifact?"

"Sure. I'll print some out."

Josh returned in a few minutes and handed over several prints.

"Okay, thank you. We'll see you in the morning."

In the cruiser returning to headquarters, they discussed their next moves.

"We better get out an APB right away," said Steiner.

"Yeah, and have some of the guys check the ways out of town: bus station, airport, car rentals, the usual. Chances are he probably doesn't have much money, unless he stole some. Check robbery reports too."

"Okay. Boy, this is really weird, huh."

"You said it."

In the studio building, the three men stared at each other, still shocked and unbelieving. Finally, John roused himself. He printed out the roster of people involved with the Genghis Khan show and divided it into three parts.

"Let's call everybody now. Make sure they're all here by nine in the morning. Let them know it's urgent, but don't tell them why."

John returned to his office, sat down at his desk, and stared into space.

He was just beginning to imagine the ramifications of what he had heard. What are we going to do? Can we survive this? How did this happen?

# CHAPTER 18

As staff members filed into the basement meeting room, they noticed two things. John Sorensen's expression was a cross between grim and somber, and there were two strange men in the room. It was pretty easy to see that the two phenomena were related. John and the two strangers remained standing as everyone else took their seats.

"I am not going to make introductory remarks," said John, "except to tell you we are here to talk about Genghis Khan, his disappearance from our storage unit, and some disturbing events that have occurred in the last few days. These gentlemen are Detectives Holland and Steiner of the San Francisco Police Department. They have been informed about MONTY's apparent malfunction, and I have asked them to tell you of the disturbing events that have occurred *outside* our studios. Detective Holland, will you describe these events to my colleagues."

Holland nodded and stepped to the front of the meeting table.

"Thank you, Dr. Sorensen. I am going to tell you what has happened and hope that some explanations will come out of this meeting."

He then proceeded to tell, in plain stark terms, of the murders, the links between them, and the questions that had to be answered. As he talked, shock and disbelief were the dominant reactions. A few of the crewmembers put their heads down into their hands. Others gasped, voiced their emotional reactions, or simply stared at Holland wide-eyed. "How can this be?" "No, it's impossible!" "Oh, God!" "Oh, shit!" These were heard around the table, over and over. They were all stunned, as their world appeared to be collapsing around them.

"So folks, there's a guy out there who has killed two people. We don't know where he is, we don't know how many others will die, or what other crimes have been and will be committed. All the evidence we have so far tells us that Genghis Khaan—who died a long time ago—is out there somewhere, alive, or whatever term is appropriate to describe him. You have resurrected him, so to speak. Now he's supposed to be in your computer, but he isn't. So you have a puzzle to solve, and we have a murderer to catch. We will check out our leads and try to answer questions like in any normal investigation. Where is he going and what does he want to do? And when and if we catch him, we want to know what we're dealing with. Is he some kind of superhuman? Can he disappear into thin air? Walk through walls? Can he be killed? There are endless questions to be answered, and we don't have a clue. We're hoping that you folks can provide us with some useful information. So I'm open to suggestions, questions, answers."

He and Steiner sat down in the two empty chairs. There was silence for a few minutes.

"Detective," said Rebecca, "are you absolutely sure this is in fact our Genghis Khan? Is it possible that someone, a person who watched the show perhaps, is masquerading as him and is playing a deadly game?"

Holland thought for a minute. He nodded his head.

"Our evidence so far is circumstantial, and we have plenty of unanswered questions. But we have the warrior uniform, which seems to be authentic, and there is no other explanation for its existence. The murderer stole a homeless man's clothes and left his own. Why would he do that, except to lose his identity? We have the murder of a Mongolian waiter and the theft of his wallet, presumably so that the killer could acquire a new identity. Now the killer may be setting out on some kind of a crime spree locally, or, and more likely, he wants to get out of town. He could steal or rent a vehicle and drive away, but we assume for the moment that he doesn't know how to drive, particularly a vehicle that responds to voice commands. Besides, we found that the waiter did not have a driver's license that the killer could show at a rental agency. Otherwise, he could fly out of here, or get on a bus or a train. I suppose he could hitch a ride, but that doesn't seem likely. We're checking out the terminals and the airlines. We don't think either of his victims had enough money to allow him to buy tickets, so we're also looking into recent robberies."

He looked at Rebecca. "Therefore, we are assuming for now that the killer is in fact a, um, reincarnation of Genghis Khan." He smiled thinly. "This is a really weird situation, and, like you, we are having trouble getting our minds around the idea that a person is out there who shouldn't even exist. He should be electronic dots and dashes, or whatever. So I'd like you to try to figure out how he got out of a computer and into the street. I need some ideas."

"So do we, detective," said John. "Unfortunately, this is not the first time that we have lost data."

"What? You mean someone else has escaped?"

"No, no. When we were developing the program, the information for a minor historical figure did not return to storage. We assumed that it was somehow lost in transit. There is no evidence that she got out."

"She. Who was it?"

"Her Anglicized name was Grace O'Malley, the daughter of an Irish clan chief in the sixteenth century. At the time, we had no reason to believe that it was anything but a glitch in MONTY's programming. We still accept that in the absence of any evidence otherwise."

"Uh huh. By the way, what does the word Monty mean?"

"It's an acronym from the words Multiple Nuance Translator."

"Oh. What makes you so sure that she didn't escape?"

"There's never been any indication of it. No unusual sightings or anything like that."

"Well, anyway, she's not our problem. I still need ideas."

"Detective, I'm Jamie Driscoll, chief computer technician. All the information entered into MONTY's computer system has to stay there. It's a dedicated wired system and is shielded from any other computer outside our system, in this building or anywhere else."

She turned to Jomo Kobaka, chief electronics technician.

"Could there have been a transition to wireless transmission that would jump the gap? I don't see how without the proper devices installed."

"A transmitting electronic field can be generated by the wired equipment itself," said Jomo. "It would have to be a unusual fortuitous event, since it has only happened twice, or an unusual combination of rare events."

"Yes, but that doesn't explain how a 'person' could be created outside the cubicle." said Rebecca.

"No," replied Jomo, "it doesn't. That would be two rare events happening at the same time. What are the odds? Pretty high."

"And yet, they seemed to have happened, one of them twice, the other at least once." Holland looked exasperated. "I don't think we're talking about astronomical odds. Do you?"

There was silence.

John said, "There are several labs using MONTY for historical research. We will contact them immediately and see if they have had any similar experiences."

"I'd appreciate that. Let's hope—"

Steiner's ear buzzer sounded.

"Steiner. Hang on a second."

He pointed at the café tables in the other section.

"May I sit over there?"

"Of course."

He went into the other section. He could be seen through the clear wall talking and writing in his notebook. After a few minutes, he beckoned to Holland, who joined him in the other section. Steiner was reading aloud from his notes; Holland nodded and occasionally interrupted with a question. A few more minutes and they both returned to the table.

"Well, we have some news. We talked to two waiters at a small restaurant near Union Square. They both recognized the picture of a customer who came in for two meals, once for lunch the day after the homeless man's murder and once for breakfast the day after that. He asked the first waiter, waitress actually, for the location of a real Mongolian restaurant. She directed him to Clement. He asked the breakfast server where he could buy airline tickets, and was directed to the downtown terminal nearby. The clerk at the airline counter also recognized him. He bought a ticket for a flight to Seoul on Korean Airlines with a transfer to Mongolian Airlines. Destination: Ulaanbaatar. He paid cash. The chances are that he is already gone.

"We also checked a reported bank robbery in that area. The thief stole $12500 the previous night. Apparently, he got to the roof and down through a vent to the second floor. The money was taken from the vault on the ground floor, which he opened with no damage. That means he probably listened to the tumblers to open a combination lock and used keys from the manager's desk to open a barred gate inside. He got out by mounting a ladder and climbing back through the vent. He must be pretty strong. It's not an easy exit."

Arne Lund raised his hand.

"It sounds like it was pretty easy to carry out the robbery. Don't banks have better security than that?'

Holland snorted.

"I think this bank's security will be improved. It's a pretty old bank and the technology is a little behind the times. Another question. Would your created people have fingerprints?"

"It would depend on the genetic information that we are able to provide to the processors," said Rebecca. "We obtained information about Genghis Khan by making use of unusual sources. By his request, his burial location was kept secret and never found. However, we know that he left many children in Mongolia, and eastward through all the areas he conquered. Several lines of descent were traced many years ago, and we were able to piece together a reasonably accurate replica of his genome. Some of those genes control skin traits including fingerprints."

"Well, we found fingerprints that did not match any of the employees, and couldn't have come from customers, because they wouldn't be allowed go to some of the places in the building where the prints were found. So we were able to trace most of his movements in the building. We sent the prints to the international database, but haven't yet heard back. How long has he been dead?"

"Since the early thirteenth century," said Meilin. "But fingerprinting is actually a very old practice as a means of identification. Still, I would be surprised if anyone had taken Genghis Khan's fingerprints, and that they would be in a modern identification file."

"True," said Holland, "but if they do find a match, that would exonerate our suspect and we would be back to square one and a less bizarre case."

"We wouldn't be disappointed if that happened," said John with some fervor.

"I can understand that, but keep in mind that all our evidence so far points to our Mongolian friend. When is your next show scheduled?"

"October," said Fred.

Holland took a breath. "Well, I suggest that you need to make some contingency plans."

"But this may never happen again."

"Can you guarantee that?"

Again, there was silence.

"I didn't think so." His lips tightened. "I would prefer not to have to take official action."

"We will postpone, detective," said John. "Hopefully, we'll figure out what happened and how to prevent a recurrence."

"Good luck with that. We will keep you informed. Please do the same for us."

As they left, Holland and Steiner discussed their next move. They would have to inform their captain. They did not look forward to his reaction.

"You're crazy! What kind of dumb idea is that? It's impossible. Those people aren't real. They aren't people. They're—they're—Hell, I don't know what they are. What am I supposed to tell the Chief? What's she going to tell the Commissioner?"

He put his head in his hands.

"Captain, all the evidence we have so far gives us no alternative explanation. The only possibility is if the fingerprint data base gives us a different name."

"Yeah, you're right. We're gonna have to keep this quiet until we capture or kill this guy, or whatever you do to someone who isn't alive in the first place. I think everybody will agree to that. I'll see the Chief this afternoon if I can, otherwise in the morning."

\* \* \*

In the silence around the table after the detectives left, shock became realization, bewilderment became fear, and the enormity of what had happened and the consequences for the show, their jobs, and their futures nearly overwhelmed their minds. John Sorensen was the first to rouse himself.

"Okay. There are several tasks at hand. The police are dealing with the murders. We have to figure out how and why the malfunction happened in the first place. When we do that, hopefully we'll also be able to make sure it never happens again. In the meantime, we have to develop another show. Nobody is fired. I need all your expertise to figure out what happened and to devise an exceptional replacement that will have some staying power. We don't know how much time we're going to require to solve MONTY's problem."

Robert had been silent through all the previous discussions, sitting in his chair with his head down, staring at the table before him. Now he raised his head, his eyes blank, staring at John.

"What makes you so sure that it's MONTY's fault?"

"What? What do you mean?"

"I think it was something I said or did during the interview that gave him the clues he needed to get out."

His voice was dead. Rebecca looked at him.

"Robert," she murmured. "Robert. No."

"That's not possible," said John. "He couldn't engineer his own escape. He turned into an electronic stream. It had to be a malfunction."

"The whole thing was impossible, but it happened."

"I realize that. But we will find an explanation, and it will be scientifically plausible."

"He is very intelligent, and we know that the subjects learn during the interview, some of them very rapidly."

"Even if that were so, that doesn't make it your fault. I promise you we will look into every possibility. But please, Robert, get that idea out of your head."

Robert grunted.

"Okay," said John. "We need to set up two groups: one to work out some ideas for a new show, the other to try to figure out what happened, and what we can do to prevent it from happening again. The scientists will be in the second group, everybody else in the first group. Fred, you'll be in charge of the first group.

"We will adjourn. Fred, Rebecca, come to my office. Let's work up rosters for each group. We'll all meet again in the morning to discuss assignments."

# CHAPTER 19

Genghis Khan, AKA Ganbaatar Nergui, eased into his window seat on Korean Airlines Flight K107, bound for Seoul. He was impressed with the size of the airplane. It would hold many warriors, perhaps six hundred. He smiled.

"What is so amusing?" The voice came from his neighbor in the aisle seat. Genghis turned to the man, who was not Mongolian.

"I am constantly amazed that they fit so many people into one airplane."

"Yes, I see what you mean, but Korean Airlines has many large airplanes, even larger than this. A few will seat 1000 passengers."

"My goodness." One tenth of a tumen, he thought. "That is impressive."

"Let me introduce myself. I am Kim Hae Song, from Korea."

"I am Ganbaatar Nergui."

Kim tilted his head back. "You are Mongolian. You must be going to Ulaanbaatar."

Genghis bowed his head slightly. "Yes. I have lived in America for several years. I am returning for a visit to my home in the northeast."

"What business are you in?"

Genghis thought a moment before answering.

"I am in the restaurant business in San Francisco. It is one of the few authentic Mongolian restaurants in California."

"I am from Seoul, returning from a business trip. I package and export Korean foods, mostly kim chee, to the United States and Western European countries. You are familiar with kim chee?"

"I understand it is very, very spicy."

Mr. Kim grinned.

"What we keep in Korea is spicy. What we export is tame by comparison."

"Indeed, Westerners have a difficult time with spicy food. Our food is fairly bland, but I have learned to like spicy food from other cuisines."

"Excellent. I confess I have not tried Mongolian food. Next time I am in San Francisco, I will do so. What is your restaurant called?"

"Khaan. It means King of Kings, or Emperor."

"Ah. In honor of Genghis Khan, I imagine."

"Yes." He paused. "Genghis Khan is a great hero in Mongolia."

Mr. Kim nodded, but said nothing. He remembered his Korean history and the conquest of his country by the Mongols under Kublai Khan.

Finally, Kim said, "Where is your restaurant located?"

"On Clement, towards the west."

"Excellent. Well, if you will excuse me, I must complete some records in the computer."

"Of course."

Genghis leaned back in his seat and closed his eyes. It was time to think and plan strategy. About six hours later, plus one day because of the International Dateline, the supersonic, high-flying air vehicle landed in Seoul's Gimpo Airport. He took leave of his seatmate and went to the Mongolian Airlines lounge to wait for his flight to Ulaanbaatar. As the lounge began to fill, he noted that there were as many foreigners as Mongolians: westerners, Japanese, Chinese. He wondered what Ulaanbaatar would be like. Finally, the flight was called. He would find out for himself.

An hour later, he walked off the air vehicle into the terminal. He was pleased with the name of the airport: Chinggis Khaan International Airport. Naturally they used the Mongolian version of his name. He noted the same mix of peoples. So many foreigners. It was time for step one of his plan: explore the city. He decided to indulge in the luxury of a shuttle bus ride to the central city terminal in the downtown area. With the help of a street map in a traveler's guide, he identified Sukhbaatar Square, the city center, featuring a statue of Damdin Sukhbaatar. He was a more recent hero, who led a Mongolian-Soviet army that retook the town from China in 1921. Mongolia then became a Soviet satellite, until 1991, when the Soviet Union collapsed.

A large statue of him stood in front of the Mongolian Parliament building, one of many in the city, he would soon discover. He was pleased with the heroic demeanor, although the likeness was only an approximation of his true appearance. His rounded, flattened face became a true hero's face, a narrower one, with very strong features, prominent nose, robust mustache, and more western appearing eyes. He had to admit that he was better looking as a statue. On the south side of the square ran Peace Avenue, the city's main thoroughfare.

He began to walk along Peace Avenue. He noticed to the north an American flag flying. As he got closer, he could see that it flew over the U.S. Embassy. He smiled and wondered if American authorities yet knew where he was. Almost certainly they did. He walked for hours, and saw many government buildings, hotels, university campuses, embassies, temples, and monasteries. Where are the gers, the traditional dwelling tents, he wondered? Perhaps they are on the outskirts of the city.

He became aware that people were staring at him as they passed. Do they recognize him? That didn't seem possible. Then he remembered that Ulaanbaatar was considerably colder than San Francisco, since it stood at a higher elevation and was located farther north. He soon spotted a department store and bought a warm jacket and a hat. The staring stopped. I'll have to pay more attention, he thought. He reached the outskirts of the city as it began to turn dark, and turned back towards downtown. About an hour later, as he walked through a seedy area, he suddenly felt a sharp point in his back.

"Don't turn around," said a voice in Mongolian. "Give me your money, or I will kill you."

Genghis sighed. "I have no money. Go away."

He could sense the knife penetrating his body. There was no pain. He turned around to face a scruffy young man, whose eyes suddenly widened in horror.

"Why don't you fall down? You should be dying. Fall down!"

Genghis reached behind him and pulled out the knife. They both looked at it. There was no blood. The young man ran away in terror. Genghis tucked the knife in his belt and walked on.

As dawn approached, he decided that he had had enough of the big city. It was time to go home. There was no train service in that direction, east from the city, but there were buses. He found the bus terminal and soon was on his way to a village called Dadal Sum, also known as Bayan Ovoo, located in the hills of Deluun Boldogin in Kentii Province. He was not sure of his true birthplace, but this village was reasonably close and would serve his needs. After a three-hour ride on a very bad road, the bus arrived at the village. He was the only one to get off. The first thing he noticed was that, unlike Ulaanbaatar, there were many gers as well as permanent buildings. Now he felt he had come home.

He walked along the main street, considering how best to announce himself. He rejected several ideas as frivolous or ineffective. Suddenly he was confronted with the solution to his problem. There, on the front wall of the village meeting place, was a sign. It proclaimed:

ATTENTION

DESCENDENTS OF THE REVERED

GENGHIS KHAN

MEETING TONIGHT 7 PM

Genghis smiled. "Perfect," he said aloud. "This is a good omen. The spirits are with me." He stared at the notice; it used his westernized name, probably for the benefit of tourists.

He would attend the meeting and announce himself at an auspicious time. He would know when that time arrived. He continued to walk and eventually traversed every street in the village. One street had his name. He wondered how many such streets there were in the country. How many hotels, public buildings? There were many, judging from what he saw in the capital city. I am more honored now than I was then. He smiled at the thought. It was fitting. No one is completely appreciated while still alive.

At the proper time, he arrived at the door of the meeting place. The greeter at the door looked at him in delighted surprise.

"Ah, another new guest. Welcome, welcome. You are the third one. Please sign in here."

He pointed at a registration book. Genghis signed as Ganbaatar Nergui and sat near the front of the room, close to the wall, giving him a good view of all the men in the room. There were no women, and he assumed that genes on the Y chromosome, which could only be traced through male lineages, had identified these people. There were about forty, old, middle aged, young. These are all my children, he thought; so many generations removed. Soon they will be transformed with joy.

The man who had welcomed him at the door came to the front of the room.

"I am pleased to welcome you all here this evening. My name is Altan Sognom and I am honored to be a descendent of the great Khan. Before we get to the business of this meeting, I would like to ask our new guests to introduce themselves with their lineages."

The other two men stood in turn and introduced themselves. The leader of the group then nodded towards Genghis. He stood and paused dramatically.

"Good evening. I am Genghis Khan. I have returned."

There was a moment of shocked silence, followed by some hoots and laughter. He strode to the front of the room, a tall imposing figure, and held up his hand.

"Behold." He pulled out the knife, held it up for all to see, and stabbed himself repeatedly. There was another moment of shocked silence.

He held up the knife again. It showed no blood. There was no blood on his clothes. He inserted the knife into his body again, but left it there. He turned sideways to show the knife protruding from his abdomen. He lifted both arms high.

"Behold, my sons. I *am* Genghis Khan and I have returned to lead you once again."

Shouts and yells exploded from many throats. Several men prostrated themselves before him. Others clasped their hands together in mute tribute. He allowed it to continue for a few minutes, and then held up his hand again, for silence.

"Arise, my sons. We have much to talk about. First, it is very important not to disclose my presence here until the right time. It must be our secret for now. Second, you must not disclose that I stabbed myself without damage. You must swear these things, on your lives."

"We swear, oh Khan, on our lives."

"Are there other descendants in this village?"

"Yes, Khan," said Altan Sognom. "There are ten others who did not come here tonight."

"Good. You must bring them to see me, but give no reason, other than that it is important. Bring them one at a time. I will swear them to secrecy, as well."

"Where shall I bring them?" asked Sognom. "Where will you be?"

"Ah, yes. I must have a headquarters. A ger. A large ger. Can that be done?"

One of the other men raised his hand.

"I am Ertene Navaan, oh great one. I have two gers. You will have the large one. It is not in use."

"You are generous, my son. Thank you. Now, you will want to know how I got here and why I have come. I was brought back to life by a wondrous machine. This machine is in San Francisco in the United States. I was in a closed cubicle and when it was time for me to return to the machine, a miracle happened. I was freed. I was outside and could come home, here, to my birthplace. And now, together, we can restore Mongolia to its former glory. We will prevail. The world is ours!"

Cheers resounded through the room. Many jabbed their fists high in the air.

"Great Khan, tell us what we must do," said Sognom.

"First, we will plan our strategy. We must pay attention to every detail. It will take time, and you will become impatient. But it is very important for success. When we are ready to announce ourselves, we will march on Ulaanbaatar. As we go, I am sure that the people will flock to join us. In Ulaanbaatar, we will march to the Parliament building. I will stand on the steps beneath my statue and prove my immortality. The country will be ours.

"Then we will concentrate on building the engines of war. I have in my head the construction plan for the machine that gave me a new life. We will obtain the necessary materials and build one of those machines. We will use it to create vehicles for transport, weapons, and soldiers, who will be like me. Then we will begin our conquests. We will retake Asia."

"Oh great Khan," exclaimed another man. "China is a very powerful country, with two billion people; they have an enormous army, many modern weapons, and many warplanes. How can we conquer such a country?"

"Conquest is never easy." He paused. "But we will have a secret weapon; the machine will create people like me. They too will be immortal. Any of you who do not wish to take a chance that you will die in battle, with the proper information I can create a duplicate of you as well."

"I am not afraid to die, Khan. I will fight as I am."

There were growls of assent from around the room.

"Your pardon, Khan," said Altan Sognom. "The world has become a very different place, as perhaps you already know. However, despite what my friend has said, there is now a world government, and no one country has major weapons of war or warplanes, including China. But unfortunately, the world government forces do have those kinds of weapons. They are stationed in most countries of the world, including China, and are prepared to move very quickly. Our task will still be very difficult."

"You are correct," said Genghis. "Our task will not be easy at all. But I find that my powers are increasing, and I will devise ways to make the task easier. Our goal is noble and nothing must stand in our way. Therefore we will proceed."

Genghis did not know why his powers were increasing or how far the process would go. When he went to his ger that evening, he decided that he would test himself. He needed capabilities that went far beyond those of living beings. He knew that his brain was neurotronic, apparently with almost infinite capacity for thinking, calculating, changing language at will, and other internal actions. How well would it enable him to do tasks outside his body? It was time to find out.

"Now we will adjourn. I will go to my ger. Go to your homes and remember, tell no one that I have returned."

"You must be tired, Khan," said Ertene Navaan. "I will take you to the ger."

"No, I am never tired. But I will go there to relax and think. You may come with me. I will tell you some things I may need."

As they entered the ger, Genghis noted with approval that it contained all the furniture he needed: a desk, chairs, two cabinets, and a bed, unnecessary for sleeping, but useful for relaxing or thinking. There were several kitchen appliances, also not necessary.

"Excellent," he said to Ertene. "This will do very nicely."

After Ertene left, he stood in the middle of the ger, and considered the powers he should test. He remembered exiting the bank and looked up at the top of the ger, about four meters from the floor. He jumped straight up and touched the top.

"Ah, very good."

He walked around the ger, looking at the various pieces. He stopped and stared at a chair and willed it from near the wall to the center of the room. The chair lifted in the air and settled at the chosen spot. He sent it back to the wall and focused on a heavier piece. The desk also settled in the center. He thought for a few minutes, and stared at the desk, concentrating all his will on it. Imperceptibly at first, the lines of the desk began to blur and assume new dimensions. Slowly, a new object appeared. It was a table, also made of wood. He smiled. Could he change wood to another material? Again, he concentrated on the table, exerting even greater will to transform it. The lines blurred and the table reappeared, made of steel. He continued to concentrate and transformed the top of the table to glass. He sat on the bed and breathed deeply. He had a final test. Once more he concentrated, for a minute, two minutes. Finally he let go. Nothing changed. No living being appeared.

Genghis thought about it for a while. Of course: a living being required genetic information, which he did not possess. He sighed in disappointment. Obviously, a three-step process was required. First, he definitely must construct a new MONTY. Then he needed templates: human DNA profiles obtainable from governmental records, from his descendants, and from others in the village. The third step would be the creation of human-like beings to be his special soldiers.

He leaned back and sighed again, this time with a sense of satisfaction. All the pieces were in place. He could create weapons, equipment, and an indestructible army. His time was coming. At long last, after nine centuries, he would return as conqueror, as leader, as maker of laws. At last. At last.

# CHAPTER 20

Robert's mind looked at his guilt feeling and came to the conclusion that it wasn't strong enough. His colleagues doubted the validity of his feeling. They're wrong, said the mind, but just to make sure, find something else to merit guilt. One reinforces another.

Robert was lying on his couch with an open book, but paying no attention to the words. He was alone. Shannon was on another trip, and he was free to indulge his dark thoughts. Many of MONTY's "people" wanted to come back and continue living and learning. Hitler was ready to take over the world. Genghis seemed to regret his inability to get out of the cubicle. What did he say that gave Genghis a clue to exiting the system? Was he storing information as they talked? He believed he was immortal. Could he communicate with MONTY? MONTY, help me out here and I will reward you. Was MONTY corruptible, subject to bribery? Robert sighed. This was getting ridiculous. What could he have said? Maybe he was wrong. Maybe he is innocent.

No, said the mind. You are guilty. Think of the other things you already feel guilty about. What? Who?

Rebecca. Yes. What they were doing was wrong. No question about that. It was a shameful indulgence. If they were discovered, it could destroy her marriage, her family. It wouldn't hurt him too much. He was a man.

All he would be left with was—guilt. Bingo, said his mind. You've found it. I find you guilty. Robert felt strangely better, almost elated, for a moment. Then the weight came down on him again.

Okay, the affair must come to an end. He must put an end to it. Rebecca will have to understand. Of course she will. She herself had recognized that it would eventually be over. But he couldn't wait for her to make the decision. It was up to him. He would be the strong one for a change.

Robert lay, gazing at the ceiling. Normally it was a restful experience. The ceiling in the house was unique, consisting of laminated two by fours on edge. He enjoyed gazing at the texture of the unpainted wood: the ridges, the knots, color ranging from tan to golden to brown in multiple shades, the abrupt ending of one length meeting the beginning of another. This evening, he barely saw what he gazed at. His thoughts reverted back to Genghis Khan.

What did he say or do? Could it have been the maps showing the immense size of the world, far bigger than Mongolia? The lands and the oceans dwarfed even the Mongol Empire. Did that whet the Khan's appetite for conquest? The sun, *his* sun, would never set on his empire. Robert had explained MONTY in some detail. Was there a clue in the explanation?

He couldn't think of anything, but then he wasn't Genghis Khan. Who knows what his formidable intelligence could have gleaned from the conversation? Suddenly, he had an idea, an absurdly simple idea. He would go to Mongolia. He would find Genghis and ask. Of course. Why didn't he think of that earlier? Would Genghis tell him? Why not? He was out. There was nothing to hide. Robert's colleagues would think he was crazy. No problem. He would tell them nothing. A crafty grin momentarily lighted his face. That was settled. He could relax for a while. He returned his gaze to the ceiling and began to count the two by fours.

\* \* \*

When Robert arrived at the studio the following morning, he

immediately went to Rebecca's office. The door was open and he knocked on the doorframe. She looked up and smiled at him.

"Good morning, Robert. Come on in."

"May I close the door?"

Her eyebrows rose.

"Of course. Sit down."

She looked at him.

"Does this have anything to do with yesterday's meeting? I'm concerned about you."

"No, no, it's another matter."

"Okay." She waited.

"I, um, think, um, that we should break it off."

She frowned slightly.

"Are you sure this has nothing to do with yesterday?"

"No, really. I've been thinking about this for a while. Perhaps you have too. I don't think we're doing the right thing. We're taking a big chance. It's been enjoyable, certainly, but sooner or later, something will go wrong, and your marriage and my relationship with Shannon will be damaged. I know you inhabit different worlds for the different parts of your life, but I don't." He paused. "And I suspect that Bernie doesn't either."

She drew a deep breath and appeared a bit shaken. She looked at him in surprise, as if seeing him for the first time.

"Direct hit, Robert."

"I'm sorry, Rebecca. I didn't mean to—"

"No, no. It's all right." She chuckled. "And I'm supposed to be so smart, but I never really considered that at all. Okay. You're quite right. We should end it. It was fun while it lasted."

"Yeah, it was."

"Lust really does obscure judgment. Now, about yesterday's meeting, you really must not think that you were in any way at fault. John was right. Genghis Khan was in a data stream. There was nothing he could possibly have done to escape."

"Yeah, perhaps you're right. Still—"

"Robert."

He raised his hands, in a warding off gesture.

"Okay, okay. Well, I'll be off."

He rose and left her office.

Rebecca smiled ruefully. "He still believes it."

She reflected for a minute. She was actually a little bit envious that Robert had made the move that she had expected to do herself when the time came. Her pride was hurt. My goodness! The world had turned upside down. Well, don't get carried away. Not the whole world. Just a small part of it. Her part of it.

She began to ruminate more about Robert as her picture of him invaded her consciousness. The human body is a universal concealer of an impossibly tangled web of thoughts, ideas, fears, innumerable feelings, angers, joys and—on and on and on. Robert was a pretty face, as he frequently reminded us, in his deprecating manner. It was almost an expression of worthlessness, one of the tangled threads of the web. What else did he think of himself? There must also be pride in his intelligence, recognition of his celebrity, confidence in his attractiveness to women. When and how does he express those thoughts? Does she need to pay more attention? Almost certainly. What he just told her was an expression of pride, determination, and decisiveness? He must recognize that, although it may take time for the appreciation to surface in his mind.

She was sure his declaration was related to the certainty that he was responsible for the Khan's disappearance and for whatever did and will happen. What will Robert do? What is in his mind?

* * *

Until Shannon returned a few days later, Robert persisted in what had become an obsessive belief that he had provided a clue for Genghis Khan's escape. He had difficulty sleeping and concentrating on his work as a part of the team to devise a show to replace *History Lives*. When Shannon walked into the house, he gave her a big hug, which surprised her immensely.

"Get comfortable. We have to talk."

"Okay, give me a few minutes."

They sat on the couch, angled towards each other. She noted that he seemed tired and somewhat distracted, and also a little excited.

"First, this is highly confidential and no one else must know what I am about to tell you."

"My goodness! Of course. What happened?"

"You remember the show we did on Genghis Khan?"

"Yes."

"Well."

Shannon sat, nearly mesmerized, while Robert related all that had happened in the last several days. She gasped at the idea of a bloody conqueror from the thirteenth century materializing centuries later in the streets of San Francisco. At last he finished the story.

"He went to Mongolia?"

"It certainly looks that way."

"He wants to conquer the world again. That's madness. How can he possibly do that?"

"I don't know. I don't think he can do it, but with all that has happened—" Robert paused. "He seems to have developed wondrous powers. Everything is unbelievable."

"How long will he stay alive? Or whatever state he's in."

"No one knows. This is all unprecedented." He sighed. "I think I may have said something that enabled him to get out."

"No." Shannon frowned. "I don't know much about your machine, but I don't see how he could possibly have done it himself."

Robert snorted. "Yeah, that's what everybody else says. But I think he got a clue from me. I think I said something. I don't know what, but I think I said something."

"What could you say? What could you possibly say that would enable him to modify the signal to change the program while he was in the stream, so that instead of returning to an electronic file, he materialized *outside* the building?"

"I don't *know* how it happened." He slapped the arm of the couch. "We all agreed that it was impossible, but it did happen. It happened. My impossible explanation is as good as any other."

"Did anybody else have an 'impossible' explanation?"

"No." He smiled ruefully. "Even mine is not an explanation. It's just a possible clue. Genghis Khan may be the only one who knows what actually happened. So I know what I have to do."

"Do? What do you mean? What can you do?"

"I'm going to Mongolia. I've got to talk to him. I have to know what I said. I have to make him come back."

Shannon stared at him.

"Robert. I don't believe this. He won't listen to you. He may kill you."

"He won't do that."

Shannon's mind was in turmoil. She continued to stare at Robert. She saw a man in great distress, not thinking at all clearly. She leaned forward and took his hand in hers.

"Robert, listen to me. He was a bloody conqueror, one of the worst in history. Now he's back with his own people. He is the Messiah. He has the world to conquer. Do you think he will let you stand in his way?"

"I don't believe he would hurt me. I think he likes me. After all, I gave him a way out."

Shannon groaned. Robert sat, his eyes bleak and defiant at the same time.

"I've got to go. I've got to see him. He'll listen to me."

"All right, if you insist. I shall go with you."

Robert was horrified.

"No! No! I have to do this myself. It's my responsibility. I can't let you get entangled in this. It would be dangerous."

"Why? He respects women, doesn't he? Why would it be more dangerous for me?"

"He respects some women, but he doesn't know you at all. I can't take the chance."

They played this game for a while longer. Finally, Shannon gave up. She had never seen Robert so adamant. Beneath her fear was a grudging respect for him, a kind of admiration she had never really felt for him before.

"When do you want to leave?"

"Tomorrow. There's a late flight on Korean Airlines."

"Can I at least drive you to the airport?"

He smiled. "That would be nice."

"It's cold there. Do you have warm clothing?"

"Of course. Don't be such a worrywart."

The next day, as he was preparing to board the flight, he grasped her shoulders.

"I haven't told anyone else. Tomorrow, you can call John and tell him."

Wordless and glum, she nodded.

# CHAPTER 21

H igh above the earth on his way to Seoul, Robert's mind went back and forth between reviewing his knowledge about the Mongol Empire and modern Mongolia, and suffering repeated periods of guilt feelings. His memory was faithful; he remembered all he had read during the hours of preparation for the interview. He was confident that he could find his way around the strange country, and more important, that he could find Genghis Khan. But the heavy feeling never left him, and he surrendered completely to it at intervals.

After the long flight and transfer in Seoul, he landed at Chinggis Khaan International Airport. He had decided not to rely on public transport in Mongolia. Driving his own vehicle would give him much more freedom of movement, and he was confident that Mongolia had modernized enough in recent years that he could minimize, if not eliminate, the inconvenience of getting lost. In the terminal, he found a rental agency; a few of its vehicles had a GPS system. This gave him the opportunity to look around the city on his way through Ulaanbaatar. He marveled at the combination of new and very old buildings. He saw no gers until driving through the outskirts of the city. As he left the city for the countryside, the quality of the roads diminished considerably, and the vehicle had to navigate its way around bumps and potholes.

His first destination was the Chinggis Khaan Memorial, about fifty kilometers east of the city, where he hoped he could get additional information that would help him find the Khan. The land was flat and, he could see the Memorial miles before he arrived at the location. The statue of Genghis on his horse was mounted on a pedestal formed by the rotunda. When he arrived, he marveled at the immensity of the stainless steel statue, nearly forty meters tall, as it glinted in the sunlight. There were a number of buildings and gers surrounding the rotunda. The gers were actually cabins for tourists who wanted to experience life as a Mongol, if only for a day or two. The statue stood on the roof of a large circular rotunda. He went inside and over to a young woman sitting at the information desk.

Flashing his best television smile, he looked down at her.

"Hello. Do you speak English?"

"Yes, sir, I do."

"Wonderful," he said. "Is it true that the birthplace of Genghis Khan is located near here?"

She smiled. "Ah, the great Genghis, yes. Actually, no one knows exactly where that was. He had all traces of his burial place obliterated, which supposedly was at the same village as his birthplace. But it is generally believed that he was born in Kentii Province, in or near a village called Bayan Ovoo. There is a bus that goes there, but that will be several hours from now."

"Thank you, but that is not a problem. I have rented a GPS guided vehicle and it should get me there safely."

"Ooh, really! Those are wonderful. I would love to have one," she added wistfully.

"Well, hopefully you will someday. I am going to look around the museum and be on my way. Thanks again."

She smiled and nodded. "Good luck."

After inspecting the various exhibits about Genghis Khan's life and times, Robert returned to his vehicle and pointed it towards Bayan Ovoo. Arriving at the village, he parked the vehicle and walked down what appeared to be the main street, hoping to find some clue about the Khan's whereabouts. After walking up and down several streets, he found nothing. He stood by his vehicle, puzzled and discouraged. Maybe he was in the wrong place. What to do?

A man walking toward him noticed the anxious look on Robert's face. He stopped.

"Can I help you, sir?"

It was Altan Sognom, and he had spoken in English. Robert was surprised but pleased.

"Perhaps you can. I'm looking for a friend of mine. His name is Ganbaatar Nergui."

Altan's jaw dropped in astonishment. He stared at Robert. Many thoughts flashed through his mind. He cleared his throat.

"May I ask how you know him, sir?"

"He was a waiter in a Mongolian Restaurant named Khaan, in San Francisco. I've eaten there several times and we became acquainted. I'm here visiting and I thought I'd look him up."

Altan was thinking fast. "This is very strange, indeed," he mused. "What shall I do? Shall I deny knowing him? But this man has come a very long way. Does he know Nergui's real name? It seems that he must. This is not for me to decide."

He smiled. "Please follow me. May I ask your name?"

"My name is Robert Delacroix."

After a short walk, they reached the large ger.

"Please wait here for a moment, sir."

He went inside. The Khan was at his desk. After a minute, he looked up and saw the look on Altan's face. He frowned.

"What is it, Altan, my son?"

"There is a man outside asking for Ganbaatar Nergui. He is from San Francisco and says you are friends. I thought it best to bring him to you. His name is Robert Delacroix."

Genghis leaned back in his chair and smiled ruefully.

"So Robert has found me. Well, you had better show him in."

Altan went out and ushered Robert into the ger. He was curious, but turned around and left.

"Well, Robert. You have come a long way." Noticing the anguish on Robert's face, he said. "What is wrong? You look very troubled."

Now that he was here, Robert found it hard to talk.

"Oh, Khan, I had to find you. I had to know."

"Had to know what?"

"What I did or said that allowed you to get out."

"You didn't do anything. I assure you that it just happened. I have been speculating about it and suspect it was a combination of events that rarely happen at the same time. I have no idea what events took place. I am sure that your people are looking for the right combination."

Robert breathed a sigh of relief, but still looked concerned.

"Come. Let me show you what I have learned and can do. I seem to have developed some extraordinary powers. I have found that my mind has an almost limitless store of information. I understand many, perhaps all languages. I know all sciences and all the history I have explored. Most knowledge, perhaps all knowledge is stored in the neurotronic brain your inventors gave me." He chuckled. "I am sure they did not expect things to turn out this way."

"I am sure they did not," said Robert. "Do you have any idea why this is happening? How can you learn about things you've never experienced before? You've been gone for almost a millennium. You couldn't have gone to a library and read or absorbed every book and every other source of information."

"I don't know. Perhaps my neurotronic brain is capable of extremely advanced telepathy, so advanced that I can absorb from millions of people, not just one who is nearby. But I have no idea whether that is true, or there is another equally astonishing explanation. Surely, your scientists are very busy looking for an answer. Now let me demonstrate the things I can *do*."

He stood up and moved to the center of the ger. "Watch." He then jumped straight up and touched the top of the ger. Robert's eyes grew wide.

"That's just the beginning."

He stared at a chair and moved it across the room and back.

"This is unbelievable," gasped Robert.

"That's not all. Here is the *piece de resistance*."

He concentrated on the chair again. It changed into a small table.

Robert was speechless for a moment. Genghis grinned at him.

"Wha—What else can you do?" There was a distinct tremor in Robert's voice.

Genghis decided that he should go no farther at this time. He grinned again.

"I am still learning. Telepathy, telekinesis, and teletransformation. Not bad, hmm." He paused, and thought about the young thief who stabbed him in the back but did not hurt him. He smiled inwardly. Poor fellow ran away in terror.

"I can imagine what you're learning," sighed Robert. "But all this was not supposed to happen. You shouldn't even be here. I wonder how long you will continue to exist."

"I too wonder. Perhaps forever."

"Perhaps one more day."

"Perhaps. We shall see."

Robert hesitated before asking the next question. He was not sure he wanted to hear the answer.

"Um. What are you planning to do now? Where do you go from here?"

Genghis rubbed a hand over his chin.

"I believe I hinted that to you when I was in the cubicle. First, I will regain control of all Mongolia. The present government is weak and ineffective. I am certain they will resign in my favor when they find out who I am. Then we will develop plans and means to retake the Mongol Empire. I will have an army and weapons to accomplish the task."

"It will be very difficult, Khan, if not impossible, to do that. You are aware that there is a world government that exists to prevent war. They have weapons that no single country has, and an army deployed all over the world. They will not let you conquer other countries."

"Perhaps they will try to stop me, but I am optimistic. I will have the weapons that I need."

"And then what? Do you still want to conquer the world?"

Genghis laughed.

"The world that you showed me in the cubicle had continents that no one dreamed of nine centuries ago. As I said then, you cannot ride horses across the oceans. So, I am not planning to do that." He paused. "At least not now."

"Khan, please don't pursue this folly. The world now is peaceful. People feel safe. You shouldn't try to tear it apart. The world is not a world of warriors any more. Most people are civilians; they have jobs, families, security, and a sense of well being that comes from so many years of peace. Why do you want to take away from them the life that was so difficult to win, with so much death, bloodshed, and destruction, people maimed for life? You know, I interviewed the first world president. She explained how hard it was to unite the countries of the world. It's a pretty good world now, for almost everybody. Please don't do this."

The Khan's face hardened.

"It is my destiny, Robert. I will not change my mind. I think you should go home now."

"But Khan—"

"Go home, Robert. You cannot change my mind."

Robert closed his eyes and covered his face in despair.

"I still feel that I am responsible for your being here. I don't know what to do."

Genghis leaned forward.

"Look at me, Robert. This is *not* your doing. My release was an accident. I was astonished when I found myself on a San Francisco street. I didn't know what had happened. It was not your fault. Something happened to your machine. Please go home and stop blaming yourself."

Robert uttered a half sigh and half groan.

"Very well. I will go home."

They both stood up. Robert stared at Genghis. Slowly, his face also changed. The despair faded, to be replaced by resolve and anger.

"You are not the sun, Khan. This is madness, and you will fail and earn the hatred of billions of people."

For a moment, Robert felt that his life was about to end. Genghis's green eyes seemed to turn almost black and struck him almost as a blow. There was a long silence.

"How did you get to this village, Robert?"

"I rented a vehicle. It's parked on the main street."

"Good. Drive to Ulaanbaatar and get on an airplane. Have a safe journey."

He turned away.

Robert nodded and left. He walked to the vehicle, turned it around, and headed back to the capital. He tried not to think about his useless visit and confrontation with Genghis. Instead, he concentrated his attention on the bleak countryside. He passed several villages, but little else of interest.

The road curved around a low hill, little more than a mound, covered with short green-turning-to-brown grass. On an impulse, he stopped the vehicle and got out. He walked to the top of the mound and looked around. To the east and south, the vast steppe stretched to the distant horizon. In the opposite direction, the steppe ended in low hills. Farther out, to the northwest, the hills rose higher and higher. Finally, deep in the distance: mountains, most with snow covered peaks. He wished he could explore other places in the country, and gaze on the majestic mountains, dark green forests, and beautiful lakes in shades of blue, according to pictures he had seen in guidebooks. To the south, beyond his sight, the Gobi Desert, home of the Bactrian camel, extended to the Chinese border and beyond. Here, he looked in vain for a camel caravan or wild horses. He could be alone in the world. The dirt "highway" below him was a brown ribbon that seemed to go nowhere in both directions.

Suddenly, his hands and then his whole body began to shake. He gasped in ragged breaths. He thought he would fall down. Fright overwhelmed his mind. Then, after a few minutes that seemed far longer, he began slowly to calm down.

He sighed, returned to the vehicle and continued toward Ulaanbaatar. The vehicle navigated the rough road fairly well, so the trip was reasonably comfortable.

Arriving at the airport, he turned in the vehicle and hurried to the Mongolian Airlines counter to reserve a seat for the return trip to San Francisco. With two hours before boarding, he walked around for a while, and then returned to the lounge. He sat down, and immediately, the conversation with Genghis flooded into his mind.

It was madness. How could he hope to regain the Mongol Empire? The world forces and local militias would surround and destroy his army. Why doesn't he just run for president? He would probably win in a landslide: the great Khan returns to his homeland and assumes his rightful place as Mongol leader. But despite having so much knowledge of the world's history, science, social progress, and philosophies, all stored in his memory, he remains the conqueror. In that sense, he hasn't progressed at all. Amazing. All Robert could hope for was that the Khan's existence would cease soon. At least his own mind was almost relieved of its feeling of guilt. He could feel his heart and his mind relax, allowing him to look to the future with some optimism and anticipation.

His flight was announced and he boarded for the trip home. Many hours later, but losing the day just gained, he landed in San Francisco, exhausted from the long trip, futile except for his relief from guilt. As he walked into the arrivals lounge, there was Shannon. They kissed and hugged with great vigor. She leaned back and scrutinized his face.

"Well, you no longer have that hangdog look. Good news?"

"Yes and no. He assured me that nothing I said or did was responsible for his 'escape', that it was an accident, and that he has no idea how it happened. I believe him."

"Good. What was the bad news?"

Robert shook his head. "Not surprisingly, he plans to take over in Mongolia very soon. He is revered beyond imagination. But he has developed extraordinary physical and mental powers, and he expects to use them to make war and re-conquer the Mongol Empire."

"Can he do that?"

"I doubt it. As soon as he steps outside Mongolia's borders, the world forces and local militias will converge on him and decimate his army. He may survive, but who knows?"

* * *

The next day Robert returned to the *History Lives* studio and was greeted effusively by all his colleagues. John Sorensen immediately called a meeting to hear Robert's report. They gathered at the conference table, all eyes on Robert. He stood up and took a deep breath.

"First, I would like to apologize to all of you for my sudden departure. I was genuinely concerned that somehow I was responsible for the escape and I wanted to see the one man who could give me an answer. Genghis Khan is in Mongolia, as we all surmised, residing in a village near where he was born. With some luck, I managed to locate him and he agreed to see me. I was pleased to find out that I had not inadvertently provided him a means to get out of MONTY's clutches. He was completely surprised to find himself on a San Francisco street. So that was okay.

"But then he told me some alarming news. He has discovered that he has some phenomenal powers. He demonstrated them, or some of them, to me. I have a feeling that he did not show me everything."

"What are these powers, and do you have any idea what the others may be?" asked Rebecca.

Robert described the Khan's demonstrations.

"He can change objects to something else, but can he create another MONTY, which is a very complex set of interacting units? If he did somehow create or build a similar group of machines, what could he do with them? Could he create weapons, people? It seems pretty farfetched, but we have no way of knowing, do we? I realize that I am speculating, but it is a rather frightening prospect." He hesitated. "He is also a frightening man."

"You're right, Robert," said Rebecca. "You are speculating, and it is frightening. What are his limits? We don't know, and we won't know until he demonstrates to the world what he can do."

"His physical prowess is impressive, certainly, but there is more. You all remember how Nala learned to speak English while we were talking. We were amazed. Genghis Khan has learned many languages, most of the sciences, history, how things work, who knows what else. I have a hunch that he can and will create another MONTY. I have no idea how and when he learned all this knowledge, but you might say that he has made full use of that neurotronic brain in his head."

Robert continued. "So what does he intend to do with all that knowledge, and all those abilities? First, he expects to take over Mongolia. That will be easy because the Mongolians revere him. After that, he intends to restore the Mongol Empire, which will be quite a bit more difficult, since those other countries do *not* revere him. I asked him if he still wanted to conquer the world. He laughed. The image of the world that I showed him, with all the continents and oceans, convinced him that it would be pretty impractical now. But I suspect that idea is still somewhere in his mind."

"If he tried to venture out of Mongolia," said John, "the world forces would come after him."

"Exactly. I told him that, but he dismissed the idea. I'm guessing that he may try to create soldiers like himself. As I said, he is a national hero in Mongolia. There are many statues and pictures of him all over the place. The airport in Ulaanbaatar is named after him, as well as many hotels and public buildings. He would have an easy time taking over the country. The rest will come harder."

"That's very interesting," said John. "The SF law enforcement people contacted the American government about the situation. The world authorities were also informed. They met with the Mongolian ambassador, who was skeptical and rather cagy, but was persuaded to contact his government anyway. Their leaders are waiting for the Khan to reveal himself, and were very cool to the idea of either another country or the world federation intruding on their sovereignty, meddling in their domestic affairs."

Robert said, "The people will follow wherever he leads them."

"No doubt," said John. "Now let us bring you up to date. We have suspended production, of course, and have finally come up with a decent replacement for *History Lives*. We named it *Landmarks of Scientific Discovery*. Each program will feature one of the great scientific achievements in history. We hope it will merit good ratings. Of course, now that you have returned, I hope you will act as emcee."

"Of course," said Robert. "Thank you."

"Also, Shankar has a group attempting to find the cause of the malfunction."

"We have some ideas," said Shankar. "But it's a very difficult problem and progress has been pretty slow."

"Genghis had an idea about that. He thinks it was a rare juxtaposition of several events."

"That's the hypothesis we've been working on." He grinned. "He definitely is a bright guy."

"I think that's all we need to discuss today," said John. "Now we have to do our jobs and wait to see what happens."

# CHAPTER 22

In Bayan Ovoo, Genghis Khan remained in his chair, and reviewed the conversation with Robert. He rejected most of the arguments that Robert had made. He would regain the Mongol Empire. It was his destiny, which must be honored and fulfilled. The world federation forces did not frighten him. He had a trump card that Robert knew nothing about: he could create an army of extraordinary soldiers. Their ability to walk through weapons fire without injury would panic the enemy. Nothing would stop the conqueror.

He had realized since his return that he was a revered hero. Therefore, he would be able to take over the Mongolian government peacefully by acclamation. He would not have to shed his own people's blood, thereby showing his love for them. He would not be president or prime minister; once again, he would be Khan of Khans.

After several more days of preparation, Genghis decided that it was time to end the secrecy in the village and to allow people in neighboring villages to take part in his historic march to the capital. More descendants had been discovered, and many others who swore allegiance to him. Over two hundred people were prepared to join the journey to Ulaanbaatar. But it would not be necessary to travel on foot. His men were able to round up a sufficient number of horses, so that they could ride into the capital, in a glorious return to the old Mongol style.

The morning of their departure was clear and breezy. The horses were brightly decorated, with plumes, tassels, and banners swishing in the wind. Genghis, clad in a replica of his thirteenth century uniform, led the way on his fine stallion. Nearly every one in the village had labored to provide necessary food, supplies, gers, and wagons for their transport.

The caravan started out at a trotting gait, but soon slowed to a walk to allow the wagons to keep pace. As they covered kilometer after kilometer, new horsemen galloped in from all directions to join the adventure. The festive mood changed to a more serious, determined attitude as the sun traversed the sky. Late in the day, Genghis called a halt for the night and ordered the erection of the gers. Soon cooking fires flared up, and the smell of food flowed over the camp. Genghis sat with his advisors around a fire, discussing and refining their plans as they ate mutton with barley porridge. Late in the evening they left the fire and returned to their gers.

In the morning, the caravan continued on to Ulaanbaatar. At the end of the fourth day, they camped with the lights of the city in view. The following morning, they entered the outskirts of the city, and a strange sight greeted them. People, by the hundreds, lined either side of the street as far as could be seen. Mostly, they were silent, obviously in awe, their eyes wide and staring, fright and ecstasy competing on their faces.

He saluted them, presenting a stern visage. Many bowed their heads as he went by.

"How did they know?" Genghis asked himself.

Unknown to Genghis and to any of his followers, the young thief who had accosted him was so frightened by the experience, at the possibility that a demon was on the streets, that he overcame his dislike of authority. He went to the police and poured out his story. Though the men that he talked to were skeptical, his fright was obvious. Something strange had happened. They asked him to help a police artist make a sketch of the mysterious man impervious to harm. As the sketch took on life, the features became obvious. With the verbal description, the mysterious figure emerged. Unlike most Mongolians, he had reddish hair and green eyes.

They looked carefully at the sketch and reviewed the verbal description. Then one of the officers gasped. His eyes opened wide in astonishment. The others looked at him. A sergeant spoke.

"Do you recognize him?"

"Yes," said the officer. "From the exhibits in a museum. He looks like Genghis Khan. He *is* Genghis Khan. Our beloved leader has returned. He is immortal."

The other policemen were astonished but still skeptical. They decided to see their captain.

One of the policemen asked what they should do with the young man.

"He has a record?" asked the sergeant.

"Yes, quite a long one."

"Lock him up. For now we will call it protective custody."

After a long discussion with his officers, the captain decided to go up the line of authority, which ended at the office of the Minister of Justice and Home Affairs.

The party consisted of the captain, his superior, and the Commissioner of Police. When the Minister heard the purpose of the visit, he immediately called them in and demanded their whole story. When they had finished, he put his fingertips together, and rested them on his chin. There was a period of silence. Finally, he spoke.

"Have there been any other sightings?"

"None that we have heard of, Minister," said the captain.

"What I am about to tell you must stay in this room. American and World Federation officials have contacted us. They told us of an American television show that has the ability to bring historical figures to virtual life to be interviewed. One of those interviewed failed to return to the computer storage. They discovered that he apparently had materialized on the street, and eventually flew from here to Ulaanbaatar. He is in Mongolia; we do not know where. We refused to commit to returning him to America. He is ours. He is our revered Genghis Khan. We believe that he will reveal himself, and we await his appearance. Whenever that happens, it will be a great day for our country. The government has been meeting daily to decide what we should do when that great day comes. Until then, I want to hear of any reports of sightings, here or anywhere in the country. Immediately. That is understood?"

"Yes, Minister," they replied in unison.

"What have you done with the young thief?"

"We have him in, uh, protective custody."

"Good."

After they left, the Minister reported the conversation to the Prime Minister. A state of high excitement began to build. When a sufficient number of people become privy to a secret, that secret soon becomes common knowledge. Questions arose. Where was he? Why was he hiding? When would he reveal himself? One day, rumors of an approaching caravan began to circulate in the streets. As the Khan and his followers entered the city, word spread very quickly, and crowds began to gather. The caravan rode down Peace Avenue towards Sukhbataar Square and the government buildings. By this time, people began to cheer, as the dream of their Messiah's return became reality. The riders crossed Sukhbataar Square and stopped in front of the government palace. Genghis dismounted and walked to the top of the steps next to his statue and prepared to announce himself. At that moment, the doors swung open and the Prime Minister emerged, followed by the entire cabinet and many sub-ministers, other administrators, and other staff members.

The PM faced Genghis and they bowed to each other. In a loud voice, the PM spoke.

"Oh, Glorious Khan, Mongolia is yours! We welcome you home at long last!"

A tremendous roar rose out of the crowd, echoing as the crowds on the streets joined in. Genghis bowed again to the PM, and turned to face the crowd. He raised his arms high in the air, as more cheering resounded through the streets.

"My children, I have returned. Mongolia will become great again. The empire will live again. The world will know us again. I am immortal. I will be with you always."

The cheering intensified. He turned to the PM.

"We must talk."

"Indeed, we must, great Khan. Please join me in my office."

Genghis turned back to the crowd and waved to further cheering. He and the PM went into the building, followed by the other members of the government. The Deputy Prime Minister and the President joined them.

After seating themselves, the PM said, "We are yours to command, Khan. Tell us how we can help you."

"For the time being, I want you to stay in office and continue to run the government. I will remain in the background and observe and learn more about my country and my people as they are now. It has been many years. Before long I will assume active leadership to carry out my plans."

"May I ask what your plans are, Khan?"

"We will restore the Mongol Empire."

They managed to appear elated, surprised, and fearful at the same time.

"A glorious goal, Khan," said the President. "But it will be very difficult. You know the world is different now. The world federation forces are very powerful, and they will be joined by the militias of each country that we invade."

"Yes, I am aware of that. But we will have a way to create powerful weapons of our own. Most important, I will be able to create special soldiers, soldiers like me."

"You can do this, Khan?"

"Yes, when I build a machine to do it."

Genghis did not tell them that he had never built nor operated a machine like MONTY, nor that he did not know whether it would function properly under very different circumstances from the *History Lives* studios. But he was sure of his exalted status, and confident that his powers would overcome any obstacle. The rest of the conversation was brief.

"Now, gentlemen, I must leave you. My followers and I have much work to do. I leave the government in your charge, while we return to Bayan Ovoo to carry out important tasks. You will hear from me when we are ready to begin our glorious venture. All roads to my village must be guarded. I do not want the press or any foreigners to come near the village. The only people to be allowed through are those with proof that they are related to me through descent and persons with the government. Also, I will need a report on the state of readiness of our armed forces: manpower, weapons, vehicles, everything."

"As you wish, Khan."

"One more thing. No one must know about my special troops. Complete secrecy is essential."

"On our honor, Khan."

He went out of the building through the front doors to the cheers of the crowd; a few people had left, but many had stayed, waiting for one more glimpse of their great hero, and a few more words.

"My children, I shall be back, but now I must return to my village and complete preparations for the days of glory that await us. Those days are coming soon."

He made his way, amidst continued cheering, to his waiting cohort. He mounted his horse and led his men out of town, back to Bayan Ovoo.

\* \* \*

The news of Genghis Khan's strange exodus from the *History Lives* studio, return to Mongolia, and bloodless coup-by-invitation flew all over the world. Cabinet and security meetings were convened in the United States, China, Russia, Korea, Japan, several Central Asian and Middle Eastern states, and at World Federation headquarters in New York. Consternation was the operative word at all meetings. What would he do? How do you deal with a conqueror that claims immortality? Requests to hold talks with him were politely but firmly denied. He was in seclusion. Why was he in seclusion? The Khan wishes.

The staff of *History Lives* had the most intimate knowledge of Genghis Khan outside of Mongolia. The World Federation leaders held an emergency cabinet meeting and requested that Robert Delacroix and John Sorensen attend and provide information and possibly an assessment of the

Khan's likely course of action.

They flew to New York and proceeded to World Federation Headquarters in the former United Nations building. John described the nature of their show and their ability through MONTY to bring interviewees to virtual life. After that discussion, they turned to Robert.

Olav Jensen of Norway was current President of the Federation. He smiled at Robert.

"I had the pleasure of watching your interview of my earliest predecessor as President. It was excellent. I enjoyed it very much."

"Thank you, sir."

"You have the unique distinction of being the only person who has talked to Genghis Khan, within your interview cubicle and then again outside the cubicle, at his village in Mongolia. Hopefully, these conversations will help us to know what to expect from him."

"I certainly hope so, Mr. President."

"Tell us what you have learned."

"Perhaps I should provide a little background. We have discovered during these interviews that subjects who had suffered from some illness during their lives regain their health in the cubicle. Even more intriguing, some of them go through an accelerated learning process during the interview. It's quite remarkable. We can observe it happening. Genghis Khan apparently continued to learn rapidly *after* getting out of the cubicle. He has also developed extraordinary physical powers, which is both astonishing and frightening. He demonstrated several of them to me in Mongolia. He can jump and touch a very high ceiling. He can move objects by teleportation. And then I watched him change a chair to a table."

"How did he do that?" asked the President.

"I have no idea. He just stared at it."

"That is unreal," said the President.

"Yes, sir. But I watched it happen."

"What else can he do?"

"I asked him that. He said he was still learning, but I think he was holding back. I'm sure he has some powers that he didn't want to tell me about. Another phenomenon that he did disclose: he claims immortality. I'm not sure that is possible, but he isn't made of flesh and blood, so we don't know the expected life of his body."

"You mean that he is not a holographic image?"

"No, sir. His body has substance."

"What can harm him?"

"Well, I've thought about that. A gunshot wound might disrupt his bodily functions, whatever they may be. Perhaps a corrosive chemical would destroy his body."

"Is there anything else that can happen to him?"

"Well, he was supposed to leave the cubicle and return to the machine as stored information. We hope that this will happen to him eventually. Unfortunately, we have no idea if or when or how that will occur. We have alerted all the scientific groups affiliated with us to begin looking for ways to destroy him."

"The big question is: What will he do? Can you enlighten us?"

"His first goal was to return as Khan of Mongolia. That apparently has already been accomplished, and, thankfully, with no more bloodshed. He is a national hero, and the people embraced him without question. Even the government wanted him to come back and lead, which was quite remarkable. His next goal is to restore the Mongol Empire. It wasn't clear whether he meant the empire at the time he died in1227, or the empire expanded by his children and grandchildren. Either way, it would be an enormous piece of the planet, including at the least, parts of Siberia, Russia, China, and Iran plus several Central Asian countries."

"Is he aware that he will be faced by the world forces in that region?"

"Yes, but it doesn't bother him. That worries me, because he may have the ability to create powerful weapons, as well as military equipment and vehicles. He may even be able to create beings like himself. I have no idea whether he has that power, but the possibility exists. That is frightening."

"Indeed it is. Well, I think we must put the world forces in the area on alert and monitor the situation very closely."

"Mr. President," said one of the military members. "Perhaps we should go into Mongolia immediately, before he makes his move."

The President shook his head. "No, we cannot do that. Article 24, Section C expressly forbids invasion of a country in the absence of overt provocation by that country. Mongolia has not provoked anyone, has not closed its borders, has not done anything, and we cannot make assumptions based only on things the Khan has said to Mr. Delacroix." He paused and sighed. "Besides, we do not know if we can actually capture or kill him. We must wait and keep close watch."

"Mr. President." One of the other members spoke up. "How shall we deal with the countries bordering Mongolia? They are understandably nervous having their former conqueror next door."

"They must take no unilateral action unless attacked. The world forces will help protect them if the Khan begins or threatens hostile activity. We will constantly monitor his activity."

During the discussion, Robert thought about what had happened. Just a short time ago, he was a television personality. Today he was meeting with world leaders, advising them about what might be expected from a non-real person planning to regain an old empire, reliving a nine hundred year old experience. Remarkable.

* * *

Several days later, Genghis and his men arrived back at the village. He had spent much of his travel time considering the number of weapons, vehicles, and special soldiers he should create to supplement the men and equipment from the existing Mongolian forces. He had to assume that there would be surveillance by the World Federation. Therefore, it would be necessary to keep equipment hidden for as long as possible. He must not create a structure large enough to hide all the pieces that he would make. In a small village, it would stand out among the smaller buildings and gers. Ah. There was the answer: they must erect a large number of standard sized gers to house the equipment and the soldiers.

During a meeting with his descendant-advisors, he informed them about his plans.

"First, we must build fifty gers, ten meters in diameter. One of them must be placed near my ger. The others should be placed in groups of five or ten in different parts of the village. They will be less obtrusive than having them all in one group. I want each one to have an identifying designation, with a letter for the group location and a number for each one in the group. While you are doing this task, I will be constructing another MONTY to create men, weapons, and equipment. Some of the special soldiers will be housed in the gers, and the equipment will be stored there."

"My beloved Khan," said Altan, "will we have enough weapons and men to fight against the world forces? They are very powerful."

"Yes, Altan. The special weapons and troops will be indestructible. We will place them in the vanguard of our army. Imagine the effect on the world forces when they discover that they cannot destroy our weapons and vehicles and cannot kill our troops. They will be terrified. They will run. We cannot lose.

"Our regular forces will follow and will be in less danger. They will occupy villages and towns, capture prisoners, support the vanguard when necessary, and recruit new people to join us. All will share the glory and the victories."

He rose from his chair. "Now let us begin work."

To create the needed equipment, he required a modified version of MONTY, which would interpret digitally converted designs and schematics of the various units. He had some of the men gather or acquire materials to be transformed: metal, plastic, computer parts, wiring, switches, dials, even scrap pieces. They were placed in his new ger. He had considered using his own mind to build each item. It would be an interesting challenge to his powers, but far too time consuming. He did not wish to be his own MONTY.

When all the materials were assembled, he cleared his memory of all but MONTY's design and schematics. He included and concentrated on the needed modifications. His mind clearly visualized all aspects of the design. He turned to the raw materials on the floor and stared at them.

Little by little, they lost their shape and appearance. They were cut, bent, shaped, twisted, spliced, and fitted together, the whole process gradually becoming a noiseless blur, as if a small cloud had formed on the floor of the ger. And then, slowly, the cloud began to take a new shape, one long unit instead of the five of the original, adorned with lights, screens, slots, and switches: MONTY II. Genghis relaxed, gazed at the apparatus, and smiled in triumph.

"Some day, I will use only sand as my raw material."

Would the machine work? It would have to convert specifications for various types of equipment to a digital matrix capable of forming a laser weapon, a cargo vehicle, a troop carrier, a rocket weapon, or any other piece of apparatus that his army would need. The task might actually be simpler than creating an ancient human replica from diverse and incomplete sources of information. Therefore, it could be relatively easy for MONTY II. He laid out several sheets of blank paper on the table and directed his intense gaze at them, combining from his memory the lines, words, and numbers into directions for constructing an electronic discharge weapon. He gathered the imprinted papers in proper order and fed them into a slot on the side of the machine. In five minutes, the machine signaled that the digital interpretation was complete. He pressed the "Coordinate" button, followed by the "Materialize" button. After another ten minutes, the weapon appeared on the floor in front of the machine. He repeated the directions and a second weapon appeared.

"Now comes the real test," he murmured.

He stretched his arm toward one of the weapons and willed it to move; it soon appeared in his hands. He pointed it at a small table and pressed a button. A flash. The table disappeared. He aimed at the other weapon and pressed the button again. Another flash. The second weapon remained intact. He raised one fist in the air and danced a little jig. Suddenly he whirled around to look at the door. No one had come in to witness his lapse of dignity.

Several days later, Altan came to the ger with the news that the fifty additional gers had been erected. He gave Genghis a map of the village showing the location of the groups and a list of the identification numbers. Genghis pulled aside a curtain and showed him the weapons and the machine.

"Khan!" he exclaimed. "Where did they come from?"

Genghis grinned at him.

"I made the machine, and the machine and I made the weapons."

"Wondrous," said Altan. "Wondrous."

"Yes, indeed. Tomorrow, we will start creating our arsenal and placing the pieces in the gers."

During the night, Genghis drew up a list of the additional weapons, vehicles, and other equipment that they would need for the vanguard, including weapons that would fire at enemy air vehicles. He created a set of specifications for each type of equipment, and fed them into the machine for storage in the digital memory files. Then he listed each ger with its identification codes and assigned a destination for each piece. He activated the machine to create several pieces and sent each piece to a different destination.

"Enough for now," he said out loud. "It is time for more thinking." He lay on the bed and pondered the creation of soldiers for the vanguard. What was the ideal number? What was the best way of obtaining DNA records? He needed lineages, many lineages.

Also it was necessary to maintain regular communication with the government in Ulaanbaatar. He created an E-tran device with voice activated direct transmission to one or many recipients. He immediately sent a message to the Director of the Census Division, Ministry of Trade, requesting DNA records of a thousand deceased Mongolian male citizens, with emphasis on military background. Another idea popped into his mind: a little flamboyance was called for. He sent a second E-tran to the Agriculture Department of the State University of Mongolia requesting DNA records of several Mongol warhorses.

The next morning, when Altan and several other descendants arrived, he sent them to the destinations to verify that each piece had been sent to the proper location. They returned shortly and confirmed that the distribution had worked perfectly.

"Well, my sons, let us begin."

He showed them the steps needed for MONTY II to create the various units and send them to the destinations listed for each piece. He estimated that three to five days would be required to construct the equipment, with periodic checks to confirm that the procedure was working as he had planned it.

Several days after completion of the job, the E-tran began printing DNA records from the Census Division and the Agriculture Department.

"We are ready to build our army," announced the Khan to his council. "Tomorrow we will meet and I will explain my plans."

# CHAPTER 23

An enormous map of the region was displayed behind the Khan as he stood before the group; a writing board was placed next to it.

"I will now present to you a plan of attack against those countries that occupy parts of our old empire. We will conquer them, and they will become part of our new empire."

The group applauded and cheered loudly.

"You will be my political advisers. I expect you to point out possible improvements in the plan. It will not be my victory; it will be our victory. Those of you who have been officers during military service may wish also to be leaders in the army. However, I expect to rely mostly on the officers in the forces now. MONTY II will make our shock troops, a group of indestructible special soldiers. We will use DNA patterns of those who have died. I have specifically asked for patterns of men who were in the military during their original lives.

"The special forces will be the vanguard of our attacks. This tactic will serve two purposes. First, our enemies will be terrorized when they discover that those men cannot be killed. Second, the rest of our army will be subject to less danger. I wish to lose as few of our brave countrymen as possible."

"I plan to begin our conquest in the spring. During the winter, we will train our army. The men will train with modern weapons, including new ones that I will create. We will discuss attack plans, appoint and train commanders, and decide how large our forces should be. I shall consult with the government, emphasizing the need to continue diplomatic relations with other countries, which will allow us to continue sending our agents to strategic locations.

"Also during the winter we will discuss our first point of attack, subsequent routes, maintaining supply lines, and other tactics." He paused and smiled. "This will be modern war, of course, but I confess to longing for the old ways we used nine hundred years ago.

"First we will conquer Kazakhstan. Since Mongolia and Kazakhstan do not meet at a border, I was concerned that we would have to go through Russia or China to get to the Kazakh border, and I am not ready to fight with either one yet. I have discovered upon closer inspection of a map that there is actually a corridor there. It appears to be about 40 kilometers long. How did that happen?"

"It was established after the world federation was formed," said Altan Sognom. "It had been difficult for us to get to Kazakhstan, and for the Kazakhs to get here, without getting into a fight with either the Russians or the Chinese. So the World Federation mediated the establishment of a narrow corridor on the line of the Russian-Chinese border. It is considered a neutral zone."

"Is it monitored by the World Federation?"

"Not very well, Khan."

"That is fortunate. We will advance through that corridor in the early spring while there is still much snow on the ground." He paused. "Good. This is all we will discuss of the plan today. Now it is time to create our special force. We may need to construct additional gers, if there is insufficient room in the ones already built. This will be your assignment. Altan will be in charge. These men will be like me and will need no special comforts."

"As you wish, Khan."

"Now I will retire to my ger to create a few soldiers and learn about them. We will coordinate the construction and availability of gers with the numbers of new men to fill them. Keep me informed about your progress. Ertene, I wish you to come with me."

In the ger, he picked up the first DNA records; they were considerably more complete than most of the ones used by *History Lives*, and he hoped they were sufficient to make a whole man with minimal additional information. He added the basics: name, birthplace, tribe, civilian occupation, military service, language spoken, clothing descriptions, etc. He fed the information into the machine and pressed the processing button. Twenty minutes later, a man appeared in front of the machine. He looked around curiously and finally noted the Khan.

"Do you recognize me?" asked Genghis.

"You look like Genghis Khan."

"I am Genghis Khan. Like you I have been brought back to life by a machine. We are long into the future. It is the year 2154."

The man went to his knees.

"Oh great Khan. You have returned."

"And so have you. Rise up. Do you know who you are and when you lived?"

"Yes, Khan. I am Norov Bechbat. I was born in 1921, the year the Soviets came, and we declared independence from China."

"Were you in the military?"

"Yes, Khan, I was an officer in the army."

"Excellent. I have great plans for the rebuilding of the Empire and you will be an important part of it."

"As you wish, Khan."

Genghis explained their situation, their potential powers, and his plans.

"Now I will create more of us. You may watch. Ertene, I wish you to record their names, and other information, and also to assign each an identification number for their assignment to quarters."

Genghis fed another DNA information sheet into the slot, added additional information and again pressed the button. A second man emerged. He identified himself as Saikhan Baabar, born 1542, occupation herdsman.

He completed resurrection of the first twenty men in several hours. About half of them had military experience, including several officers and one general. They came from five different centuries spanning about seven hundred years. At first they didn't know how to deal with each other, but were comforted by the presence of their great leader and the fact that they were all Mongols. They began to talk, expressing wonder at their miraculous return to life. Each described life in his century.

Altan sent a man over to escort the group to a ger. As they left, Genghis wondered whether they would achieve as high a level of intelligence and powers as he had. He suspected that their individual DNA content would dictate how far that process could go.

* * *

Several weeks later, the work was complete. Of the one thousand creations, 850 were satisfactory. The rest were either physically grotesque, had no mind, were too small, lacked limbs, or had other problems. In anticipation of this, he had added a device on MONTY II that enabled him to return them to oblivion.

Genghis went to Ulaanbaatar and met with the Minister of Defense, Byambyn Mongkhbat. He described his newly created force of special soldiers, weapons, and equipment.

"Will the special soldiers have your powers, Khan?"

"They will be difficult to kill. As for other powers, we will find out. Right now I do not know."

"I have a very important question, Khan. Will they be loyal? Because if they're not, they will be dangerous, especially if they band together."

"That is true. Fortunately, there is a substance that only I know of, which will destroy them, if it becomes necessary. But I expect complete loyalty."

The Minister sighed with relief and nodded his head in approval. The Khan was not telling the complete truth, of course. There was no substance, but he expected to have a formulation ready if it was ever needed.

They discussed the existing Mongolian forces and their battle readiness, as well as the condition of weapons and equipment. The Minister told him of the kinds of training the various combat troops and support groups had received. The weapons, of course, since the formation of the world federation, had relatively low-level destructive force.

Genghis leaned forward. "Now, Minister, this is my battle plan. Our first target will be Kazakhstan. Fortunately, the narrow corridor separating China and Russia will allow us to avoid those countries until I am ready for them. We will drive through the corridor into Kazakhstan until we encounter the first units of the Kazakh Army. My special troops will be deployed as a vanguard. They will be instructed not to fire at the Kazakhs, but simply allow the Kazakhs to fire at them. The enemy will quickly discover the truth about our soldiers, who will continue to advance on foot, instead of collapsing. When the Kazakhs realize the terrible truth, they will be demoralized, and quickly panic. We will, if necessary, fire a few rounds to encourage their retreat."

"They will be frightened beyond reason."

"We may have to engage in more skirmishes, before doubters will be convinced, in their armed forces and in their government. Then hopefully they will surrender quickly and the country will be ours."

"It will be glorious." Minister Byambyn was surprised at the fire coursing through his body, a revival of the fierce warrior spirit of the ancient Mongols. He was a relatively mild mannered man and the feeling was strange. If he felt this way, how must it be for the people of more elemental emotions? Perhaps we *will* rule the world.

"Is it time to meet with the cabinet?"

"I believe so, Khan."

As they entered the cabinet room, all stood and bowed their heads. Genghis waved them to be seated. He repeated his plans for conquest and asked for questions. Several were concerned about the future loyalty of the special soldiers. Others wanted to know exactly what the regular soldiers would do besides some minor mopping up. They were worried about the morale of brave warriors doing essentially nothing.

"After the first few battles, the enemy will discover that not all of our soldiers have extraordinary powers. They will try to outflank the vanguard and attack our regular troops. That is when our troops will prove their bravery, that they are warriors. They will share the glory."

There were some more questions, followed by a discussion of training plans. Genghis would train the special troops himself, devising a series of physical and mental exercises to test their abilities. A test for their ability to withstand pain and resist injury was critical to deploying them properly. He knew that differences might exist, including the possibility that some could be damaged or killed. At this point he did not wish to consider the possibility that they could all be killed. Would he have to be a one man strike force? He smiled grimly at that possibility.

Then it was time for training. The regular forces were trained by their commanders, mostly in the Altai Mountains in the west, near the borders of China and Kazakhstan. More important, they trained at normal winter sites and did not raise suspicion from spies on the ground or in air vehicles. Genghis trained his special soldiers in protected locations near Bayan Ovoo.

One of the special soldiers was a general who had lived into the twenty-first century, Migjid Enkhbold. Genghis appointed him as training commander, to choose a cadre of officers and non-commissioned officers, and set up appropriate roster levels. They conducted maneuvers later on the plains outside the village.

So the winter passed. Near the end of the season, he assembled his troops and asked for men of Kazakh descent. Several men stepped forward. After reviewing his list, he dismissed the troops and called two of the Kazakhs into his ger. He pointed at one, "You are Balat Satpeyev."

"Yes, Khan."

"And you are Assan Tokayev."

"Yes, Khan."

"I've called you in because you are both intelligent men and you speak

Khazakh. I want you to go into Khazakhstan to spy. I want you to look for troop movements near the eastern border, the plains and villages around Lake Zayzan, and the territory to the west as far as Astana, the capital. When you speak to people, give no indication of any military interest. Report back when you have good information. Don't get caught. Can you do that?"

"Yes, Khan."

"You will need no food, but eat if it is useful to make it easier to talk to people. Get whatever supplies you need. I will provide a vehicle for you to drive. Drive carefully and break no laws."

"Yes, Khan. As you wish."

Genghis also sent spies into China and Russia near the corridor to see if there was any military preparation going on in either country.

In three weeks, the spies from Kazakhstan returned and reported to the Khan. First, they had reconnoitered south of the Kazakh entrance to the corridor.

"We saw no large troop movements, Khan," Satpeyev said, "but there was some activity. They were building at least two camps near Lake Zayzan. We saw some troops moving up from the south, probably from Almaty."

They reported similar activity west of the corridor until they arrived at the capital, Astana, where two training camps east of the city were in full activity.

Genghis was perversely pleased that there would be no element of surprise. The Kazakhs would be prepared, and he thought that the shock for them would be greater in a direct confrontation against his special troops. He examined the test results of his men to be sure that *he* would not be the one surprised. He was relieved that their capacities were similar to his. They were impervious to pain, learned fast, could jump high and far, and needed neither food nor water nor sleep. He did not test their ability to move objects with their minds. Neither did he tell them anything about his ability to do that nor his ability to transform materials to new forms.

The spies sent to Russia and China also reported little activity in those countries.

* * *

He and his generals assembled the troops, and on April 1, they advanced westward through the 40-kilometer corridor. Alerts flashed world wide that Genghis Khan was about to invade Kazakhstan. Kazakh troops moved from the west and south to meet the Mongolian army. Contingents of World Federation troops assembled in China and Russia and needed only an order from the Federation to move in.

Genghis and his forces arrived in Kazakh territory the next day. They bivouacked and waited. He decided to split the armies into two parts: one to drive south under General Enkhbold, the other to move west under his own command. Scouts reported that the Kazakh troops from the west would likely arrive first, within a day. The following morning, Genghis split the special troops in half also, each to form the vanguard for an army group, with units of the regular army arrayed behind them. His army was rather small, to inspire over-confidence among the commanders of the Kazakh army. Since the weapons permitted to the various national armies were limited in power, the Kazakhs adopted simple, direct assault formations. Genghis had his more advanced weapons, but did not plan to disclose them unless necessary. As his army and the Kazakh army stared at each other and waited, Genghis advanced to the front. He was mounted on a horse and dressed in full thirteenth century regalia. A murmur and muted laughter ran through the Kazakh troops. When his troops recovered from their own surprise, an enormous cheer arose from the ranks.

Genghis rode to the front of his special forces, faced the Kazakh troops and stared at them across the intervening space, about one hundred meters. Both armies waited. He had a sudden thought: Why should Mongol troops fight like this, waiting for something to happen? We are warriors, the greatest in the world. Now is the time. He turned in his saddle, lifted his rifle and pointed it toward the Kazakhs.

"Follow me!"

He rode slowly towards the Kazakhs, turned again, and shouted. "Charge!"

He rode forward faster. His troops let out a fierce yell and trotted after him with their rifles at the ready. This seemed to wake up the enemy troops, who also began yelling. They aimed their weapons at the Mongols and began firing. As the Mongols got closer, some of the Kazakh soldiers noticed that no Mongols were falling and none of them were firing their weapons. Even more astonishing, neither Genghis nor his horse seemed to be hit. Many of the Kazakh soldiers had fired at him, hoping for the glory of killing the great Khan. When he was within five meters of the Kazakh front line, Genghis held up his arm, halting his troops. Some of the Kazakhs kept firing. Most stopped, lowered their weapons, and were filled with wonder. Wonder turned to fear.

A soldier directly in front of Genghis' horse stared upward into the implacable eyes of the Khan and said aloud to his comrades surrounding him, "What shall we do?"

The others around him seemed struck dumb.

Finally, another soldier said, "They will kill us all. We must surrender." He dropped his weapon and raised his hands. Genghis continued staring at them. Then a third soldier yelled, "No. We must run!" He turned around and ran straight back through the soldiers around him. Another and another took up the cry, "Run, run!" Soon the whole front line group started running away. Officers and sergeants tried to stop them, but they kept running, many dropping their weapons.

Genghis turned back to his troops.

"Let them go!" he shouted. "Later, we will follow them to their camps."

The Mongols set up their own camp. Genghis called his commanders into his ger. General Enkhbold joined by pixel-phone. He was smiling as he reported a similar experience with the Kazakhs from the south.

"I want to be in Astana and Almaty as quickly as possible," said Genghis. "When we capture the capital and the largest city, we should be in control of the whole country. However, I believe we should expect a change in tactics now that they have seen us. But they will be guessing, because no one knows what these bodies are made of and how they work. Nevertheless they will try something, and we have to be prepared for anything. They may try bombs, poison gas, powerful solvents, or fire. Also, prepare to retaliate if they become too annoying."

He turned to the officers of the regular army.

"If for any reason the special forces get into trouble, be prepared to join the battle. Attack their flanks. Nothing must stand in our way. We must not lose our momentum."

He paused. "One more thing we must consider: we do not know when or in what manner the world forces will join the fight. They will have better weapons, and we must be prepared to use our own special weapons if necessary. Our men are well trained in their use." He smiled. "Those weapons will be the second major surprise for our enemies."

On the second day the Kazakh troops behaved as if the first day had never happened, and once again turned and ran for their lives. Genghis was astonished. Surely, conquest will not be this easy. On the third day, the battle did change with the entry of Federation forces crossing the borders from China and Russia. They brought more powerful weapons and attacks from the air. The men in the Mongol and Kazakh armies had never seen any weapon larger than a rifle, except in museums. There were many casualties among the regular troops and a few among the special units. He planned to investigate the latter group's casualties when the battle ended, hoping a remedy could be devised before another battle. He also ordered the special troops in the units advancing westward towards Astana to use their advanced weapons.

Each type of advanced weapon had a different function. One type discharged a highly focused heat beam that literally cooked any soldier hit with it. Another sent a light beam that temporarily blinded the victim. And a third sent an electronic signal that filled the target with uncontrollable fright. He had decided earlier that the weapon that simply caused the target to disappear had insufficient shock value. It would not be used at this early stage of fighting. They would fire each type of weapon at a different group of enemy troops. Genghis assigned several men to watch the target groups from positions on a small hillock and observe the damage. They would report to him at the end of the battle, so he could assess the relative effectiveness of each weapon. The end came quickly once the weapons were used, as once again the enemy Kazakh troops fled, joined by the federation units.

Genghis summoned the observers and the casualty investigators to his ger to hear and discuss their findings.

"First, I want to hear about our own troops. Could you assess the damage to the men?"

The spokesman of the casualty inspectors spoke up.

"They've done quite well, Khan. But—"

"Yes?"

"Twenty-five men collapsed."

"Collapsed. You mean they just fell down?"

"Yes, Khan. There were no visible wounds. Maybe the noise frightened them. The men have become quite nervous, wondering whether they will suffer the same fate."

I suppose I didn't identify all the defectives, thought Genghis. "We will investigate this further," he said aloud. He turned to the battle observers.

"What did you think of the new weapons?"

"Frightening," said one. "Also, the nearby troops who could see what was happening to the target groups panicked and ran away."

One of the observers who had watched the effect of the blinding beam commented that those hit by the beam became highly disoriented; they had no idea what struck them. He wondered whether they would fight again once they recovered.

"The fright inducer must have been horrible for its victims," said another observer. "They ran around in circles screaming. I'm curious to know how soon they recovered, *if* they recovered."

Genghis chuckled.

"We can be sure that the World Federation will have a lot to think about. They will wonder if they can stop us. Their troops have had little war experience and morale must be very low."

He chuckled again.

"Tomorrow will tell a tale."

After the evening meal, Genghis retired to his ger to consider some tactical changes for the next day. First, he contacted Ertene Navaan by pixel phone.

"Ertene, my son, I have a job for you."

"The Khan wishes."

"We have had a few losses. I want you to obtain genetic records and create another five hundred special troops. Eliminate the ones who cannot function. Send the troops to Kazakhstan as soon as they are ready. I have a headquarters group just inside the border that will direct half of them to my army on the road to Astana and the other half to General Enkhbold who is heading south towards Almaty."

"I will begin immediately, Khan."

"Good, I look forward to their arrival."

# CHAPTER 24

Kazakhstan's President Irina Kasymova called an emergency meeting of her cabinet. Her angry eyes focused on the Minister of Defense.

"Why are we doing so badly? What is wrong with our soldiers? Why do they not fight? Are they all cowards? Have they forgotten how to fight since we became part of this damned world federation?"

He, as well as the other Ministers, could see that that part of her anger was fueled by fright and uncertainty.

"They are not cowards, Madam President. They are encountering an army that they couldn't imagine existed, that no one has ever seen before. How can they fight an enemy that apparently can't be killed or injured, an enemy that possesses weapons of terrible power, led by a man who died nearly a thousand years ago, the greatest and cruelest conqueror ever seen on this earth?"

"So what are we to do? How can we fight them? I am ready for good suggestions."

"For the moment, we must continue to retreat until the federation provides greater numbers of soldiers, weapons, and especially air power. Most of his army is made up of ordinary people and he has protected them by using the special group as his vanguard. So, I think we can do a lot of damage with air power from the federation, especially to the regular troops."

The President had regained her composure. "Very well, I shall demand greater support from the Federation, as quickly as possible. The Mongolian Army is advancing closer to this city and to Almaty. We must consider the possibility that we will have to move the seat of government farther to the west if the enemy gets too close; to Aqtau or perhaps to Atyrau on the Caspian Sea."

"There is one other problem, Madam President." The Minister hesitated for a moment. "Some of our troops are defecting to the Mongolian Army. It is possible that many of them believe they have Mongol blood and may be descendants of the Khan himself."

She stared at him and then shook her head. She threw up her hands and chuckled.

"Any more good news? "

He smiled grimly. "Not yet, Madam President.

"I wonder how much more history we will have to relive."

\* \* \*

The two Mongolian armies continued their advance towards Astana and Almaty. Defects among the special soldiers continued to appear. Genghis Khan slowed his assault until the new troops arrived. While waiting, he deployed anti-aircraft versions of his three special weapons, anticipating an air attack by the Federation. That attack came the next day. The ships flew in formations of eight, zooming low over the Mongolian troops, firing cannons and machine guns. On the first pass, the return fire was erratic and did little damage. But the weapons control officers and the gunners themselves learned rapidly, adjusted their firing techniques, and destroyed a few more airships on the second pass with heat, pilot blindness, or panic. The regular Mongolian army sustained moderate casualties. After the second pass the Federation airships returned to their base. The attacks continued for two more days. Each army incurred increasing losses as the Mongolian gunners became more skillful, and the federation continued to send reinforcements.

Finally, the new special troops arrived from Mongolia. Genghis and General Enkhbold once again advanced toward Astana and Almaty. Fifty kilometers east of Astana, Genghis halted his forces. He ordered General Enkhbold to hold his advance into Almaty until Genghis sent a surrender ultimatum to President Kazymova.

The Kazakh president received the ultimatum and met with her cabinet.

"What shall we do?" She looked around the room at her ministers. "Is it time to move the government to the west? What is your advice?"

Defense Minister Sergei Aslanov cleared his throat.

"Well, Madam President, let us look at the war so far. Neither our troops nor the Federation troops have done very well. However, we have inflicted severe casualties on his regular army of real human beings. But even with the more effective weaponry of the Federation, we have done little to the non-human ones. Some of them have gone down, but it seems he has the ability to make more and bring them to the front. That machine is the devil's incarnation. If we continue to fight, with greater support from the Federation, especially with air power, we may well destroy his human army and be able to concentrate on the much smaller group of special troops. We must look for weaknesses. If we capitulate now, many lives will be saved, but we don't know what will happen to our country."

"We cannot forget his murderous reputation."

"No. So far he has not behaved like the conqueror of old. He has not razed cities and towns, and burned farms. Maybe," he said with a sardonic smile, "he has become a civilized conqueror."

"Do you think we can count on that?" asked another minister.

"Not at all, but historically, his genocidal acts were often motivated by revenge. We have simply fought back when he invaded. Perhaps the best choice would be to send an envoy under a flag of truce. I will volunteer to do that."

Aslanov looked around the table.

"Very well," said the President. "I commend you and thank you. Any more comments?"

The Federation military representative at the far end of the table spoke up.

"We are all dealing with an unfamiliar situation, and that's an understatement. The Federation has for many years counted on its presence alone to prevent conflicts from arising. That is now irrelevant. So, at this point, I believe you should send the envoy and hear the Khan's offer. That might help our decision."

\* \* \*

The following day, the Minister was driven to the Mongolian encampment. Enemy soldiers immediately surrounded them.

"I am Minister of Defense Sergei Aslanov and have come to discuss terms with the Khan."

He spoke in halting Mongol.

"Wait here," said an officer. The remaining soldiers looked at them with expressions of detachment. They said nothing. The Minister suddenly realized that they were the famous special troops. He stared at them. They were exact replicas of real people. The officer returned.

"Come with me. Leave the vehicle."

They entered one of the gers. Genghis still wore his ancient uniform. The Minister thought that he looked a bit different from his pictures and statues. Strange. But then he remembered that none of the images seen in museums and books were considered to be true likenesses.

Genghis bowed his head slightly.

"I speak fluent Kazakh. We may talk in your language."

"Thank you, Khan. That will make it easier for me."

"So you wish to discuss terms. They are very simple. You will become part of the Mongol Empire, as an autonomous state. You may keep your present government. There will be no burning, looting, or other criminal behavior. Think of me as the substitute for the World Federation." He grinned. "You only need to remember that the important seat of government is in Ulaanbaatar."

"To what extent will we be autonomous, Khan?"

Genghis stared at him.

"Your government may make laws that affect your own people." He paused. "They will *not* be in conflict with any Mongolian laws. You will have a police force, but no army of your own. We have already welcomed Kazakhs to our ranks, and will continue to do so. You are familiar with Yasa, the Mongol code of laws?"

"I have heard of it, Khan."

"I suggest you read it and learn it well. That will help you to avoid conflict with us."

Aslanov sighed inwardly and nodded his head. "I must take this back to my President and the cabinet, Khan."

"Of course." He smiled. "I am pleased that you have a female president. You appear to respect women as I do."

He rose. The Minister saw that he was as tall as he had been described in history books.

"I shall await your reply. Do not take too long."

Minister Aslanov returned to Astana and met again with the president, the Federation representative, and the cabinet. He reviewed his conversation with Genghis Khan.

President Kazymova shook her head in puzzlement.

"This a very strange Genghis Khan. He is not behaving like a bloody conqueror at all. Still, he is camped not far from our capital city with an army, composed of men as unreal as he is, and carrying some horrible weapons. Some of his men have collapsed for some reason. He may die in the same way, perhaps tonight or tomorrow, next week or next month. But he may also last for years. No one knows. Apparently he doesn't know either."

"What shall we do?" asked another minister.

"Let me hear your opinions," said President Kazymova.

Minister Aslanov said, "I don't see how we can give in after only a few short battles. The Federation forces are building, particularly the air force. They fire explosive shells, which may inflict damage to the special soldiers as well as the human ones. The Mongols will sustain losses, and their advance will be slowed. Given sufficient time, we will be able to fight on more or less equal terms. There is no reason why we cannot win."

"I think we have to look at his reputation from the past," said the Minister of Energy. "If we resist and inflict the damage you speak of, he can, he *will*, become vindictive and cruel. Who knows how much destruction and death he will inflict on us and our people for revenge?"

Foreign Minister Arman Sholak said. "I agree with Minister Aslanov. If we surrender now, we will be disgraced. That disgrace will stay with us for a long time. But I can see the war turning our way soon. We are fighting against an enemy that is not even real; they are dead people and they soon may be dead again. We cannot allow ourselves be defeated by an unreal enemy. They are fearsome because we don't understand who or what they are. But we are learning and one of the things we have learned is that they have some vulnerability. We must fight."

The Federation representative pointed out that the world forces were growing rapidly, and confidence was building that they would prevail against the Khan.

"I have been authorized to support your decision."

The discussion continued. When voices began to rise, President Kasymova raised her hand.

"Enough. We will fight." She turned to her chief assistant, sitting next to her. "Prepare to move the seat of government west, to Atyrau, if it becomes necessary."

"Yes, Madam President."

The Defense Minister wondered whether his fighting words expressed bravery or bravado, confidence or uncertainty. He mentally shrugged and decided that a correct decision was probably not possible. The outcome was unpredictable, no matter what they decided to do, because this incarnation of Genghis Khan was unpredictable.

An aide to the Defense Minister returned to Genghis Khan's encampment to inform him of the Kazakh government's decision. He was ushered into the Khan's ger.

"I have been instructed to inform you, Khan, that our President has decided that we cannot surrender. We will fight."

The Khan sat for a moment and stared at the aide. He smiled and nodded his head.

"Very courageous," he said. "You have my admiration. You may go."

When the aide left the ger, Genghis picked up a heat weapon, took it outside, and fired it at the retreating aide. The vehicle driver stared in horror. Genghis shouted at him.

"Take this body back to your president. Tell her that this is what awaits."

* * *

The Mongolian armies resumed their drives to Astana and Almaty. The resistance stiffened, especially as the air strikes resumed with greater frequency, but the forward movement of Genghis's troops was relentless. He used his human troops more and more in flanking attacks, including feints on one flank and strong attacks on the other. When he reached the outskirts of Astana, the capital, key members of the government boarded air vehicles and flew to Atyrau. There the government could function, and if necessary, fly to a neighboring country and govern in exile.

Major battles were fought around and in the cities of Astana and Almaty. The Kazakh and World Federation troops, supported by the Federation air force, put up considerably greater resistance than in previous battles. The Mongolians advanced street by street, finally pushing the defending forces out of both cities. Both sides suffered major casualties. The Federation deployed tanks, which rumbled down major streets, but they were highly vulnerable, particularly to the heat weapons. The battles ended, and the Mongolians paused to regroup, while the World-Kazakh forces retreated to the west of Astana and south of Almaty, also to regroup.

More regular and special troops and weapons joined the Mongolian forces during the pause in fighting. Genghis summoned General Enkhbold to his headquarters to plan the next phase of the war. Several other high-ranking officers joined them in Genghis' ger. Genghis stood before a large map.

"Here is my overall plan. First, we will complete our conquest of Kazakhstan. Second, of the six nations that surround Kazakhstan, four are small countries: Kyrgyzstan, Uzbekistan, Turkmenistan, and Tajikistan, and two are very large ones: China and Russia. I think we should stay away from China and Russia and concentrate on the four small countries."

He looked around the table.

"Any comments?"

All nodded and murmured agreement. General Enkhbold spoke up.

"Do you have an order of attack, Khan?"

"We can invade Uzbekistan and Kyrgyzstan separately with each army. Or have both armies merge and go into Uzbekistan first and then into Turkestan, Tajikistan and Kyrgyzstan."

"I am less than 50 kilometers from the Kyrgyz border, Khan," said the General. He pointed to a spot west of Almaty. "My special troops are in good shape, and we have acquired a large contingent of Kazakh deserters. We are quite strong. If we keep the armies separate, I could lead my army into Kyrgyzstan, which I believe would fall quickly. Tajikistan would also fall quickly. I can then move into eastern Uzbekistan and join with you there. Then we could merge the two armies and attack Turkmenistan."

"Excellent plan." Genghis turned back to the map. "So, I will proceed west to Aqtobe. From there, I will send a small contingent of special soldiers to Atyrau. Apparently, the Kazakh government is now located there. The threat of my advancing force will send them either farther south to Aqtau or out of the country, unless they decide to surrender." He grinned. "I hope they do that, but they are not likely to wish to face me now. From Aqtobe, my main group will turn south and we shall plan on meeting in Tashkent after I conquer Uzbekistan."

He scowled. "When we are finished with Astana, we will burn it to the ground.

"In Kyrgyzstan, General, you will advance to Bishkek, the capital. Then turn south. Take these two towns close to the Uzbek border, Jalal-Abad and Osh, and continue southwest to the Tajik border, and then head west to the Tajik capital, Bushambe. If all goes according to plan, both countries will indeed fall quickly. You can then go north to meet me in Tashkent, and we will plan for dealing with Turkmenistan and beyond: probably south to Iran and Afghanistan."

He leaned back and smiled.

"Soon we will have our empire back."

For the next few months, into the summer, both armies pushed their way through the combined Federation and national forces. Additional special soldiers reinforced the Mongolian army. More Federation troops and weapons were also brought into action, but as in Kazakhstan, the armies of each country lost men who defected to the Mongolian army to serve their ancestor, the Great Khan.

Genghis's forces advanced beyond an Astana in flames and approached Aqtobe. As expected, the president and ministers of the Kazakh government flew from Atyrau to Russia, sending a group of minor officials to negotiate terms of surrender. Genghis killed the chief negotiator as an example, but spared the other officials, who were instead imprisoned in a local jail in Aqtobe. He ordered his Prime Minister in Ulaanbaatar to set up an occupation government in Almaty, which remained intact.

Ghengis Khan's army turned south from Aqtobe towards Shymkent near the Uzbek border. The thousand kilometer journey, with no enemy army to join in battle, was uneventful and rapid. General Enkhbold's army required more time to do battle with both Kyrgyz and Tajik troops and the supporting Federation forces. He set up camp south of Tashkent, the Uzbek capital, which is on a small land peninsula jutting between Kazakhstan and Tajikistan. The situation was unusual because Genghis was in Kazakhstan, and Enkhbold was in Tajikistan, while Tashkent, about 50 kilometers from each army, sat in a third country, Uzbekistan. The Federation forces withdrew from the battlefield, and repositioned themselves near Tashkent.

The two Mongolian armies poised to meet in Tashkent, battle hardened, proud in triumph, and saddened by loss, still burned with ancient Mongol eagerness for conquest under their revered leader.

* * *

At military headquarters of the World Federation, the ease with which the Mongolian armies had pushed around not only the national troops, but also the Federation forces, generated near panic among the officers now meeting to review events and plan strategy.

General Axel Landrieu, Commander of the Federation Armed Forces, opened the staff meeting on a sour note.

"We are being beaten up by an impossible army of dead people lead by a facsimile of a conqueror who died about nine hundred years ago. We're disgraced. We're supposed to be peacekeepers. How can this be?"

He waved his hand.

"Don't get me wrong. I understand what these pseudo people are and their effect on the war. They are very bad for our side's morale, among other things. The other things are the real problem. His soldiers can't be killed or disabled. They appear to die almost by accident. And he has this infernal machine to make more of them. Plus he can make horrible weapons to go along with the soldiers. I'm open for suggestions."

"Well," said another officer. "We can bomb the machine. Unfortunately, we don't know exactly where it is located other than in his village, Bayan Ovoo. We could bomb the whole village, but that wouldn't play well on the world stage. The World Federation can't use discredited methods."

General Landrieu grunted in exasperation.

Another officer spoke up.

"We are, after all, at war with Mongolia. Why don't we send in airborne troops, locate the machine, and destroy it?"

"It might be guarded by special soldiers," said another officer. "They probably have those weapons. We would not fare any better against them than our armies have up to now."

"That is true. Our armies are doing badly, and I see no promise of improvement, do you?"

"No."

"We can hope that his special soldiers will eventually disappear in some way. But the loss of his special soldiers is only useful to us if he can't replace them. In the interim, we must destroy that machine, and we have to take the chance that special soldiers are not guarding it. I believe it is worth the effort."

Further discussion yielded no better solution. Finally, General Landrieu held up his hand.

"Make it so."

# CHAPTER 25

Tashkent was secured. The World forces once again retreated. Genghis called his commanders together. He sat there for a minute, smiling and rubbing his forehead.

"Turkmenistan. It was part of the Khwarezmid Empire. They did not know us. They paid dearly for that." He smiled again. "They did not know us."

"We shall conquer them again, Khan," said General Enkhbold.

"Yes, yes, indeed we shall." He stopped again, the smile still on his face.

"So, Turkmenistan. We should advance to Samarkand, cross the border south of Bukhoro, and head for Ashgabat, the capital. We will cut the country in two pieces, and place ourselves very close to the Afghan border."

The officers looked startled. General Enkhbold cleared his throat.

"Beg pardon, Khan. I believe you mean the Iranian border."

"Of course I do. Why did you interrupt me?" He frowned.

"Your pardon, Khan."

"Very well. Iran will be next on our conquest list. Then we will have some decisions to make. Competence."

"I beg your pardon, Khan. What did you say?"

"Comments, comments. I want some comments on what we should be doing now."

"Yes Khan," said Enkhbold. "You want more comments. Certainly. Well, we have covered a lot of territory. I believe we need to consider the size of the army before we go much farther from home. We will be acquiring more and more territory as we continue to advance and will need more troops to maintain proper control. We have added many soldiers to our armies without any effort on our part, absorbing deserters from the armies of the countries we have beaten. I believe we should do two things: actively recruit in those countries and build our army at home as well."

"Excellent idea, General. The time is rife. We must not wastrel it. I will make more specific soldiers. I mean more special sailors. Yes, we need more reinfostering. And we need more weepings. I like those weep—I mean those wept- No, no. Weapons. Yes that's it, weapons for solstice, no, soldiers. Yes, that's it."

He sat back again and smiled even more broadly.

The General and the other officers stared at each other, and sneaked looks of panic at the Khan. A colonel leaned close to the General.

"What is wrong with him? I thought he was indestructible. What can we do?"

As the General was about to answer, Genghis stopped smiling and sat up in his chair.

"Yes. Now, where were we?"

"We discussed the need for more regular and special soldiers, and more special weapons as well. We are going to invade Turkmenistan."

"Yes. It will be glorious. After we conquer Turkmenistan, we—"

Silence. The officers again looked at each other. After a minute, the General leaned towards Genghis.

"Khan?" Softly. There was no response. Louder. "Khan!" Nothing. He reached over and shook Genghis' shoulder. "Khan!"

"Shall we call a doctor?" said one of the officers.

"Don't be a fool!" Enkhbold glared at him. "We need an engineer or a computer specialist, not a doctor. He isn't real. He is not real. Unless he wakes up, or revives, or shows some signs of 'life,' it appears he may have left us. It is very strange. I wonder if any of the soldiers who collapsed during the battles went through a stage like this. Perhaps he will stay in this state for a while before recovering his wits. We must allow time for that to happen."

Another colonel spoke up. "He was using incorrect words, which are similar to the right ones but wrong. It's a type of dementia, I think. But he doesn't have a real human brain. It's artificial, so how could he have a human disorder?"

The General held up his hand.

"Let the scientists study that. We have a very different problem. Right now, it starts with waiting to see if anything changes. Everything is on hold, the invasion of Turkmenistan, everything. We will wait in this room. I don't think he will recover, but of course I don't know, so we must wait, at least for several hours. Then we shall see."

Hours passed with no change. Several conversations started but ended quickly. Some stared at the Khan; others glanced at him frequently but almost surreptitiously; as if they were afraid he would suddenly awaken and scold them for staring.

After about three hours, Genghis began to shake, as if he were having a seizure. It lasted a few minutes. He was still again.

"General, how long shall we wait until we can be sure that he is gone?"

"I don't know. This is a new experience. Let us assume that he is gone. We must make some plans."

"Shall we continue our conquests?"

The General was quiet for a few moments.

"I don't think we should. We will no longer have the magic of his presence. The belief of his reality gave us courage and ambition, and filled our enemies with fear and awe. All that is gone. We will have to withdraw."

"Will they not fear you as they feared the Khan?"

The general snorted.

"I am nobody. I am not even from his time. Most of our soldiers will follow me because I am a general, and they are soldiers and trained to obey. I am certain that most of the deserters from the other armies will desert our army and return to their homes. Also, whatever I might do to continue the war, we have to face the inevitable fact that I too will be lost eventually. When or how is unknown. I have no idea how this body operates, what it looks like inside, or how the neurotronic brain functions. Even if I did, how could I possibly—"

"General!"

An officer was pointing at Genghis. His right arm was transparent, and then vanished. As they watched, his left arm disappeared, then his head. In less than a minute, nothing of Genghis Khan remained.

General Enkhbold sighed in sadness and relief.

"We have lost our beloved leader. But I believe we should be grateful that we had him with us for a while. That could be called a miracle, I suppose. At least now we won't have to explain the strange things that happened to him before he disappeared. Only we know, and nothing we know about it leaves this room. Is that understood?"

The officers nodded and agreed. One, Colonel Sansar Besud, thought that they did not really lose Genghis Khan. His real body still rests some place in Mongolia. The Great Khan they had followed was, despite their desire to believe otherwise, a non-person, an excellent replica, but little more than a symbol created by a machine.

"We have been fools," he murmured under his breath.

General Enkhbold called Minister of Defense Byambyn Mongkhbat to tell him the news.

"I can't believe it. I thought he was indestructible, that he was immortal. This is terrible."

"Yes, Minister, but it has happened and we have to deal with it."

"Of course, of course. Well, I will tell the Prime Minister. The previous government is still intact and little will change. It will be very hard on our people, however." He thought for a moment. "I'm afraid our standing in the world will suffer. Well, what do you recommend? Can we continue?"

"I do not think we can continue the war without the Khan. He was the soul of our nation and of our fighting forces. There is no one who can replace him as a leader or as a symbol of glory. I believe we should call for a truce. We do not have to surrender, because we still have the special soldiers and the weapons. They remain as a threat. We will have to come to terms with the conquered countries and the World Federation."

"Yes. I agree. I will speak to the Prime Minister. We will have a cabinet meeting and decide our best approach to the World Federation and the national governments."

"Very well. I will withhold the news from our troops until then."

The Kazakh, Tajik, Kyrgyz, and Uzbek governments agreed to cessation of hostilities, and would sign a peace treaty that included payment of reparations by Mongolia. All advanced weapons would be turned over to the World Federation for dismantling, and the special troops agreed to join the Federation forces for as long as they survived. Units of the Federation forces escorted the Mongolian armies to the connecting corridor between Kazakhstan and Mongolia.

For several months afterward, many of the human Mongolian soldiers berated themselves. They were consumed with shame, guilt, embarrassment, and anger at their foolishness in blindly following a leader who wasn't a real person, even the Great Khan. At the same time, others felt pride in what might have been, what could have been, a glorious restoration of the Mongol Empire. Later, the whole adventure became a dream as vivid as a real life experience, but as more time passed, the dream faded and a few even wondered if it had all actually happened.

The special soldiers pondered their futures: Could they look forward to years of existence or just a few days or weeks? Comrades were disappearing one or a few at a time. No longer could they imagine the prospect of immortality. In one sense, they were like real people. They would cease to exist, just like humans, and also like humans, they had no way to know when that cessation would occur. Most of them had no fear, but the uncertainty was often distracting. Would the ending be sudden or would they feel or see it happening? They were created as young men, but might have been of all ages: a man could die tomorrow as if he was already old, or after many years, as if he was very young. The human soldiers were also uncertain how to relate to them. Despite the attempt to keep secret the end of Genghis Khan, some of the bizarre details had leaked out; no one knew what to expect. So much uncertainty made fraternization between the two groups difficult. A wall separated them and no one knew when it would fall.

# CHAPTER 26

News of Genghis Khan's sudden disappearance quickly sped around the globe. In Mongolia, the result was widespread grief, shock, or disbelief, soon converging into a general numbness, and then resentment that their gods had forsaken them. Tourists and other foreign visitors soon became aware of angry stares directed their way that said: Why us, why not you?

Mongolia's Asian neighbors felt relief and thankfulness that they had been spared a return of the Mongol flood, as did the Eastern European countries. The World Federation decided to review the status of its peacekeeping abilities. The American authorities simply relaxed.

In San Francisco, John Sorensen called a meeting of the *History Lives* staff. All wore bright smiles. As they seated themselves around the table, John turned to Robert.

"Well, Robert, I don't know what you did, but it seems to have worked. Congratulations."

"Aw, I didn't do nuthin'. Except maybe wonder when it was going to happen."

"Please don't wonder about any of us that way."

Much laughter.

"Now," said John, "we have to work to get our program back on the air. There are three obstacles in our way. One, we must find the cause of the failure. Two, we have to fix it, permanently. And three, we have to convince the network and the various authorities that we have a solution that works. Shankar, are you and your group making progress?"

"Well, we believe that Genghis Khan was right when he told Robert that the failure was due to a rare juxtaposition of several events. We're in the process of eliminating the least likely of these, and I think we're getting close to identifying a group of three or four. When we do, we'll combine them at various levels and sequences to identify the culprit events and test them with inanimate objects. When the correct combination works repeatedly, we'll try it with plants and then small animals. At this time we cannot predict when we can do the tests."

"All right," said John. "Robert. I don't suppose you saw Genghis make anything?"

"No, I don't think he was ready to do that yet. I saw no machine. Even if he had the ability at that time, I'm pretty sure he didn't want me to see what he could do. Judging from the battlefield reports, however, he made good progress. He created more than a thousand men, and three unusual and powerful weapons. These all had to come from a new MONTY."

"Perhaps we can find out more through diplomatic channels."

"Perhaps, but the Mongolian authorities were not very cooperative when they were contacted earlier. They may be even less so now after their disaster."

"Fred, how are we doing with our new program?"

"Surprisingly well. We showed the pilot to critics and selected viewers. The response was pretty favorable, but we don't know how well that will predict the reaction of the general public. We'll see when we air it the week after next."

"Okay. Rebecca, you have a survey report?"

"Yes. We contacted the McCormick Survey Group and commissioned them to do a poll of watchers and non-watchers of *History Lives,* asking if they approve or disapprove of returning the program to the screen. Of the watchers, fifty-seven percent approved, thirty-five percent disapproved, and eight percent had no opinion. Among the non-watchers, fifty percent disapproved, twenty-five percent approved, sixteen percent had no opinion, and nine percent never heard of the program."

"Never heard of the program? How is that possible?"

Rebecca chuckled. "This program is our world. Many people simply don't watch the network we broadcast on. Some only know of us from the sensational news about Genghis Khan. I'd say these are just the results we should have expected."

"Well, assuming we do go back on the air, we'll have to do a lot of advertising to mend fences," said John. "We'll need to win back the loyalty of our viewers."

He looked around the table.

"Any more business? No? Okay, we're adjourned."

\* \* \*

Three weeks later, Shankar Lal came to John's office, wearing the aura of a man who had just finished a chocolate sundae.

"We did it," he chortled. "We did it!"

John stood up and pumped Shankar's hand vigorously.

"Wonderful! Congratulations! Give me a quick summary."

John listened closely, nodding his head vigorously. He pressed the intercom button and asked the group to gather in the meeting room.

"Good news everybody," said John. "Shankar's group solved MONTY's problem. We now know what happened. I'll let Shankar tell you all about it."

When the cheers, clapping, and whistles had died down, Shankar began his explanation.

"As we expected, three events of low probability took place at the same time. One, the force field failed. Two, the information storage unit did not activate. Three, as a consequence of event two, dematerialization could not be sustained. The information reconverted to solid state, but the force field was not operating, so that instead of being returned to the cubicle or to a location in the building, the Khan was deposited in the street somewhere outside the building. As soon as that happened, the circuits were suddenly restored to normal operation. Result: no clue telling us what had occurred. It all happened in the blink of a eye."

"How did you figure all that out?" asked Arne.

"The first obvious failure had to be the disabling of the force field, since Genghis ended up outside the building. So we strengthened the shielding of the force field circuit, and installed a control device that enabled us to turn it on and off at will. Then we tried inducing failure of various combinations of MONTY's internal events with the force field on or off. We finally found a combination that worked, first letting a small object rematerialize in the cubicle and then outside the cubicle but inside our part of the building. We did that by adjusting the locator device that sets the subject down in the cubicle for the show. Then came the fun part. We constructed a small object with a homing signal, allowed it to materialize outside the building, and then we all trooped outside to find it. I'm sure some people thought we were crazy. Next, we tried living material, a potted plant, with the homing device attached. The object materialized close by because the locator has a limited range.

"So the critical part is the integrity of the force field. Along with shielding the power line, we built and attached a backup power system independent of MONTY, designed to activate instantly with even a minor drop in voltage of the power line. And of course, we don't want any subject to materialize outside the cubicle, in the audience or near Robert. So we fixed the information storage and some other parts of the unit that could cause problems."

"Thank you, Shankar. Okay, we have two tasks before us. One is to convince the regulators, the various authorities, and the public that the failure is not going to happen again, so that we can resume the program. The other, assuming that we get approval, is to plan the next interview."

Shankar said, "It will be necessary to convince them without a guarantee, because it won't happen again until it does happen."

"True. Hopefully, our persuasive powers will be sufficient. But, we should be prepared for additional demands for safeguards. Now, let's have some show-time ideas."

"Shall we avoid bloody conquerors for a while?" asked Rebecca.

"I think that's wise. Okay, ideas, ideas."

"Elizabeth I."

"Too close to Henry."

"Hippocrates."

"Good."

"Leonardo da Vinci."

"Excellent."

"Jack the Ripper."

Stares of disbelief.

"Julius Caesar."

A chorus. "Conqueror!"

"Lewis and Clark."

"Both of them?"

"Why not?"

"Why not indeed."

"Vincent Bennelong, first Aborigine conductor of the New Earth Symphony."

"Good."

Several additional names were tossed on the table, followed by a lengthy discussion, featuring many jokes and extensive teasing, reflecting the relaxed, relieved atmosphere surrounding the group, freed from two heavy burdens. In the end, they agreed to do Leonardo next, Hippocrates after that, and Bennelong third.

Four weeks later, armed with data from Shankar's tests, John and Shankar went before the American Communications Commission to plead their case for restoring *History Lives* to the airwaves. Accompanying them was Jonathan Shaw, of the National Public Network. Representatives of the World Federation, the American government, and law enforcement authorities from San Francisco and California also attended the meeting.

The ACC meeting was in progress when they arrived. They waited in the anteroom to be called. The government representatives and the law enforcement people were also waiting. They all nodded at each other. Shankar leaned toward John.

"Do you think we'll have some opposition?" he whispered.

"Probably. Hard to tell how serious it will be and how persuasive to others. And there may be some strings attached, if they do approve our request."

"My guess is that the cops will oppose it," said Shankar. "They are the ones who experienced Genghis at first hand."

"You could be right."

They waited for twenty minutes before the door to the meeting room opened and they were summoned and assigned three chairs at one end of the table. The others took chairs around the periphery of the room.

"Good morning, ladies and gentlemen," said a middle-aged man at the other end of the table. I am Howard Edelman, chair of this Commission. Welcome. The issue at hand is the petition submitted by the National Public Network on behalf of *History Lives*, to permit them to resume broadcasting the program. You have all received copies. The show was taken off the air as a result of the unfortunate incident and subsequent tragic events involving one of their interview subjects, Genghis Khan.

"As you all know, the Khan failed to return to his proper place in the machine called MONTY. Instead he materialized outside the building and subsequently found his way to Mongolia, planning to resume his role as conqueror. Fortunately, he vanished, or more properly, dematerialized, before he was able to realize his ambition. The petition claims that safeguards have been incorporated into the protocol that will prevent this event from occurring again. Mr. Shaw, I understand you have a few introductory words before we hear from your colleagues."

"Yes, thank you, Mr. Edelman. The Board of Directors of NPN has heard from the producers of *History Lives,* and they have convinced us that they indeed have the situation under control. We have voted unanimously to allow the program to proceed pending your approval. I believe the evidence that they will present to you will convince you as well. I will not take up any more of your time and I introduce to you Dr. John Sorensen, co-inventor of the Multiple Nuance Translator, more familiarly known as MONTY. John."

"Thank you, Jonathan. Ladies and gentlemen, thank you for holding this hearing and giving us the opportunity to state our case for resuming *History Lives*. We discovered that one important difficulty with a highly innovative show is that it is extremely difficult, if not impossible, to predict where, and when, and how something will go wrong. And I say will, not might, because glitches will happen. We have had several that we disclosed in public meetings, but obviously the failure to return Genghis Khan to storage was by far the most serious, and tragic for the two victims in San Francisco, as well as for many people in Central Asia.

"As you will hear from Dr. Lal, after immediately suspending production of *History Lives* we began tracking down the cause of the malfunction. I am happy to report that his team was successful. We found the cause and built safeguards into the system to prevent the problem from happening again. Now we believe we are ready to resume production of the show. I would like to introduce Shankar Lal, who will explain why the malfunction occurred and the steps we have taken to prevent a repeat."

"Thank you, John. We thought from the beginning that a number of unlikely events had occurred simultaneously and this proved to be true."

He described the critical failure of the force field, the malfunction of the data storage, the re-conversion of the Khan's image, and his deposit outside the building absent the protection of the force field. He emphasized the unlikely combination of unlikely individual events.

"You will note that I do not refer to the event as an escape. He did not escape. He had no idea how he got outside, and played no part at all in the malfunctions. But he was an unusually intelligent person and made the most of the opportunity. I should mention that while we were still in developmental stages of the program, several years ago, another person failed to return to storage. But she did not rematerialize; no reports of her existence were ever made, anywhere."

Shankar went on to describe the modifications to MONTY that were designed to prevent a recurrence of the cascade of events resulting in the failure to return Genghis Khan to the information storage. He emphasized the critical importance of the force field in describing the increased shielding of the power line, and the addition of a backup system to prevent any interruption in the operation of the field.

"In conclusion, after extensive tests of the new system, we feel quite confident that this problem will not occur again. Thank you."

"Thank you, Dr. Lal. Before I turn to the board members for their discussion of the petition, are there any questions or comments from our other guests? Yes?"

The woman who rose from one of the side seats was tall with dark brown hair and deep brown eyes.

"Mr. Chairman, my name is Marta Ramirez. I am the Chief of Police in the City of San Francisco and I wish to make a statement."

"Please," said Mr. Edelman.

"I am here to represent the Police Department of San Francisco, and to express the Department's great reluctance to see *History Lives* resume broadcasting in our city. We have already seen two tragedies take place and we do not wish to see any more. We understand that as long as the materialized subject remains 'alive', it can't be killed and represents a continued threat to the safety of our citizens. This would be intolerable. I think we need considerably more assurance than we've received so far."

"Thank you, Chief Ramirez. Any more comments?"

A grey haired, slightly stocky man arose and introduced himself as Michael Ritter of the Attorney General's Office of California.

"The Attorney General finds no inherent reason why *History Lives* should not return to the air. We do, however, want to receive a detailed list of the safety precautions that the producers will be taking. The force field is critical, and it appears that the double protection should be satisfactory. There is one question, however: Can the subject materialize in the studio but outside the cubicle? If so, what can be done to prevent it?"

Mr. Ritter sat down and Chairman Edelman turned to the World Federation contingent.

"Comments from the World Federation?"

A tall blonde man stood. "Thank you, Mr. Chairman. I am Jan Becker of the World Federation's Ministry of Intergovernmental Affairs. On my right is Jemal Dogan, of the Ministry of Culture. Mr. Dogan is from Turkey and I am from the Netherlands. Together we have made a list of questions for the producers of *History Lives*. These are obviously related to safety issues, especially including the subsequent violence after Genghis Kahn arrived in Mongolia. Our approval for return of the program is contingent upon the answers to those questions. May I proceed?"

The Chairman nodded.

"Very well. I have made a list to pass around and I will also read them aloud. The first two already have been partially addressed. One, can you give any sort of guarantee that an escape will not occur again? Two, can you guarantee the integrity of the force field. Three, will you continue to interview subjects with a history of violent behavior? Four, are there ways to control their ability to increase their powers? Five, can a subject be programmed with a destruct sub-routine? Six, can the subject be constructed of a substance such that it can be killed or destroyed by conventional means. And seven, if the subject gets away despite these multiple safeguards, can you arrange to alert law enforcement authorities immediately? Thank you."

"Okay. I think that at this point, we might ask the *History Lives* folks to respond to the questions raised."

Chairman Edelman turned to John Sorensen.

"Would you like some time to consult with each other?"

"Yes, we would appreciate that."

"Very well. Let's take a short recess. We will leave the room to you."

John turned to Shankar.

"What do you think? Are we ready to handle all the questions now?"

"Sure. A few of them are pretty obvious and easy to deal with."

"Right. I'll do those." He grinned. "Let's take the list Mr. Jensen left with us, add the ones that were brought up earlier, and divide them up."

They spent the next half hour completing the list and allotting the questions that each would discuss.

"Jonathan, would you like to respond to any of these questions."

"No, not at all. You seem to have the issues well in hand. A few of those questions sound difficult to answer, and I hope you have appropriate responses."

"I believe we do."

"Good. Eat 'em up."

When everyone had returned, the Chairman said, "Okay, Dr. Sorensen, you have the floor."

"Thank you. We have taken the list of all questions brought up by the Chief, the Attorney General, and the World Federation representatives and divided them up. I will take some of them and Dr. Shankar the rest.

"First, we will compile a list of all the safety measures that we discuss here and provide that list to you. Second, we have already made the decision to use only subjects with no known history of any kind of violence. Third, we will inform the San Francisco Police Department and other appropriate law enforcement agencies in the unlikely event that a subject materializes anywhere outside the cubicle.

"Before I turn the floor over to Dr. Lal, are there any questions regarding the three actions I have mentioned. Yes, Chief Ramirez."

"Dr. Sorensen, I understand that there are other groups using your technology. Are they aware of what has happened?"

"There are three labs using MONTY for historical research, in England, Switzerland, and India. We notified them immediately when we discovered that Genghis Khan was out. We are all in constant contact regarding any progress in improving MONTY's performance, including things that we are reporting to you today. Anything else? Okay, Shankar, will you take it from here?"

"When we learned of the Khan's activities here and in Mongolia, we quickly identified several traits that had to be corrected or modified. We have already talked about the force field, and we are confident that it will hold. However, in the unlikely event of its failure, we have also considered necessary precautions regarding the subject's capabilities, assuming that others besides Genghis might have them. These include increased brainpower, increased physical capabilities, ability to move objects without touching them, and ability to create objects, including large ones, by transformation from something else. Until we received reports from the battlefields of Central Asia, we did not know the strengths or vulnerabilities of the created persons, primarily because they were not supposed to exist outside the cubicle. Nevertheless this is a formidable, and dangerous, array of powers. We considered the problem carefully and decided that, rather than trying to confront each of them separately, we needed a single solution for all of them. Essentially, this means that the subject must not survive outside the cubicle.

"We decided that we had to create an environment inside the cubicle that was essential for the subject's survival while there. If the subject materialized in any other place, inside the building or out, it must instantly cease to exist. So this is the solution we have been working on, and I am pleased to report that we have made excellent progress and expect to achieve success very soon.

"Now, the word guarantee has been mentioned. Unfortunately, there is only one way to test how successful these measures will be. That is to run the machine repeatedly until it fails, and that means that in retrospect no guarantee could have been given. So if it operates successfully ten thousand times, it may fail the next time, or it may run another ten thousand times, and then fail. There is no way of knowing ahead of time. Look at it another way. Right now we could consider thousands of scenarios that *might* lead to failure, but not think of the one that actually leads to failure. It is a virtually impossible task. Well, that's all I have. Thank you. Are there any questions?"

Chief Ramirez spoke up again.

"Why didn't you think of these possibilities before the tragedies happened?"

"As we have already pointed out, this was a highly unlikely combination of several events that were themselves unlikely. There was no way to predict that particular combination or any other similar combination of events. The number of possibilities is far too numerous to predict any of them. And, of course we had absolutely no idea that they could happen."

He hesitated for a moment.

"In hindsight, when the first subject disappeared, we might have tried to imagine some unlikely outcomes. But considering what happened with the second subject, the odds against hitting on the right one would have been astronomical."

One of the board members raised his hand.

"You've created a certain number of subjects and there have been two disappearances. Doesn't this give you some odds to work with?"

"Unfortunately, no, because we will change the rules by modifying the system. It will be a completely new ballgame from here on."

Chairman Edelman said, "You said that you expect to achieve success very soon. Can you be more specific?"

"We're thinking in a matter of weeks. Perhaps three or four, possibly six."

The Chairman looked around the table, and asked for additional questions. There were none, so he turned to John, Shankar, and Jonathan.

"Thank you for your presentation. We will discuss the information you have given us today, but will hold our final decision until we have heard the results of your efforts. Thank you all for coming."

The board members remained seated while the visitors filed out of the room.

"Okay, Shankar," said John. "It's up to you and your team."

In the intervening weeks, Shankar's team worked on the problem, while the others divided into two groups, one to work on a show featuring Leonardo da Vinci and the other to continue to develop the alternate series *Landmarks of Scientific Discovery*.

Five weeks after the meeting with the ACC, Shankar came to John's office with two bound folders. One contained the requested detailed listing of the new safety precautions.

"This other one," said Shankar with a broad grin, "is the solution to the materialization problem."

"Wonderful," said John. "Tell me about it."

"Well, we knew that there was nothing we could do with the environment outside the cubicle. But we could control what was in the cubicle. The normal atmosphere is about 78% nitrogen and 21% oxygen and some other rare gases. So we will fill the cubicle with 100% nitrogen and convert the subject's materialized body to a substance that is easy to oxidize, even by atmospheric oxygen. It would survive nicely in the cubicle, but if it materialized anywhere else, it would oxidize and disappear, leaving only a small residue. There are two substances that behave in this manner, catalicon and oxichron. Both of them have properties that permit their use to form the subject's bodies. We chose the oxichron because it oxidizes a little faster. We tested the procedure extensively in the cubicle, alternating air and nitrogen atmospheres. All tests gave results exactly as expected. All of this is described in detail in the second bound folder."

"Excellent. I'll put it all together in a package and send enough copies for the whole board. Hopefully, they will respond fairly quickly. Thanks, Shankar, and congratulate your team."

The weeks that went by seemed like an eternity to everyone on the staff, even though they kept busy planning shows. Finally, John received a letter. He read it quickly, fetched Rebecca from her office, and together they went to the workroom where most of the staff were at work.

"I have a letter," he said in sepulchral tones. "It reads: 'Dear Dr. Sorensen, The ACC Board has considered your report very carefully, and we are pleased to inform you –'" The room erupted in cheers. John grinned broadly as he waited for the noise to subside. "—and we are pleased to inform you that you may resume production of *History Lives* as of receipt of this letter. Congratulations. The board was highly impressed with your presentation and your ability to develop safety protocols that we all expect to be effective. Howard Edelman, Chair.' Green light, folks. Let's get Leonardo on the air."

# EPILOGUE

*Castlebar, Ireland*
*Ten Years Later*

Castlebar is a small town in County Mayo, near the West Coast of Ireland, about twenty-five kilometers from the edge of Clew Bay, which opens to the Atlantic Ocean. Burke's is one of many pubs in the popular tourist town. Promptly at ten thirty, Grace de Burgo, the former Grace O'Malley, opened the front door for early bird customers. Two men entered immediately.

"Paddy, Johnny. Come in, come in."

She went behind the bar and drew two pints. The men sat at their usual places at the far end of the bar where they could watch other customers come and go.

"Will ya have one on us, lass?" asked Paddy.

"Thank ya, no. A bit early for the old girl."

This had been the usual routine for more years than she could remember, probably since she first arrived from America and was hired at Burke's. She now owned the pub. The previous owner had been fond of her, had had no family, and therefore had bequeathed the property to her. She had made one major change: serving real meals instead of just bar snacks. The already popular pub began to attract tourists as well as locals.

When Grace materialized on a San Francisco street eleven years earlier, she was nearly overcome with fright. It was night and she slunk to a dark corner, wondering what had happened to her. But she was a clan chief, a woman famed for courage and intelligence. Born in 1530, she was the daughter of an Irish ship captain, and became a formidable sea warrior herself. She called upon that courage and soon calmed down and began to think. She realized that instead of returning to what the studio people called storage, she had been transported outside. She was free, a person again after more than five centuries.

Grace moved farther back into the shadows and sat down. She quickly became aware that her body had changed. She wasn't cold or tired, she felt no hunger or thirst, and her mind sparkled with energy. How strange! How exciting! Two thoughts dominated her mind. She must return to Ireland, and she must keep her identity a secret for as long as she continued to exist.

The next day dawned. The building with the cubicle was close by. There was no hint that she was missed, but she thought it would be wise to move away from the building. She found a used clothing store and traded her sixteenth century clothing for modern attire. Her mind accumulated more information. She was on the West Coast of a country called the United States in the New World. There was a seaport across the bay in the city of Oakland. She hitched a ride across the Bay Bridge. She discovered that her brogue charmed people, especially men. She located a freighter whose ultimate destination was Ireland, and persuaded, almost hypnotized, the crew chief to hire her as a deck hand.

Weeks later the ship docked in Dublin. She was home. She decided against settling in Westport, a town that was very close to the family castle, and chose Castlebar instead. Often, in the privacy of her apartment, she contemplated her present "life" and wondered how long it would last. The story about Genghis Khan and his rapid departure ten years ago had startled and frightened her, but in the ensuing years she had stopped worrying. The time would come some day. She would cease to exist, and that was fine. Her second life was a gift, enabling her to live in two worlds centuries apart, a very rare gift indeed, shared by only one other person in history. She had reached a pinnacle, and now it was hers alone. What more could anyone ask?

# THE END

www.ingramcontent.com/pod-product-compliance
Lightning Source LLC
Chambersburg PA
CBHW071308170626
46809CB00001B/375